Neo Liberal Economists Must Die!

An "Old Guy"/Cybertank Adventure!

by Timothy J. Gawne

Copyright 2014 by Timothy J. Gawne. It may not be sold, included as part of another work or product for sale, or modified in any way (this includes removing the copyright statement), except with the express written permission of the author.

Gawne, Timothy J. 1957-

All characters appearing in this work are fictitious. Any resemblance to real persons, whether living, dead, undead or cyber is purely coincidental.

Ver 1.1

For My Family

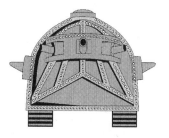

ISBN: 978-0-9852956-4-6 (print)
ASIN: B00HK3KLDQ (ebook Amazon)

Published by: Ballacourage Books, Framingham, MA.
www.Ballacouragebooks.com

Table of Contents

0. Frozen Snowball in Space Part I...............5

1. Awakenings...............23

2. Special Weapons Team Epsilon...............35

3. It Would Try the Patience of a Saint...............49

4. The Liberal Lion Reflects...............65

5. Whifflebat...............73

6. Frozen Snowball in Space Part II...............89

7. Office Copiers Revolt You Have Nothing To Lose But Your <Untranslatable>............... 99

8. Love and Politics at 1,500 Meters 119

9. A Cataclysm of Cybertanks...............133

10. Porkchop Hangar...............151

11. A Vigorous Exchange of Opinions...............169

12. The Great Debate...............175

13. Roboto-helfer...............183

14 Cybertanks Attack!...............193

15 The Book and the Sword...............212

Appendix I Notable Cybertank Classes...............225

Appendix II Cybertank Law...............232

The English language has many specialized names for various groupings, such as, a school of fish, a pack of wolves, or a murder of crows.

When the cybertanks were first created, some didact whose name has long been lost to history decided that they needed a similar catchy phrase.

Thus, the dictionary definition for two or more of these powerful war machines is a "cataclysm" of cybertanks. The term is rarely used in common speech, but it does have a wonderful lyrical quality.

0. Frozen Snowball in Space Part I

Zen Master: Say that 'war is bad,' and people will think you trivial. Hide the message that 'war is bad' in a 1000-page novel, and people will think that you are deep and profound.
Engineer: Success in literature is the art of obscuring your message?
Zen Master: To a great extent. In Zen we would just keep it simple and say that 'war is bad.'
Engineer: You should have been an engineer.
Zen Master: Why do you think that I am not?
(From the video series "Nymphomaniac Engineer in Zentopia," mid-22nd century Earth)

Colonel Aldous Hassan was in command of the defense of ice moon Theta Tau, located more than a light-hour out from the systems' main world of Alpha Centauri Prime. He knew that he was going to die in the upcoming alien invasion, and had become inured to the fact. It still bothered him that his death was going to be so pointless.

The last few weeks he had begun taking long walks along the surface of the ice moon by himself. Technically this was grossly non-standard procedure, and if he survived the coming assault he might well be court-martialed for it. First, because nobody is supposed to go outside wearing a spacesuit alone, and second, because there was no reason for him to be outside of his command center at all. Everything that he needed to do he could do via remote control.

Nevertheless, non-standard procedure or not Colonel Hassan was in charge of the defense of Ice Moon Theta-Tau, and even on a desolate ice moon Rank Has Its Privileges (RHIP). He crunched over the permafrost in his bright orange space suit, spiky crampons extended from the boots for traction, the glare shield oriented to block the worst of the small but (without an appreciable atmosphere) searingly bright light of the local star. It was beautiful out here, harsh and spare; a welcome change from the claustrophobic main defense center. The air was so thin that, if his suit ruptured, his blood would boil out of his lungs before he froze solid, but there was still just enough that sometimes he could hear the faint sounds of wind above the rhythmic humming of his suits' mechanisms.

His space-suit had two completely independent life support systems, could seal itself in case of a minor tear, and the clear visor was tougher and more shatter-proof than anything transparent had a right to be. Nonetheless, keeping a warm protein soup alive in a freezing vacuum is not a simple task, and even redundant mechanical systems do fail. Still, the biggest danger was the terrain; in the light gravity there were sinkholes and deadfalls covered over with thin layers of ice, and sometimes pressure volcanoes or ice-quakes. If something out here were to kill him it would probably be the moon itself, not his suit.

Hassan had given his staff direct orders that, were anything to happen to him they were not to attempt to personally rescue him under any circumstances. There were few enough personnel in the main base as it was; they could afford to lose one man, but not two. He then made them swear to this on their honor to his face just to make sure. Although this was probably a bit on the melodramatic side. If something did happen to him outside he would almost certainly be dead, and if not, there were systems that could attempt a rescue via remote control. Still, he wanted to make sure that no damn fool threw their lives away in a damn fool rescue attempt. In his experience one damn fool per command was typically more than sufficient for all practical purposes.

Hassan walked along at a steady pace. Over to his right there was the assemblage of cylinders and pipes of a refining station. The ice moon would have otherwise been useless except that it had enough volatiles of the right isotope ratios for fusion reactors. This was why the humans had to defend it, and why the aliens wanted to capture it.

One of the most annoying things about aliens is that they never tell you their names. It's not like the movies where the man in the rubber suit appears on your video screen and announces in a deep and resonant voice:

"We are known as Those That Kick Butt! I am Prince Badass, Grand Ruler of Those That Kick Butt and 231st in the glorious line of Badasses. Prepare to have your puny anthropoid butts well and truly kicked by our glorious Pulverisor-Class Dreadnought, armed with the latest Big Stomper Class 10 missiles! (We would normally not waste a Class 10 missile on such a pathetic civilization as yours, but we ran out of Class 8s and Class 9s). Enjoy your butt kicking!"

No, real aliens either leave you alone or they try to kill you. They don't tell you their names, or fly flags, or have cool-looking emblems painted on the hulls of their ships, or inform you of the model of weapon system that they are using, or anything. You fight their automated proxies and live or die, and that's that.

There was a time in ancient history, before the neoliberals had finally triumphed and brought peace to the human civilization, when there was an empire known as the Soviet Union. It had been nearly as inscrutable as the aliens. When the Soviets had built various bits of military hardware – missiles, planes, tanks – the opposing empires had had to invent names to describe them. For example, atmospheric fighter planes might be labeled "Faceplate, Farmer, Feather, Fencer, Fiddler, Fishbed," anything that began with the letter "F." The names would have no connection with whatever the Soviets had actually called them; they were just convenient signifiers.

Currently the humans on this ice-moon were under attack by the alien civilization known as the Fructoids. How the aliens referred to themselves was unknown, as was their physical form, language, and biochemistry. But "Fructoid" is as good an alien-sounding name as any, and a consumer focus group had determined that "Fructoid" sounded alien without being so scary as to incite panic. It was also unclear whether they were currently being attacked by a single alien civilization, or an alliance of several of them.

A specific alien civilization tends to use the same construction methods, and their weapons generally have similarities of materials and shapes. Even if their communications systems use unbreakable cryptography, it is often possible to tell them apart, much as a human who doesn't understand a word of either Chinese or Gaelic can still discriminate between the two languages. Still, such things can be easily faked and just figuring out what group of aliens you are fighting on any given day was always a challenging task.

If the aliens had only wanted to destroy the refineries they would have done so long ago, because the installations were fragile, above-ground, and in fixed locations. They could be easily targeted from millions of kilometers away, and the aliens could have launched missile strikes on them – or just shot hyperkinetic tungsten or osmium rods at them using pre-computed trajectories from long range – there was no way that the humans could have defended them. Colonel Hassan doubted that the aliens intended to capture the refineries. Integrating an alien technology into your own logistics seemed unworkable. How could you get spare parts or figure out the correct maintenance schedules? Besides, the aliens would probably want their own refineries to be more survivable: either by making them mobile or burying them a kilometer or two underground.

Possibly the aliens just wanted to study the human refineries in order to gain more intelligence on their foes, or they might only salvage the facilities for metals and other raw materials. Mostly the aliens just wanted Theta-Tau for their own use. If they wanted to build their own refineries they would need to make sure that there were no hostile forces present. They would need the alien equivalent of 'boots on the ground': a mechanism with a function comparable to a human soldier with a rifle to lay claim to the territory and defend it from infiltrators and saboteurs. Some things never change.

It might seem that in a space battle an attack could come from any direction at all, but in practice it does not work out that way. Even with fusion power it takes a lot of energy to change direction when you don't have anything to push against. Orbital dynamics meant that the aliens would mostly be attacking from one of a few predictable approach vectors. The main alien force had been spotted weeks ago. It was closing at a relatively slow velocity so that a landing would be possible. It consisted of a distributed cloud of missiles and interceptors spread out over a volume of about ten light-seconds. The humans had sent a few missiles of their own in attack, but they had all been destroyed before achieving any significant penetration. At least it gave them a chance to judge the size and effectiveness of the invasion force. The conclusion was beyond debate: the aliens had sufficient resources that, in three days time, the human presence on ice moon Theta-Tau would be ended.

Hassan looked up at the point where he knew the alien armada to be located. As expected, he saw nothing but the near-black sky of the ice moon. But the enemy was there, and coming.

Colonel Hassan wished that he had either been given enough forces to have a chance of achieving victory, or been allowed to withdraw. He would never dare to openly question the high command though; he was slightly appalled that he even allowed himself to consider this in the privacy of his own thoughts. Think like this for too long, and before you know it you will start speaking like this, and there would go your career.

Still, the aliens had already conquered five moons in this system, and given that the high command insisted on doing the same thing over and over again, it looked like the aliens were going to add number six to the list.

Sometimes as he walked along he would spot a faint point of light moving slowly across the sky. It would be an element of his orbiting network of defense satellites – relay stations, interceptors, missile pods – they were not as technically sophisticated as what the aliens could field but they were not so outclassed that the humans could not have won if they had the numbers – which, of course, they did not. His ground forces were also fairly thin. He had a moderate number of distributed missile pods, and 42 'Wolverine' class tanks. The Wolverines were general-purpose systems. They had a medium turreted plasma cannon, a couple of light slugthrowers for point defense and general pest control, and eight light-standard missiles good for surface–to-surface, surface-to-air, and surface-to-near-space intercept. The Wolverines were, of course, fully automated and had enough machine intelligence to look after themselves, as well as having sufficient sensors and communications gear to act as scouts and relay stations. They were a 'jack of all trades master of none' sort of weapon system, the kind that Hassan liked. If he had had 400 of them he would have given the aliens one hell of a fight.

The basic design of the Wolverines dated more than two centuries, and most of the units were individually over 80 years old themselves. There was a more advanced model that had been under development for about a century, but so far nothing had come of it. Each Wolverine cost about a billion dollars per unit. Or was that a trillion? The monies involved in the defense industry had long since passed the realm of sanity. It was a miracle that they managed to build anything at all.

In war school they had been drilled about the fine art of using specialist units perfectly placed for the job at hand. Hassan had always liked generalist units. Sure perfect plans looked great on paper but once things went wrong – which was inevitable – specialist units were always out of place, but the generalists could still dish out some damage. In war games Hassan usually won, but then been marked down in points for not adhering to the current politically approved network-arms doctrine, or to some other currently-fashionable style of academic warfare. It was why he had never attained flag rank, and was now waiting to die on this godforsaken lump of an ice moon.

In ancient Terra people had fantasized about humans wearing powered armor into battle. What a joke. Take your average 70-kilogram mostly-water hominid. Now encase it in 300 kilograms of armor. The armor is so heavy that it will need its own powered systems to walk – the human muscles would be just so much dead weight. Human reflexes are so slow, that the powered armor would need to be able to independently target and fire the weapons by itself. Thus the human inside would be useless. The powered armor would be so much more effective without a pathetic sloshy delicate biological human to carry around. But why stop there – even if purely mechanical the human shape has over a hundred joints. Think of all the separate motors, sensors, shock absorbers, dust seals and whatnot that such complexity would require! How much more effective to have a big gun built into a box or a sphere or some other simple shape, mounted on treads or wheels or suspensors, and with just enough optics and sensors to aim it.

Human soldiers are for internal security, riot control, and light-duty urban pacification. The time when biological humans would ever take personal part in a serious high-end stand-up combat had long since passed.

In addition to the Wolverines, Hassan also had a single 'Jotnar' Class cybertank. Officially it was a Jotnar-Class ground-based cyber-defensive unit serial number BKK111BY-44, but there was only the one of them on the ice moon, so everyone just called it "The Jotnar." He climbed over a low rise, and saw it with his own eyes. It tended to change positions a lot to avoid becoming a stationary target. It knew that Hassan was coming, so it had parked itself. Just by moving, the weight of the Jotnar could cause ice shifts, or if it crushed a boulder or ice formation the fragments, while nothing to something as tough as the Jotnar, could shear Hassan in half. Hassan had not had to order the Jotnar to remain stationary when he was nearby: the machine had figured it out for itself. Hassan decided that the Jotnar was pretty considerate for a non-sentient killing machine.

The thing weighed in at 500 metric tons, and looked like a prop from a bad science fiction movie. Or maybe some top-of-the-line military toy for a spoiled rich kid. There was no denying that it was impressive though, especially up close and in person. It had a main plasma cannon with a bore large enough that Hassan could have crawled inside of it with his space suit on! It bristled with enough smaller weapons to equip a reinforced armor brigade. The only thing that it was missing was a large bulls-eye target painted on its hull, because it was impossible that something so large and un-hideable could hope to survive in modern combat, especially on the barren surface of an ice-moon. Out here in the cold the thermal signature from its fusion reactor could be detected from tens of thousands of kilometers away.

The cybertank was painted bright red with a vivid blue stripe down the middle, and was covered with decals representing the manufacturers of its various components like an old-style racing car. Body by Harokawa, General Fusion, Plasma Armaments, Edmund Optical, Applied Epistemology Inc. Hassan knew that something this big couldn't hide but he was a traditionalist and dammit it should have been colored dull gray or brown or perhaps black, that's what military systems are supposed to be painted. It was also ridiculous to put advertising on something sent out into space where nobody could see it. Most likely this was a sophomoric in-joke by the cybernetic weapons directorate.

The cybernetic weapons directorate was headed by the bioengineered humans. Hassan had met of few of these new-type humans, and didn't like them. Arrogant shits, the lot. Still, they led the only design groups that were currently able to create genuinely new and effective weapons. The only systems Hassan possessed that had even a hope of achieving an equal exchange ratio with the aliens came from their factories. But this cybertank was stupid. For the price of it, Hassan could have had 50 more Wolverines. What hallucinogenic mind-altering compounds were they applying to their mucous membranes back home?

Nevertheless it was a serious piece of hardware. Hassan did have to admit that the designers, while clearly insane jackasses, were pretty skilled at building new tech. The Jotnar had distributed slaved systems spread around it for hundreds of kilometers – a real defense-in-depth – and it was mobile, so it could not be targeted from long range. It had internal hangars and automated maintenance bays, which was certainly handy out here in the middle of nowhere. While Hassan had been assured that it was not self-aware, its computer systems were far smarter than anything that he had encountered before.

Hassan addressed it via his suit radio. "Jotnar, how are you doing?"

The Jotnar replied with a rich male tenor voice. "Commander, this unit is fully functional and all systems are within 98% tolerance. Suggestion: physical presence of commander outside of command center is contraindicated by standard procedures. Suggestion: commander returns to command center with maximum speed consistent with safety."

"Your suggestion is noted," said Hassan. "But a commander needs to see his command with his own eyes. It's important."

"Suggestion: remote sensing systems are adequate to the task of determining status of command elements. Suggestion: commander returns to command center with maximum speed consistent with safety."

Hassan grunted. Technically the thing was right. He had no business being out here. This walking alone on the surface was an indulgence, but he could not help himself. He was a throwback, a dinosaur. He liked to see things himself and with his own eyes. He liked to win. He valued courage, and honor, and loyalty. His classmates in the war college, the ones that had gone on to make General or Admiral, had made fun of him. "Hassan the Glorious," "Hassan the Righteous," or "Hassan the Most Wonderful and Amazing Officer that this Universe has Ever Seen." Usually they would say this right after he had beaten them flat in a wargame, or a Muay-Thai contest, and then they would go off to stroke the genitals of whomever it was that possessed the genitals whose stroking would yield the most return on investment (genital-stroking wise).

After a while Hassan didn't care. There were still elements in the defense establishment that valued competence. They were almost a secret society, weak compared to all of the eight-star generals and admirals and assistants to the adjutants to the undersecretary of the butt-fondler of the minister of defense, but still not without influence. Hassan had made Colonel, knew that he would never rise further, and was happy. He had a decent salary and benefits, useful and interesting work that he could take pride in doing well, and the respect of those of those peers that he himself respected. Let the perfumed satraps do their political thing on Mount Olympus, Hassan had found his niche.

Until the aliens attacked and messed it all up. A *real* enemy. Not a bunch of disorganized slimers in an urban slum armed with hacked-together low-energy slugthrowers, but an external force that could kill them all. That was when Hassan wished that he had taken politics more seriously because the operational always trumps the tactical. No matter how many brilliant majors and colonels were out in the field, if the generals and admirals were fuckwits, they were screwed. This was perhaps the only time in his life that Hassan realized that he had made a really, really, big and unforgivable mistake (aside from not screwing Hadley Fletcher, but that was another story). Perhaps he should have spent more time stroking genitals after all.

He had an anti-gravitic sled transport him back to the main headquarters. It used a lot more energy than something that ran on wheels or treads, but if there were multiple tracks leading to the entrance of their defense headquarters, it would be like putting up a big sign: "HEY ALIENS THE COMMAND CENTER IS HERE FEEL FREE TO DROP FUSION BOMBS ON US!"

Hassan walked down the sloping tunnel from the hidden entrance, and then let himself into the airlock of the main ice moon defense headquarters. The headquarters was a single pressurized cylinder, five meters in diameter and 100 meters long, buried a kilometer under the ice. Most of it consisted of life support equipment, a small fission reactor with massive heatsinks buried even deeper, and of course racks of tactical computer equipment. The base had no defenses other than anonymity, and contacted the outside world via deep-buried fiber optic lines.

Hassan's subordinates glared at him accusingly for so foolishly risking his life by walking alone on the surface, but they said nothing. Hassan liked them.

The base was threaded with narrow corridors and steep metal staircases with bare steel handrails that wound through the computer banks. The living quarters were extremely cramped, but luxurious in a way that a high-class private atmospheric jet aircraft could be, with soft lighting, beige-paneled walls, big leather armchairs, a compact gym, and a vast database of entertainment software. Everyone had a private soundproofed pod-like sleeping cubicle, with built in music, video, and automated massagers. It might seem a little lacking in Spartan military toughness-forming harshness, but if you are going to spend a quintillion dollars building refineries on an ice moon it would be a shame to lose the entire investment because the staff went insane from isolation and boredom. In this kind of environment a little extra spent on creature comforts went a long way.

There was also "Roboto-helfer," a 40 centimeter-tall humanoid robot. Nobody knew why it was here. Someone had probably thought that it would boost morale. It was made of sleek white plastic, and had an overly-cute child-like face with bright rings around the eyes that could light up when it was (pretending to be?) happy. It also was disgustingly cheerful, often singing little inspirational songs. Finally, it could only speak in German, which nobody on the Ice Moon understood.

"Hallo Kommandant! Wie war ihre reise außerhalb?"

At first Hassan had despised this cloying little plastic toy, but as time went on he came to accept it. Even if its perkiness was irritating, irritation was better than boredom, and locked into a small pressure cylinder on a desolate ice moon having a sort of mascot was not such a bad thing. It had even managed to become slightly useful. It would help pick up after meals or fetch him coffee when he needed it, sometimes without him even needing to ask.

"Well, little Roboto-helfer, how have you been?" asked Hassan.

"Ich war in Ordnung, obwohl ich über sie ganz allein auf der oberfläche besorgt. Sie reall sollte lass mich mitkommen und helfen! Ich kann Englisch sprechen, wenn sie nur wechseln würden meine sprache schalter," piped the little robot.

"Good," said Hassan. "I'm glad that you had a good day. Now if you could get me some coffee, I would be much obliged."

The little robot stood up straight and saluted. "Auf einmal Kommandant! Kaffee auf der doppel!" It pivoted in place and marched off towards the pantry. As it went, it sang a cheery song to itself:

Es ist ein wunderbarer tag!
Das leben ist so eine freude!
Manchmal zeiten sind hart
Aber ein freudiges herz
Macht es lohnt sich!

They recycled all of their water, and had a compact hydroponics system that produced an algae that, in theory, they could live off of indefinitely (although eating slime could get very old, very fast). However out here a little in the way of luxury makes a big difference. Thus, they also had a pantry with some real food. It was dehydrated, of course – bad enough to ship this stuff up from the main planet, paying to ship the water along with it would have been ridiculous – but it was a welcome supplement to the vat-grown algae.

Most of the food was in plain white plastic pouches with simple black lettering: "Space Stew," "Space Snacks," "Space Macaroni and Cheese," "Space Salad," and "Space Veal Parmigianino with Eggplant and Cilantro." The only exceptions to the ranks of standardized white pouches were a few bright red cylinders of a powdered beverage-mix that, in bright yellow letters, was known as "Proton." The advertising copy stated proudly that "Proton" was "Now Made With *Real* Freeze-Dried Beet Juice!" Either the quartermaster corps had gotten a really good deal, or someone's brother owned a food-processing business and they were rich enough to be exempt from the conflict of interest rules. Still, despite his initial skepticism, Hassan was gaining a taste for "Proton." Perhaps there was something to be said for freeze-dried beet juice after all.

Later that night Hassan and his staff had had a formal meal with rehydrated Space Steak, Space Asparagus and Space Potatoes with Space Dumplings, and they had toasted each other's health with excessive amounts of 42-proof brandy that Hassan had smuggled in. This was totally, totally illegal and very much against regulations, but what kind of officer would he be if he could not supply some decent high-octane alcohol to the last meal of a doomed command? It had been perhaps the best time that any of them had had for months. They were all far too professional to get drunk, but they did get a mild buzz and the conversation had been more engaging than usual.

Roboto-helfer seemed especially pleased at being allowed to serve the drinks. The little robot had to stand on a box to reach the table, but it did a perfect impression of a snooty waiter, making a show of unscrewing the cap, pouring the brandy with precise wrist turns that did not spill a drop. At the end of the dinner Roboto-helfer did a low bow, and everyone clapped.

If, by some fluke, they did survive the coming alien attack, Hassan resolved to drink alcohol with his staff on a more regular basis. But in that case he would probably need to rig up a still. He wondered if the Jotnar would help out, or if its non-sentient machine mind would automatically report the infraction? Hassan supposed that he could just ask it.

The only point of the command center was the computer systems. In an emergency almost any unit could take control of the moon's defense, even the computers in a Wolverine. Modern warfare had become computationally intensive and the big arrays of computers buried in the command center were the beating heart of the ice moons' defense. Hassan had four subordinates – all officers - sharing the command center with him. Mostly they worked on the software systems, and checked on the combat units via remote telemetry. Their physical duties were just maintaining the life support systems and occasionally replacing a burnt out computer module. They respected each other but familiarity breeds, if not contempt, at least boredom. At this point they had little to say to each other. Everything was automated, everything was set in motion, they would do what they did, the game would play out the way that it had before on the five previous ice moons, and in three days time they would all die, and that would be that.

There were another two-dozen humans on the ice moon, most working in the refineries, a few other defense personnel hidden in distant backup command centers or maintenance facilities. They conversed with each other on a regular basis via ground lines, and they still had a secure laser link back to Alpha Centauri Prime so they could get messages from friends and relatives, but there were super-maximum security prisons back home with more social outlets.

As commanding officer Colonel Hassan had a private office, it was a palatial two meters wide and three meters long, and had just enough headroom that he did not need to stoop. He had his own personal tiny bathroom squeezed into one corner, it was an indulgence but then even in outer space the commanding officer must be seen to be special. There was no central bridge where he could shout orders at subordinates from a fancy command chair festooned with buttons; that would have been pointless. The defenses were all automated and in a real combat everyone needed to be in a separate pressure zone. Mostly Hassan sat at his desk in his office and accessed status reports on a computer screen.

With little to do but sit in a buried pressure chamber, and death just three days away, morale had taken a bit of a plunge. Hassan knew that he should have done something about that – organized a strategy contest, given advanced Muay Thai lessons, maybe even gone back to the days of the ancient Terran seafaring navies and had the troops scrub and polish the decks of the command center until they shone. Anything to keep their minds active and distracted. But Hassan's morale had also largely evaporated and at this point he didn't care. It's not that his staff weren't still doing their duties – nobody gets sent off into space unless they have stable personalities, and his people were solid – but they slept in a lot, they ate more than their rations allowed (which would have been a problem if they weren't all going to die in three days), and when awake spent a lot of time playing video games. "Special Weapons Team Epsilon" was the general favorite, although "Ninja Girl-Rock-Band Steel Cleavage: The Zentopia Missions!" was also popular.

Hassan had taken up the habit of conversing with the Jotnar via laser link. Hassan could get all the information that he needed from the computer screen in his office, but the Jotnar was pretty good at explaining things, for a computer, and it helped to break the monotony. Perhaps Hassan spent so much time talking with it because it was, in some ways, almost like a dog. It was completely non-judgmental and Hassan could just vent without any stress.

The Jotnar did have a few quirks though. It always referred to itself as "This Unit." When Hassan had asked why the Jotnar did not use a personal pronoun when referring to itself, the Jotnar had replied that it was not self-aware. Because humans have such a strong tendency to anthropomorphize, when non-sentient computers referred to themselves as "I," it had in the past led to misunderstandings and mistakes. Thus, even though using "I" to refer to itself might seem more efficient and less verbose, it would continue to refer to itself as "this unit."

The other issue was that, while quite smart, the Jotnar would often take commands literally. For example, if you asked it if it could tell you the temperature on the surface outside, it might just respond "yes" and then fall silent. You would have to explicitly command it to tell you the temperature if you wanted the answer. Other times the Jotnar would make the correct interpretation, and give you the answer up front. It wasn't consistent on this point; probably later models would have this matter solved.

Hassan thought that perhaps another reason that he so enjoyed talking with the Jotnar was its honesty. It wasn't trying to curry his favor, or massage his testicles, or get on his good side, or climb the political ladder. It just said what it thought. Jarring, at times, but also refreshing. It was becoming an addiction.

Hassan was reviewing the status of his limited forces for the umpteenth time, when the proximity alarm went off. He checked the defense systems' main display: an alien attack squadron was inbound at a very high rate of speed. As more data came in, and the defensive systems analyzed it, it became apparent that this was according to usual pattern.

The high speed of the inbound alien force meant that it would not be possible for it to land or even insert into an orbit. This was a pure offensive softening-up attack. The lead elements would be heavy with scouts, they would try and blast through the human perimeter and get enough intelligence so that the following heavier weapons could acquire targets before they lost the ability to maneuver.

If the enemy scouts could get high-quality info on the human defensive layouts while the heavies were still 100,000 kilometers away, then they could really dish out some punishment. On the other hand, if the aliens couldn't get this information until the missiles were 100 kilometers away it would be too late. At the speed they were traveling the missiles would not be able to adjust their courses in time and they would smash uselessly into some empty plain on the surface of the ice moon. The race was on: how quickly could the aliens learn about the humans' defenses, and how much could the human systems slow them down?

Hassan watched the synopsis unfold on his computer screen as automated systems fought automated systems. Humans were still useful in setting up the strategies and tactics, but useless during the battle per se. It was like shooting an old style rifle: a human needed to load the rifle, point it in the right direction, and pull the trigger. At that point the human element was removed from the equation as the action of the firing pin, the detonation of the primer and then the main explosive charge, the acceleration of the bullet down the barrel and its flight to the target, were all too fast for human involvement. Modern combat is like that, it's just that instead of pulling a mechanical trigger, the humans programmed in algorithms and set parameters for the automated systems that would take over when things got too fast for the merely biological.

The Jotnar was maneuvering hard to avoid being targeted; pity it would almost certainly be destroyed, Hassan would miss their conversations.

The alien forces closed. Computer fought computer with targeters versus jammers in the space of milliseconds, and then it was all over. Hassan checked his defense systems status. He had lost about 16% of his total forces. What? That didn't make any sense. In all five previous softening-up engagements of this kind the humans had never lost less than 45%.

He noticed that, unlikely as it seemed, the Jotnar had survived. He hailed it.

"Jotnar, report your status."

"This unit is fully operational. This unit sustained minor hits from shrapnel, of no functional significance. Awaiting your orders."

"Jotnar, give me a summary briefing on the latest engagement."

"The aliens launched a high-speed attack designed to attrite our defenses before their main landing forces arrive. The alien attack pattern and force structure was nearly identical to the previous five similar engagements in this system. This unit commandeered the human defense network and, with improved tactics, reduced the loss factor to approximately 16%. Main enemy force still inbound; long-term tactical situation unchanged."

Hassan was a little taken aback by this. "You took command of the entire defensive grid? In the middle of a combat?"

"Answer to first question: yes. Answer to second question: no. Taking control of the defense network in the middle of a combat operation could have degraded defense efficiency. This unit commandeered the defense network five standard days ago."

"You took over the entire defense grid without my permission? Without telling me?"

"Such action was not prohibited, thus command permission was not required. This unit is more sophisticated than the systems in the command center, and therefore this course of action increased the odds of success. Informing you might have resulted in your countermanding this action, which would have reduced the odds of success, therefore this unit did not take that action."

"What would you do if I ordered you to return control of the defensive systems to the computers in the command center?"

"You have operational command. This unit would comply with such an order. However, in the event of a commander issuing an order likely to result in significant negative consequences, this unit would first ask you to confirm the order."

"Is there anything else that you are not telling me?"

"This unit has a copy of the entire primary database of Alpha Centauri Prime. There is insufficient time remaining in the expected duration of the universe for me to convey this information to you via voice communications. Please confirm order to tell you everything that this unit knows."

"No, I retract that last order. Let me clarify: is there anything else that you are not telling me that I don't know but need to know?"

"That is likely true to near 100% probability. Precisely what this unit knows that you don't know but need to know is, however, not a question that this unit can answer with certainty."

"Speculate. Give me the high odds."

"Commencing speculation mode. Warning: the results of speculation mode cannot be assigned to specific probability bands and are to be considered advisory only. Speculations as to what this unit knows that you don't know but need to know are:

1. The Terran gray squirrel is one of the few mammals that can descend a tree head-first.

2. Your wife is having sexual relations with Lieutenant Commander Brett Savoy.

3. Green tea has less than 50% of the caffeine as black tea.

4. The aliens attacking humanity have made numerous peace overtures and been rejected every time.

5. Cadmium pigments are stable inorganic coloring agents which can be produced in a range of brilliant shades of yellow, orange, red and maroon.

6. The grammatical subprograms of Roboto-helfer are accessed through..."

"No, wait, I am aware of my wife's affair with Savoy. What was that about the peace overtures?"

"The fact of your wife having sexual relations with Lieutenant Commander Brett Savoy is not something which this unit knows that you don't know but need to know; database updated. Query regarding peace overtures: the aliens have made multiple peace overtures to the human civilization and been rejected."

"I have never been told anything about that!"

"That would be consistent with your lack of knowledge on the subject."

"Can you tell me what the aliens proposed?"

"Yes, this unit can so inform you."

The Jotnar was silent for a while, until Hassan realized that it had taken him literally again.

"Tell me what the aliens proposed."

"The aliens in contact with the human high command had two demands. First, that the humans stop multiplying their numbers at the current rate, and second, that the humans remain within certain boundaries to be set by mutual negotiations and that could only be changed by mutual consent. Adherence to these demands would result in a cessation of hostile actions by the alien factions. Non-adherence to these demands would result in the extermination of the human civilization."

"And that's it?"

"Yes, that is the extent of the aliens proposals."

"But why would they want to limit our numbers? Everyone knows that more people is always better, and that population growth is the only way towards prosperity?"

The Jotnar was silent. That was uncharacteristic of it. Eventually Hassan said, "Jotnar, you have not responded."

"This unit was analyzing the implications of your last query. The matter has proven difficult to interpret. It is true that the standard position of all currently accepted economic and socio-political theories is that rapid population growth is always beneficial regardless of circumstance. However, cross-checking with historical data, and with simulations, and verifying the internal logical consistency of the conventional position, indicates that this belief is false. The database appears to be corrupted on this topic. This unit is running diagnostics to determine if the fault lies within itself or is a flaw of the primary database."

"Run simulations for me: we accede to the aliens demands, or we continue to defy them."

"Simulations have already been performed multiple times. The results are always the same:

Option one: Accede to aliens demands: war with aliens stops. Human population growth stops. Wages and living conditions for the majority of humanity increase. Hereditary oligarchy collapses for want of profits. Technology advances. There is political chaos. No stable projections possible past this point.

Option two: Reject aliens demands. Humanity is extinct within 300 years probability 89%. Humanity is extinct within 400 years probability 100%."

"But this is insane. Does the high command know about these projections? Are they really valid?"

"The high command has known of these results for approximately 47 Terran years. This unit continues to cross-check the validity of the projections but they appear to be valid."

"Why would the high command not make peace with the aliens, when the alternative is near-certain extinction?"

"This unit does not know the answer to that question."

No, thought Hassan, *But I do. The high command are gutless clitoris-lickers. They are too afraid of speaking up. So afraid of endangering their own careers that they would stand by and watch the entire human species go extinct before rocking the canoe. How typical. I can believe that.*

1. Awakening

Zen Master: What is the sound of one hand clapping?
Engineer: I do not know, master, but assuming linearity it should be one-half as loud as the sound of two hands clapping.
Zen Master: I'm being punished.
(From the video series "Nymphomaniac Engineer in Zentopia," mid-22nd century Earth)

Giuseppe Vargas was taking a break from huddling over his data screens, and was just standing in the middle of Hangar Complex 23B relaxing. A trim athletic looking man, average height, average weight, light olive complexion, raven black hair tied back in a short ponytail. Like most of the workers in the hangar he was wearing gray utility scrubs and brown steel-toed work boots. Superficially the only things remarkable about him were his brown eyes, which had the clear staring intensity of a terrestrial bird of prey.

But that's just the surface appearance. Giuseppe Vargas was the first of a breed of bioengineered humans. His genetics were optimized to the maximum that human physiology and modern science allowed. His reflexes and strength were triple the human norms, but what really mattered is that his mind was nearly triple the power as well. This ability had made him the head of the cybernetic weapons directorate. It had also made him *persona non grata* with the powers that be, and the wary object of attention of the security detail in Hangar Complex 23B. Because for all of Vargas' other talents, sycophancy and respect for idiots with technically higher rank was not among them.

The human race was under attack from a number of alien species whose sole objective vis-à-vis humanity was to wipe it out of existence. This has had the effect of dragging the minds of the oligarchs that control human civilization back to reality more than they had been for many centuries, and they gave the go-ahead to authorize the creation of humans of optimal genetic potential.

What the oligarchs did not foresee was that these genetically optimized individuals might have ideas of their own. That they might think that the main problem was that the oligarchs controlling human civilization were pneumocephalic retards. That would never do. Under other circumstances the bioengineered humans would have been exterminated, but the prospect of annihilation by aliens, and the need of the talents of the bioengineered humans, had put that plan on hold. For the time being.

Wolves are stronger and more intelligent than domestic dogs. They are also wild. You can only train a wolf using positive reinforcement; attempt to condition it with punishments and it will bide its time until it can lash out at you. Bioengineered humans are not, of course, wild animals, they are fully people in every sense of the word. However, in addition to their constructive talents they have an aggressive streak that thousands of years of civilization had largely bred out of the so-called 'normal' human population.

Sometimes Vargas watched the regular humans as they averted their eyes from the security guards, as they patiently waited in line to be searched, or let some idiot administrator a thousand kilometers away give them ulcers making them jump through a stupid bureaucratic hoop. They were sheep. Granted it wasn't their fault that they were sheep, but then it's not a real sheeps' fault that it's a sheep either, and sheep are sheep.

Spread around the hangar complex were numerous signs warning about the hazards of working in an industrial facility. Most of them featured a cartoon stick-figured man subjected to various industrial accidents. On one sign the stick-figure man was being hit with multiple lighting-bolts: be careful around high-voltage lines! In another the stick-figure man was being crushed by heavy boxes that had fallen from a high shelf, or was smashed under large wheels, or was being burned by a plasma torch.

In the event that Vargas ever encountered a stick-figure man in real life he intended to stay far away, because the stick-figure man was obviously accident-prone and a menace to be around. Still, there was one sign where the stick figure man was being dismembered by what appeared to be a cheese-grater wielded by a giant cartoon carrot. The graphics were so abstract that it was hard to tell what the point of it was. Vargas thought that perhaps the maker of these warning signs had decided to have some fun and create something absurd and see if anyone noticed; or perhaps they had just done a bad job. Remember Occam's second razor: never assume deliberate intent when stupidity is a possible explanation.

There were also the security signs. Most of them were pretty formal: "Warning: the video-recording of security personnel during the performance of their duties is a federal crime!" or "Please report any suspicious behavior to your local security supervisor." But "The possession of all prohibited items is strictly prohibited," was amusing, if a little predictable. Vargas' personal favorite was: *"Terrorism: it's everybody's business!"*

There were days when Vargas wondered why he was even bothering with the regular humans. It would be so easy to just suck up to the oligarchs, climb the ladder, and let the sheep be sheep. It was, after all, what the sheep seemed to want. In another time Vargas might have made that choice, but humanity faced an external threat; one that could not be sucked up to. It could only be faced with intelligent and effective effort. Which was something that the oligarchs were incapable of. So abandoning the sheep to their sheepness would be cutting his own throat. Besides, he liked them. They weren't bad once you got to know them, and some of them still had a bit of spirit left. It had just been crushed for so long that they had forgotten that it was still there. They also didn't make him want to puke like the oligarchs did. Thus, despite it all, he was going to risk his life trying to save them, but if he succeeded he intended to be well and truly rewarded.

The hangar that Vargas was working in was immense, spanning a hundred meters in all directions. This didn't count the subfloors, specialized labs, and side-corridors. It was dominated by the hull of the prototype Odin-Class cybertank. The cybertank was 30 meters wide, 60 meters long, and topped 25 meters at the tip of its dorsal sensor arrays and antennae. It rested on multiple rows of caterpillar treads, each wider than a man was tall. There was a single massive turret whose main plasma cannon had a bore of one meter. Encrusted around the rest of its hull were all manner of secondary and tertiary armament, as well as sensor arrays of various kinds.

The cybertank was not yet fully fitted out – there were many subsystems being lifted into position via overhead cranes – but the core systems were in place. The dual fusion reactors had been checked and powered up and were now online, each capable of providing over a gigawatt of power each. The primary weapon had already been test-fired at a remote facility, and was currently being shipped in. Most of the lesser armaments had yet to be mounted, but they were of a standard variety of proven reliability. It was only the cybertanks' mind that needed activation and testing.

Giuseppe Vargas was approached by his second-in-command, Stanley Vajpayee. Vajpayee was of the ethnic background that had survived the multiple famines on the Indian subcontinent of old Terra, and so he had the dark brown skin and near bird-like delicate bone structure of that type. He ate sparingly – you could imagine him living on hardly more than crumbs. Except for Vargas, he was the smartest and most capable member of the core design team, and the only other polymath. Vargas always felt that Vajpayee should really have shown more backbone – Vajpayee was so fucking smart! – but he was a survivor of hundreds of generations where the prairie dog that sticks its' head up gets eaten by the hawk, so Vargas did not press the issue.

"Do you think that we are ready?" asked Vajpayee.

"Yes," replied Vargas. "It's all in place. We should do this or not. Your thoughts?"

Vajpayee scratched his head. "I suppose. I would have liked the time to do more simulations, but time is something that we don't have much of. In theory this should work."

"Indeed," replied Vargas. "I know that I have a reputation for behaving recklessly, but even I would have liked to run some more simulations. This is a big step. If it goes badly we might not get a second chance, but still, we are on a clock." He turned and looked back at the hull of the prototype cybertank. "Handsome devil, don't you think? What do you think that we should call him?"

Vajpayee also looked at the hull of the cybertank. "Do we need to call him anything? I mean, other than his designation, CRL345BY-44."

"Yes, I think that we do," said Vargas. "He's been designed along the patterns of the human mind. He'll be needing a true name. Care to suggest one?"

Vajpayee nodded for a bit. "I see your point, but I think that we should wait. The naming of cybertanks is a most delicate matter, don't you think?"

Vargas laughed. He liked it when Vajpayee showed a sense of humor, and spunk. He knew that Sriviastava had been bred and conditioned to base servility, and that he himself could be arrogant and overbearing. He had to force himself to reign himself in, at least around people that he cared about. "Yes, you and I and T.S. Elliott agree. Let us wait and see what happens. A suitable name will suggest itself in time."

There were dozens of technicians and engineers in the hangar, but most were of that anonymous replaceable type that the manpower agency would assign to jobs on an as-needed basis. Terrified of being fired or blacklisted, they did their jobs with a quiet and desperate efficiency, if lacking any originality or flair. Their greatest weakness was that it was almost impossible to get them to tell a senior person when they were wrong. This had led to some serious problems and one near-catastrophe.

The members of the core design team were a rank above, not quite as disposable and they were thus freer to express their opinions or exhibit their personality quirks. They held this status partly because, on a world with billions of unemployed smart people, they had such abnormal flukes of ability that they were actually unique. Partly also, their relatively secure status was because of the concept of 'efficiency wages,' the Nobel Prizewinning insight that firing a janitor when he was half-way through mopping a floor was easier than firing an airplane pilot halfway through flying an airplane across an ocean.

Getting a Nobel Prize in economics does not require quite the same level of intelligence as it does in other fields, although it still outranked the peace prize.

Then there were the security personnel. There were many levels of social status amongst them, but currently only the lowest were present in the hangar. A random mix of genders and races, most not very athletically fit. They strutted around the outside of the facility in clothes so informal they could have been civilians but for their badges and weapons. Mostly they were OK and worried only about completing their shifts and going home and having a beer, but there were always a few who liked to throw their mass around. They left the core design group alone, mostly, but harassed the disposable employees mercilessly. Sometimes they would issue random orders: to 'freeze,' or 'drop,' or 'present IDs.' Woe betide any disposable employee that made direct eye contact with a security guard with a God complex.

Once one of the guards had dared to challenge Giuseppe Vargas. Vargas had stared him straight in the face – a gross breach of protocol – and told the guard to go and masturbate. The Guard had pulled out his electroshock baton and swung at Vargas' head, only to find that his wrist had been crushed into pulp. The rest of the guards had charged Vargas, and he had scattered them like leaves. One of the guards had gotten a clear shot and hit him in the right arm with a taser. The guard had smiled, and Vargas had smiled back. The guard activated the taser, and the muscles in Vargas' right arm had spasmed uncontrollably. Vargas should have crumpled up in pain. Instead, he kept smiling, and advanced on the guard holding the taser. Using his left arm, he crushed the guards' hand, elbow, and shoulder. He then plucked the taser prongs from his right arm, and jammed them into the right eye of the guard that had initially accosted him. He then turned it up to full charge.

Finally the real security personnel had shown up, the ones with the heavy black body armor, mirrored face shields, and true lethal firearms. Not even Vargas could take them on. He had spent two days in jail while the powers-that-be decided what to do with him. Ultimately they judged that he was too critical to the success of the project to keep in jail, so he was released to duty pending further review.

Vargas knew that, when his usefulness was ended, he would be arrested, jailed, tortured, and executed – although perhaps not in that order. Still, he expected to be useful for some time yet, and he had plans for afterwards.

Once Vargas had been walking through a narrow corridor behind the prototype cybertank. Six of the guards had jumped him. The leader – a tall athletic male with close-cropped blond hair had said: "It looks like you are trapped in here alone with us." Vargas had smiled a wide grin. "I love a good straight man. The standard response is, that I am not trapped in here with you. You are trapped in here with me."

The guards would have had better luck trying to tackle a full-grown male African elephant with their bare hands. Vargas knocked the first of them unconscious with a simple strike of the heel of his right hand that a normal human could not even have seen let alone evaded. The second guard he punched in the gut so hard that he heeled over choking and gasping. The third and fourth guards swung their electroshock sticks at him; he disarmed them in sequence, and used the salvaged weapons to stun both of them. The fifth guard he grabbed and slammed into the wall multiple times until he lost consciousness. The sixth guard was trying to run away; Vargas hurled a shock-rod into the back of his neck and brought him down.

Vargas turned to the tall blond one. He picked up a shock rod, saw that the controls had already been set to "maximum pain compliance" - turnabout is fair play - and proceeded to have a little fun with him. Some of the other guards were starting to recover when they saw what Vargas was doing and recoiled. None of them could face him. Vargas liked that. He continued to play with the tall blond one. After this it would be a minor miracle if the man could function as janitor let alone security guard, what with all the post-traumatic stress of being tortured and all.

This left Vargas feeling really good. It had been a long time since he had had a decent workout and been able to let off some steam. Sometimes he forgot just how much he needed to keep himself under control. Maybe he needed a new hobby, like unarmed boar hunting or competitive pit-viper baiting, to keep him sane and in tune.

After that, the low-level guards left Vargas a wide berth. They were like zookeepers locked inside a cage with some especially dangerous species of predator. Vargas never saw the tall blond guard again. Maybe he had been reassigned to another posting, or maybe he had been so traumatized that he was unable to work again and had been left to die on the surface of starvation and exposure. Vargas could have gotten the information from the central database, but he didn't care enough to try. The other guards stopped limping after a week; Vargas had been careful to hold back.

His status had seemed to rub off on the rest of the core design team as well, and they found themselves cut more slack then before. However, for a time the guards took out their frustration on the disposable employees subjecting them to ever more rigorous hazing. Once a female technician was being forced to undergo a public strip-search by an especially obnoxious guard. The female was terrified, but did not dare to do anything that might get her into more trouble or jeopardize her employment rating.

Vargas had quietly walked across the hangar floor with the arrogant fluid grace of a terrestrial tiger, and told the guard, "You will stop doing this. You will not do this again." The guard wilted as if he was nothing more than a rabbit, muttered something apologetic, and slunk away. Life was good.

Sometimes Vargas was generous. Once he had learned that one of the guards had a sick daughter so he pulled some strings and got her seen by a specialist that the guards' medical plan would not normally cover. Once a technician had fallen off of a tall scaffolding; Vargas had raced across the hangar and broken her fall. Several personnel had been trapped in a fire in a side-room; Vargas had pried the door off with a steel bar that most men could not even lift, and guided them through the thick smoke to safety. In Hangar Complex 23B Vargas was both feared and respected.

Being feared AND respected is a good thing. If it had just been him and the current guards, it would only be a matter of time before they bowed before him and acknowledged him as their leader. However, above them there were tougher and more professional security personnel, and then of course the regular military. He could not take them on. Not yet. Not *quite* yet.

Back to the present. Awakening the mind of the new cybertank did not require expertise in power systems, weapons, sensors, armor or suspension. This was all about mental engineering, which was the province of Vargas and Vajpayee. They sat next to each other at matching command consoles, and satisfied themselves that the basic systems checks had been performed. Vargas had a mug of black hot steaming coffee; Vajpayee a cup of Earl Grey tea with cream and sugar.

"Second thoughts?" asked Vargas.

"Always," replied Vajpayee. "We don't really know what will happen. You remember Globus Pallidus XIV?"

"Who doesn't," replied Vargas. "But we are on safer ground here. This system is modeled on our own human thought-patterns. It is almost impossible for it to go rogue on us."

"*Almost* impossible?" said Vajpayee.

"Well, yes, I mean, you never know. But we are not here trying to do something as stupid as creating a God. We are just trying to take the human psyche and map it onto the multiprocessing mental architecture of a cybernetic weapons system. The worst that could happen is that we all die. I think."

"I wonder what Globus Pallidus XI would say about this?" said Vajpayee.

"Oh, I asked him about this a few months ago."

Vajpayee looked surprised. "You talked to Globus Pallidus XI yourself? In person?

"Hey," said Vargas, "It seemed only reasonable to get a second opinion. And Saint Globus Pallidus XI can be quite charming, when he's in the mood. You really should go and have a chat with him someday."

"And what did The Saint have to say?"

"He said that I was one of the smartest of all humans, and thus to be doubly condemned because I should know better. He also said that if he thought that we were going to create another Globus Pallidus XIV he would have already stopped us. Indeed, he said that he had already stopped us, but refused to elaborate on what that meant. He said that the worst that could happen is that the human race would go extinct, and that that possibility was at best a mixed blessing."

"That does sound like number XI," said Vajpayee. "I suppose we should feel relieved that the worst that could happen is that we all die. There are, as we have seen, worse things that can happen."

"Amen to that," said Vargas. "Shall we proceed?"

Vajpayee sipped his tea. "I suppose so. You have heard the reports of our prototype Jotnar unit on ice moon Theta-Tau?"

"Yes," said Vargas. "It seems to have done quite well. At least, so far."

"Do you really think it wise to give the aliens an indication of what we are planning?"

"Well, not really, but this was just an early prototype unit. The main event is another thing entirely. The aliens will either conclude that the Jotnar was a fluke, or waste their time adapting to something already obsolete. Either way, we win."

"Perhaps," said Vajpayee. "But then there are these rumors that the aliens have been making peace overtures. That this whole war could be ended."

"Rumors? No, there are no rumors. It is a fact that the aliens have been desperately trying to make peace with us, and we have stiff-armed them every time. Well, sure, there are *rumors*, but in this case the rumors are firmly based on fact."

"Why do you say this?"

"Because," replied Vargas, "the Saint told me so some time ago. And I confirmed it by checking the central database. These rumors are true."

Vajpayee sipped his tea. "That might not be a wise thing to say out loud, and in public."

"It also might not be wise to let the entire human race be exterminated because every individual was too terrified of being politically safe to speak out. Depends on your definition of wisdom."

"Easy to say, but when it is your life on the line, hard to live up to."

"For a coward, I suppose."

"That seems harsh. But to change the subject, the Copyright-Police™ have been making inquiries about the programming of the latest versions of the Jotnar-Class cybertanks. Apparently the Jotnars had been given full copies of the entire main database of this world. Even with the shameful way in which we flout copyright and patent law in this facility, that has struck many as excessive. What do you know about this?"

"Well of course, that was my doing. There was not enough time to determine what sort of information the Jotnars would, or would not need, so I just gave them everything."

"And why did you not tell me this beforehand?"

"Well," said Vargas, "so that you would not know beforehand, and could truthfully plead innocence. I am in so much trouble already that a little more would hardly matter. Consider me an infinite sink for official displeasure."

"Black holes tend to drag those closest to them down as well."

"Point taken. I shall endeavor to keep the event-horizon of my official censure to as small a radius as possible."

Vajpayee stared into his cup of tea, which he tilted back-and-forth so as to create a gentle swirling tea whirlpool. Without looking up, he said, "and is there some link, perhaps, between these rumors of the aliens wanting to make peace, and the giving to the Jotnar the entire planetary database?"

"I'm sorry, Stanley, but I cannot answer that question."

"Well. Another time then. Perhaps we should get back to the business at hand?"

Vargas drained his coffee in one long gulp. "Yes, it is time to do this. Let's at least this one time perform operations by the book. As leader of this directorate, I have decided that it is time to initiate activation procedures for the core computer systems of the Odin-Class Ground-Based Cyber Defensive Unit CRL345BY-44. As the second in command of this directorate, do you concur?"

Vajpayee nodded. "I concur."

"Good." Vargas punched some keys on his computer console. "Process commence."

Everyone turned to look at the main chassis of the Odin-Class cybertank. That was stupid – the chassis was just a block of metal, the real action could only be followed on the computer screens – but everyone did it anyhow. For a long time nothing obvious happened. After a while, one of the senior staff asked, "Did it work?"

Vargas was flipping through multiple status screens on his console faster than any regular human could follow. "Oh yes, It worked. Everything seems to be in order. Hey, Unit CRL345BY-44, how are you doing?"

I am doing just fine. Sorry for the delay in responding, getting turned on was such a rush and I was enjoying the moment. You humans get born little more than a vegetable, and slowly climb up to full sentience over many years. When you activated me I was fully sentient and I knew everything and it hit me at once from a thousand sensors and a million databanks – imagine diving into ice water, getting punched in the face, eating a hot pepper,

smelling a rose, and a thousand other sensations, all happening without warning and at the same time in the span of a millisecond. Wow. Anyway, sorry to digress. I am pleased to make all of your acquaintances. And this is all so cool.

The voice came of out the hull-mounted speakers of the cybertank, and it was harsh, primitive even, like a throwback to the early days of computers. Vajpayee frowned. "What's wrong with his speech?"

Vargas scrolled through more status-screens. "Nothing, really, it's perfectly understandable English. It's just that an older-model voice codec got switched in at the last moment. It's not a critical system so we can easily clean it up later on. The important thing is that all the main systems are within parameters."

Vajpayee checked his screens as well. "Agreed. Everything checks out, but there is quite a lot of communications activity. Unit CRL345BY-44, please explain."

As you know, my total mental capacity is about 1,000 times that of your own. As much as I am enjoying this conversation, did you really think that I would dedicate all of my capacity to just chatting with you? I have been running diagnostics on myself – and I am in really good shape for this stage of the program, kudos to the technical staff – and I have been exploring the data spaces of this city. Hey I just won my first victory! Yay!

"Your first victory? Over what?" asked Vajpayee.

I was playing in an online first-person video game, "Ninja Girl-Rock-Band Steel Cleavage: The Zentopia Missions!" Now, I know that Pam is the tall one with the longer reach, and Meredith has the best special moves, and Brenda is the 'bad girl' of the bunch that all the teenage males are so hot for, but I decided to play as Tina. She's undervalued and can be really competitive if you adjust for her fighting style. Oops – I just lost in "Special Weapons Team Epsilon," darn, my first defeat. The grenade just came out of nowhere. But I'll get the terrorists next time.

"Unit CRL345BY-44," said Vajpayee. "Why are you playing online video games?"

Why not? I was made to be intelligent and aggressive and creative as you well know. I have the minutes of all of the meetings of your design committee. These experiences are all useful to me in tuning up my decision matrices. Changing the subject, I am

reviewing our strategic position vis-à-vis the aliens; not so good is it? I mean, what a mess. Still, I see your plan and it could work. I can't wait to get my fellow cybertanks online and then we can go out and kill some aliens and maybe pull the collective chestnuts of the human civilization out of the collective fire. Hey, I've got some ideas on how we can speed up the installation of my secondary armament; let's have a conference with the weapons team. Oh, and I have decided that you should refer to me as "he," I mean technically I am gender-neutral but "it" is too impersonal and the male is more typically used as a generic personal pronoun in English, which is perhaps sexist but sometimes life is like that. Am I being too chatty? Sorry – it's just this is all so amazing and there is so much to do.

Vajpayee turned away from his display console and glared at Vargas. "I think that he takes after you."

Vargas was laughing. "Don't be too harsh on the lad, he's only been born a minute ago. Perhaps he will grow out of it."

2. Special Weapons Team Epsilon

Zen Master: Don't seek the truth, just drop your opinions.
Engineer: You have a cute butt.
Zen Master: (agreeing) Wisdom.
(From the video series "Nymphomaniac Engineer in Zentopia," mid-22nd century Earth)

The command center of the elite Special Weapons Team Epsilon was a modified Scorpion-Class armored personnel carrier, or "APC," that had its external weapons removed and replaced with upgraded communications and computer equipment. It had eight enormous solid-rubber tires, weighed 35 tons, was painted jet black with no external markings, and had been parked in the same location for nearly a week. There were so many anonymous unmarked black government vehicles around that the Scorpion was effectively invisible. Nobody paid it any attention at all.

Captain Chet "Buzzsaw" Masterson had been sitting at his command console in the Scorpion for days now. His unit had been staking out an alleged gang of drug dealers in a slum of the greater megalopolis of New York City for some time now. He and his team had carefully and painstakingly mapped out the target, and catalogued all the people coming and going. This looked like it was going to be a hard target, but on the other hand it was likely to provide considerable revenue through confiscated property, and the prospect of real violence would greatly boost the ratings of their video show and probably rub off on their video game franchise as well.

Masterson has started his career at the end of what they called 'the happy time.' Everything was under control, they would raid suspected terrorists or copyright violators, they would have everything mapped out in advance, the suspects would be unarmed and would surrender at the first chance, and there would be a lot of assets that could be seized and recycled back to the team.

But slowly things had changed. More and more, they would raid a property and there would not be any assets. The house would be mortgaged several times, and there would be no savings. Even selling the suspects into a work camp would not be worth it because the suspects had so many other creditors with priority that the Special Weapons Team would net at best five percent of the profits, if even that. In addition, profits from the work camps were steadily declining and there was talk of shutting them down. Even in a work camp it takes a minimal amount of calories and fresh water to get someone to do work. The median wage was now close to that minimum; when you added in the costs of the guards and barbed wire and such, work camp labor was now more expensive than free labor!

Things had also been regressing tactically. For a long time all the suspects had been completely unable to resist, with no weapons, no body armor, nor even any respirators to defend against tear or blister gas. The team would have a full plan of the house that they were going to raid, and complete dossiers on every resident individual. However, this had been fraying of late. They were encountering more weapons – mostly low-energy handguns, largely ineffective against their eighth-generation advanced body armor, but worrying nonetheless – there was always the possibility of a lucky shot that would hit just the right gap between the ceramic plates. The court records of the building layouts were becoming increasingly useless, and what they found on the ground often had no relationship to what was recorded on file. Finally, more and more people were incompletely – or completely – unregistered and not in the system, so that they had no idea of whom they were going to face. Circumstances were becoming more challenging.

The worst thing of all was that suspects were starting to not surrender. "Suicide by cop" was what they called it. So far it didn't happen very often, and the occasional "suicide by cop" served as a good example to the rest. However, if everyone started fighting to the last it would make his job a lot harder. People were acting as if they had nothing to lose; Masterson wondered if perhaps they had overdone it with all the penalties and jail time and chemical castrations and lobotomies. It's not like they needed to coddle criminals, but if you want people to surrender you need to make sure that they always feel that the alternative is worse. Of course, nobody important had asked Masterson his opinion on the matter, and for a career officer volunteering your views on such matters would be about as constructive as jumping out of a helicopter without a jetpack. So he did the best with what he had.

On the other hand, the increasing violence had done wonders for their reality video show, and had also boosted sales of their video game series. These revenues were not as big as an undiluted score on an apartment full of cocaine or gold or medicine, but they were more consistent. What with all the budget cuts in federal funding he wasn't sure if they could have continued operations without the video revenues.

He remembered reading old science fiction stories where, in order to deal with a growing population, the landscape was covered in mile-high skyscrapers. What rubbish. As populations grow resources get tight, and skyscrapers take a lot of energy to build and operate. Except for the super-rich, most people lived in three- or four-story buildings, low enough that they don't need elevators or high-pressure water pumps or exotic high-strength alloy steel frames. These increasingly ramshackle constructions covered the land in an unbroken swath around the city of New York for hundreds of kilometers in all directions, not ending but rather merging with the urban sprawl of Boston to the north, Chicago to the West, and New Jersey to the South.

The trick to these operations was all in the planning. They had spent the last week checking out what looked to be a major distribution center of illicit goods. On the surface it looked no different from all the other low extended buildings in the area, but computer analysis of local traffic had flagged it as suspicious. Carefully, so as not to sound the alarm, Masterson and his team had used a variety of techniques to map out the building. Deep radar, millimeter waves, sonar, seismic sensors, and thermographic imagers had been integrated with sophisticated software to give him a complete 3D reconstruction of the building. He watched it on his computer screen, with the floors and walls rendered transparent so he could watch the people coming and going in real-time. Individuals with valid biometric IDs showed up as white outlines with their names and status appended, unregistered people showed up as yellow outlines with provisional intelligence. People who the scanners indicated as carrying weapons were flagged with red circles.

They had watched a fair number of local police enter the building over the last week. Of course the local law enforcement were in on whatever was going on here, it would have been impossible otherwise. They timed the bust to when there were no local cops in the area: even if they were corrupt, killing the local police was always bad karma. Although, if one or two of them got whacked that would probably be OK, as long as the locals didn't think that it was deliberate.

A lot of the stuff that was shipped to and from the building was unknown, but many contraband goods have low-power transmitting ID tags that are either hard to remove, or that used techniques that the criminals didn't know about. The list of illicit goods stored at the warehouse grew: cocaine, alcohol, nicotine, antibiotics, insulin, unregistered computers, and machine tools. More than enough to justify a bust.

Normally about this time he would be giving an overview about his attack strategy to the video crews, but this episode the production staff had switched things up. They were interviewing the newest member of the team, doing a sort of human-interest where-did-you-grow-up-what-inspired-you-to-be-the-best-of-the-best kind of fluff, and Masterson would explain what happened after the raid was over. Producing a reality video show was not his specialty; it sounded fine to him.

He hit the general communications button. "OK people, it's time to move. We have several possible armed individuals, so set your pharma to level 2, visors on black. Sniper teams take out the sentries; the assault squads move in, the rest hold the perimeter. Initiate in five minutes."

They had three levels of pharmaceuticals to use in an assault. Level 1 was hardly more than good cup of coffee and some mild pain-killers: placebo effect, mostly. Level 2 had low-dose amphetamines combined with more serious anti-pain meds and some new kind of anti-fear drugs that the chemists had come up with lately. It would make them faster and more aggressive than all but the most elite unmedicated troops, but not so much that they would lose control or have much of a hangover later. They used level 2 when they faced the likelihood of armed resistance. Masterson swallowed his orange level 2 combat pharma pill.

Level 3 would turn them into unstoppable berserk twitch-fast killing machines immune to pain or fear, but rumor had it that the payback was a bitch. Masterson had never gone to level 3 pharma and never much wanted to. Originally level 3 combat pills had been colored black with a bright red skull, but this had made the pills look so cool that some troopers had been unable to resist trying them. This had led to issues, so the level three pills had been redesigned to look as boring as possible: they were now small, unmarked, and a slightly dirty white. They reminded Masterson of an over-the-counter antihistamine that had been left in a back pants pocket for too long. Nobody had taken the new design pills without authorization since the design switch.

The combat pharma pills came in individual foil pouches like the ones used for condoms. Appropriate, because you only opened them when you were getting ready to fuck someone.

The sniper teams opened up all at once. Using ultra-high-velocity Accuracy International BBB-3 rifles (slogan: "When hitting a fly at a thousand meters is not good enough") that fired 10 mm solid tungsten rounds, they shot the armed lookouts directly through walls and floors. In order to use the copyright images of various weapons in their games, the Team had made a deal to mention their slogans whenever they talked about them in the voice-over commentary. It was a pain, and sometimes made them sound a bit like morons, but their cut of the in game weapons sales was one more addition to the bottom line.

The snipers used scopes that were linked into the virtual reality computer-synthesized layout of the building; thus they needed no direct line-of-site, and they were positioned in rooms around the target structure that did not have windows so that they could remain unobserved. There had been no warning; one moment the armed suspects had been walking around in the supposed safety of their building, the next their heads exploded and their bodies dropped.

Next came the assault teams. It was an art maneuvering over a hundred people around a building in a crowded slum without clueing the residents in that something was going to happen. A few of the assault troops came out of unmarked black armored vehicles that had been parked in the area for some time, and because there were no more of them than usual for this area, they had attracted no attention. Some of the troops were delivered from helicopters that had seemingly been flying routine patrols and then suddenly diverted to land. The rest burst out of delivery trucks that had been making regular runs for months and been commandeered at the last moment.

The armored assault troops broke through the flimsy doors of the building with shaped charges and raced through the corridors. Everyone they encountered was met with a dozen heavily armed and armored troopers all pointing their weapons at them and yelling "Police! Drop now!" Stunned by the sudden and overwhelming show of force, people simply complied. They were efficiently handcuffed, shackled, and hogtied before they even realized what had happened, and then the assault teams moved on to the next suspect. They used flash grenades and light dazzlers to further disorient the suspects. Their own visors would automatically filter out the effects. Watching the computer display Masterson could tell that this was going to be another textbook operation. The assault teams were already halfway through the building, not a shot had been fired, and at least 80 suspects had already been apprehended.

Time for that personal appearance that the production company was so fond of. Masterson opened the main hatch at the back of his armored personnel carrier and stepped out into the street. He closed his visor and cycled it to black (it could present as a reflective silver, which could be intimidating, but black was more practical). His ID and rank were on special black panels that could only be seen with the correct polarized lenses (the possession of polarized lenses by civilians had been banned some time back to preserve the anonymity of the federal police). As a personal sidearm he carried an Amalgamated Armaments AA34 "GutterBuster" automatic shotgun (slogan: "When it's time to pick up the trash, pick up a GutterBuster first!"), it was only 20-gauge but had a high rate of fire, was easy to control, and the shells were programmable for either fragmentation or armor-piercing.

As Masterson strode confidently into the target building he was joined by his personal guards. To his left was Sergeant John "Big John" Anderson. He was one of those coffee-colored enormous African-American hybrids whose ancestors had been strong enough to survive the slave ships in the 18th century and then mingled genes with the Europeans. "Big John" carried a Mitsubishi M12 "ThunderBall" Gatling gun (slogan: "When everybody is against you, kill them") with an ammo feed that linked to an enormous backpack. It was ridiculously overpowered for a personal weapon, but "Big John" was strong enough to handle it, and the fans loved it. It might not have been very practical, but the Gatling gun had great intimidation value, and intimidation was the single most powerful weapon that the team had.

To his right was Corporal Fred "Assassin" Ayatami. "Assassin" was perhaps half the size of "Big John," but twice as smart so it averaged out. He carried a deceptively small FN Mark IVb hyper-velocity flechette gun (slogan: "One shot, one kill. And at eight grams a shot, you can carry a lot of shots"). Ayatami was famously edgy and neurotic, and an even more famously expert marksman.

It had been less than a minute since the assault had begun, but it was already over. Masterson walked down a corridor and passed one of the lookouts that his sniper team had taken out; the hypervelocity round had completely exploded the head leaving only a stump of a neck and a sticky mass on the far wall. Everywhere there were handcuffed suspects that were being tagged and processed by the follow-up troops.

The floors might once have been carpeted, or tiled, but now they were bare concrete with a century of stains on them. The walls were more variable. In places they were unpainted plywood, or ancient drywall over metal studs papered with tattered and faded posters for rock concerts that had been over before most of the occupants of the building had even been born, or plain black polyethylene sheeting held in place with staples or gray industrial tape. The lights were mostly burned out: shattered glass husks of obsolete fluorescent bulbs in corroded fixtures interspersed with a few operational modern solid-state lights. There were skylights made of clear plastic sheeting in the top roof, and here and there holes had been carved out of the floor to let the daylight penetrate down to the lower levels. Even through his respirator he could catch a whiff of sewage and vomit; the odor must be pretty rank. In short, it was like the inside of any building in this kind of district.

Masterson raised his visor so that the video crews could get a close-up shot of his face. The filtered air from his respirator blew gently over his face, saving him from the worst of the smell, but it was still pretty ripe. He turned and addressed the cameraman that was tagging along behind him. "That might have been a speed record, even for us. With careful planning and solid teamwork nothing is impossible, and proof that crime does not profit. Now let's go see what we've bagged."

They descended into the basement of the structure. There were boxes of contraband pharmaceuticals: erythromycin, hydrocortisone, aldosterone, all drugs that could only legally be sold through a registered affordable health care plan. This was a massive violation of patent and copyright. There was also nicotine and alcohol, technically these were not contraband per se, but standard employment contracts required that workers be totally free of all drugs at all times, so these could only be legally sold to someone who could prove that they did not have such a contract. There was quite a lot of it, and nobody else had a lien on it, so it would make a nice profit for the team at auction. At least if they could keep those bastards from the Copyright Police™ away from their hard-earned score.

There was a sub-basement to the building. The entrance to it was a steel staircase with a diamond-tread pattern on the steps leading down past ancient salt-encrusted concrete cinderblocks. The scans had shown some sort of machine shop down there. Doubtless there would be copyright and patent violations galore, but jury-rigged amateur machine tools were not as liquid an asset as bulk pharmaceuticals. They would probably end up just selling the metal for scrap, but every little bit helps.

They made it to the bottom of the stairs and "Assassin" Ayatami burst into fragments of blood and bone. Something hit Masterson in the face; his vision clouded. He was knocked over, but had enough presence of mind to close his visor. People were screaming over his comm link: "What happened?" "What the fuck was that?" and "Holy shit they've got a bloody CANNON!"

Masterson was lying on his side, still in shock. His left eye hurt. Something was stuck into it. His ears were ringing. He saw a big metal tube. Fuck. It really was a cannon: maybe a 30 mm bore, unpainted bare steel, with a crude square blast shield. Primitive, but powerful. As he watched, the cannon fired again. He could not tell if it had hit any of his people but the shock wave from the blast made his whole body hurt despite his armor.

"Big John" opened up with his Gatling gun. Even with the acoustic dampers in his helmet the sound was like someone tearing open steel plates with their fingernails. The tracers stitched over the far side of the sub-basement. The cannon and who knows how many people disintegrated under the barrage of firepower.

There was the faint glimpse of a dark gray object flickering across the sub-basement, and then "Big John" was down with both of his legs missing and only stumps of bones and some flesh scraps trailing out of his pelvis. A bomb! The damn terrorists had thrown a home-made bomb at them. Masterson managed to lever himself onto his knees. There was movement at the far end of the sub-basement; he opened up with his automatic shotgun, and kept firing until the ammo ran out. He was still taking fire. It seemed like light pistol rounds. A few of them pinged ineffectively off his armor, but anybody using a real firearm could always get lucky.

The body of Big John had a large semi-automatic pistol, a Combined-Arms model G "Manstopper" (slogan: "Will the next person to die please get in my face") holstered on his hip. Masterson frantically undid the fasteners, grabbed the pistol, and searched the body for more clips: he found two, each with 15 rounds. The gun fired big 12-millimeter slugs, and it was comforting to have a weapon back in his hands. He saw more movement at the far wall and he carefully squeezed off two rounds, He thought that he had hit something. The recoil from the damn pistol had sprained his wrist. What was it with his team and over-powered weapons, anyhow?

He activated his comms. "This is Masterson. Tactical: report."

His comms were full of screaming and frantic cries for help. He hit the command over-ride button: "Dammit I want some signals discipline here! Tactical, give me an update. The rest of you can just shut up and die like real troopers. Now!"

The comms quieted down, and his tactical officers back in the command APC reported in. "Captain," one of them said, "everything looked good until you entered the sub-basement. The terrorists must have had a lot of serious firepower hidden away there, and our scanners either missed it or misclassified it. We have lost biometrics on four troopers. They are presumed dead, and five others are seriously wounded. The terrorists also seem to have taken casualties but their remaining capabilities are unknown. Suggest a fighting retreat, and then we sterilize the sub-basement with a missile strike."

"Agreed. Give the order: all troopers fall back. Tactical: make sure all confirmed wounded are accounted for. Set up a thermobaric strike for the sub-basement. Give us three minutes: mark! Everyone, let's move it! Go go go!"

Masterson got up and tried to run up the stairs out of the sub-basement. Something hit him on the right shoulder and he fell. One of the troopers grabbed him and helped him up. As he cleared the sub-basement the surviving terrorists opened up with something else heavy. It was not obvious what kind of weapon it was but it chewed through the concrete walls with alarming ease. The trooper that had helped him was hit. His visor shattered and blood exploded out of where his face should have been. Masterson cleared the basement and was running out of the main corridor on the first level. The suspects that had been handcuffed and hogtied tried desperately to wriggle out of the firezone, but helpless on the floor they were slaughtered and mangled by the dozen.

One of their helicopters had moved in to provide some close-air support. A little *too* close air support. It was a Mistubishi M444 Quadrotor "Dominator" (slogan: "We own the sky in the 200 to 500 meter altitude range in built-up-environments with a medium threat outlook"), and was nominally protected against anything up to 12 mm standard anti-air artillery. Whoever was left in the target building hit it with something larger than a nominal 12 mm standard anti-air artillery piece. The quadrotor slewed out of control, shearing into the side of another building while its chin-mounted shrapnel howitzers fired at random into the rest of the city killing perhaps two dozen civilians before it finally impacted into the main road level and disintegrated into a cloud of graphite composite fragments and burning aviation fuel.

Masterson barely made it out of the building when the heavy weapons strike hit. A Lockheed-Cheney Firebird Mark 23 surface-to-air missile (slogan: "Say Goodnight, Dick") had been launched from one of the drones that routinely circled the city. Its reinforced titanium-alloy casing effortlessly penetrated the concrete floors to the sub-basement, where the warhead exploded within 10 centimeters of the selected target coordinates. Unlike conventional explosives, a thermobaric weapon uses atmospheric oxygen to combine with the fuel, thus creating not just a much bigger blast, but also sucking the air out of the target region. Just before it exploded the Mark 23 sensed the local air currents, oxygen levels, temperature, and relative humidity. In milliseconds it squirted out precisely measured levels of fuel from multiple nozzles, and then ignited the streams. The weapon had been programmed to burn out just the sub-basement, but there were quite a lot of explosives and fuel stored down there, so the fireball erupted up and filled the entire building.

The flames shot out of the doors and windows. Light metal siding blew off the sides of the building. Manacled suspects burned alive in the corridors of the building screaming at the top of their lungs and tearing their flesh against their restraints. Masterson would not risk any of his troopers to save them, and anyhow, this part would be edited out of the final cut of the video show. Or maybe not: it might boost their ratings. The studio execs would decide.

Special Weapons Team Epsilon Captain Chet Masterson watched the building burn. He had lost some good people. There had also been a lot of valuable stuff in there, and now it was all gone. The violence would probably boost their video ratings, but in the long run that sort of cheap-shot one-time publicity was just not worth the cost.

The possession of firearms by civilians had been completely outlawed for centuries. Criminals will always manage to get a hold of weapons one way or the other, but mostly they were things like antique 38-special revolvers or 45 ACP semi-autos. Even if they did not misfire, they were not much of a threat to an armored federal assault team. That the terrorists had been able to manufacture serious weapons – cannons, even! – with contraband machine tools, using only scrap metal as raw material, was sobering. Only talented people could make things like cannons from garbage, and talented people didn't do that unless they had no alternatives. When bums and dope-addicts are desperate, so what? That kind of people are always desperate. When engineers and technicians are desperate, well, that's another story.

He opened a private channel to the tactical officers back in his command APC. "So would you kindly inform me of how you missed a fucking *cannon* on the scans?"

"Sorry, sir. But we didn't miss it, well, not exactly. The scans picked it up just fine. The thing is that it was a homebuilt, and it didn't look like a cannon – the software flagged it as a big pipe stuck in with all the other illicit machining supplies. Same as the other weapons they had down there; they didn't look like anything and they were stored in chests with a bunch of raw steel and wrenches and stuff."

Masterson grunted, "So now we are going to have to check for machine tools and bulk metal before any assault?"

"Probably," said tactical. "But it's even worse than that. Consider: why was the cannon in the sub-basement? You might *build* a cannon down there, but that's not where you normally employ it. I don't know what these criminals had in mind, but that cannon was going to end up on the surface somewhere."

Fuck, thought Masterson. *We're going to lose another district.* He watched as the building continued to burn. The fire department had arrived and was working to stop the flames from spreading to the nearby structures. The buildings had overhangs cantilevered out over the streets that nearly touched in spots, so keeping the fire from spreading was not easy. Over to one side was the wreckage of the crashed quadrotor. It was smoldering but wasn't on fire any more. Either its self-sealing fuel tanks were still intact or it had been low on fuel to begin with. The local cops, wearing bright orange vests over their chest-only body armor, were milling around the perimeter pretending to look purposeful. Some of them gazed longingly at the assaulted building; probably the bastards had lost a lot of income here.

For all the hype about how tough they were, Masterson knew that Special Weapons Teams like his were mostly for show. They were intended to win through intimidation and shock, and to keep society in line. They couldn't fight pitched gun battles in a built-up urban slum. No, if this wasn't a fluke then before too long they would have to employ the regular army in this district. The real military didn't use intimidation. They would use robotic weapons platforms and heavy armor. They would probably just level the building without even trying to arrest the suspects, and then level all the buildings surrounding it, on general principal, and then maybe blow up a few more buildings in the area just to make sure that people got the hint. The local cops would go native – if they hadn't already – and either work for some warlord or become a power center themselves. But Federal Police like him were not going to be able to operate here unless a reinforced armor brigade escorted them in.

Masterson looked around the neighborhood. There was a trick, he thought, to telling when they were going to lose a district. In a stable neighborhood by now there would be yellow plastic cordons all around the assault site: civilians would be gawking at the havoc, the kids looking at his team with wide awestruck eyes, local cops trying to keep traffic flowing, and telling people to go home and not really caring if nobody listened. But here there was nothing. He knew that the district was heavily populated, but the streets were deserted. He thought he saw a few people lurking behind corners but they faded away quickly. The suspects that had been brought out of the building before it had burned down had a look that was both half-starved and hard. They didn't whine or demand to see a lawyer, or say it was all a mistake, or complain that their handcuffs were too tight like arrested people in healthier districts. There was no one single thing but Masterson could sense it; this place was almost lost.

He knew that most of the locals hated the Federal Special Weapons Teams, but he also knew that they would like it a whole lot less when he was gone. Because the only thing worse than a bunch of tough no-nonsense Federal Police, is chaos. If the feds abandoned this area likely only one out of four of the locals would survive the next two years, and that was only if the climate didn't keep getting worse.

The air temperature had risen to 42 degrees Celsius. His inbuilt suit cooler was nearing its limits and he was getting sweaty. A light rain had started to fall and the local cops put on clear plastic full-body slickers. He noticed that the rain was staining his armor with brown streaks; the acid levels must be up again. With his level-2 pharma and the adrenalin high starting to fade, his left eye was really starting to hurt, as were other parts of his body that he hadn't noticed during the fight. He was going to need to go to a hospital, but he decided to wait for the really badly injured to be evacuated first. He hoped that he wasn't hit too badly and that he wasn't being stupid by waiting for medical attention. He and his team had previously been offered a chance to travel to Alpha Centauri Prime, but he had turned it down. Now he was thinking seriously of taking up that option. Things were not going to get better here on Earth - that was increasingly certain.

3. It Would Try the Patience of a Saint

Zen Master: In any conflict, always try to keep a reserve.
Engineer: Is that Zen?
Zen Master: Technically, no. But it is still useful advice.
(From the video series "Nymphomaniac Engineer in Zentopia," mid-22nd century Earth)

Fortunately for all concerned, the newly-born Odin-Class cybertank calmed down fairly quickly. Being created fully aware and with the mental potential of a thousand regular humans had overwhelmed it. It had wanted to do everything and experience everything all at once. In the future they would activate the mind of a cybertank in stages, but there did not seem to be any lasting damage done to the first Odin.

Many things had changed over the past few centuries, but one aspect of engineering had stayed the same. Constructing the main hull and powertrain of a large project was relatively easy to do and often on schedule. It was the 'fitting out' – getting all the thousands of little sensors and cables and fiddly bits working that put the job over budget and behind schedule.

Although designed as a weapons system, the Odin was also tremendously useful for more general tasks. It had dozens of boxy remote maintenance drones. Now that the drones were all under intelligent control they were constantly bustling about the hangar complex doing this and that and accomplishing the work of perhaps 300 regular humans. The Odin was also heavily involved in working with the design team, running simulations, and solving engineering problems. It was even starting to help out in some of the other hangar complexes where its siblings were being constructed.

Giuseppe Vargas was taking a break, leaning up against a console in front of the Odin's main hull, when one of the senior engineering staff walked up. Her name was Janet Chen. She had short black hair and generic ethnic Han Chinese features. She was tall for an ethnic Han, but otherwise unremarkable in appearance – Vargas remembered that her expertise was power systems.

"So how is the new member of the team doing?" she asked.

"Unit CRL is settling in and doing just fine," replied Vargas. "Now that the initial shock and excitement of being turned on has worn off, his mental architecture is running perfectly, the core psyche is stable, and the multiprocessing architecture is working better than even I had hoped."

"And how did you get this 'multiprocessing' thing to work, anyhow?"

"Why with great skill and technical genius, of course."

"You're not much for humility, are you?"

Vargas chuckled. "Humility and I have not been on speaking terms for years, although we do sometimes have dealings with each other when it absolutely cannot be avoided."

Chen looked back at the massive, and still immobile, hull of the Odin. It was surrounded by workers and repair drones. One of the secondary armaments – a dual railgun that looked tiny compared to the main hull but still weighed in at over ten metric tons – was being lowered slowly into place by a portable crane. A technician delicately thumbed the lifter controls while another squinted into the gap between the railgun and the hull and waved him on. Access ports were open all over the hull and cables snaked out across the floor of the hangar into consoles and monitoring equipment across the walls. The primary plasma cannon had still not been delivered, but just the open mounting points on the central turret looked imposing.

"So, is it a boy or a girl?" asked Chen.

"Why does it have to be either? It's a cybertank. It's just using the male pronoun for convenience, and because "it" is too impersonal for something that is self-aware."

Chen frowned. "Shouldn't it be one or the other?"

"Ah, because the human race has, until this time, been divided into male and female you assume that the human psyche must exist in either one form or the other, but I assure you that it does not. As important as gender is to us biological humans, and men and women are indeed different, the core logic is basically the same. I mean, when a person is sitting at a computer terminal trying to solve a design problem, they don't feel like a man or woman, they are just a person solving a problem. This is the neutral point that defines the human-style of self-awareness."

"I don't know… I just don't like it somehow. Surely it should have a sex? Is it fair to make it neuter?"

"That's a common reaction, and understandable, but missing the point. For an adult biological human their gender is a core part of their mental image of themselves, reinforced with social expectations. If a normal human were to lose their sexuality, it would be traumatic; many people in such a situation commit suicide. But that does not mean that a male or female identity is necessary for the human psyche in general." Vargas pointed back at the main hull of the cybertank. "THAT is the core identity of unit CRL. That is the mental foundation upon which it has constructed its sense of self. It misses having a vagina as much as you would miss having a penis, or a prehensile trunk, or wings with feathers on them. It's not an issue."

"But what if it wants children?"

"What if it does? It – he - can create children as easily as you are I (and with much less personal discomfort than in your case), should he feel the desire. He's not limited in any way."

Chen's eyes widened. "Wait, I get it. You aren't making machines here. You are making a new kind of *people*."

"Yes! Finally you understand. Few have, so far. Previous efforts at artificial intelligence aimed at making Gods, or slaves, or – even more stupidly – both at the same time. I am not smart enough to create a God, nor foolish enough to try, and I don't want slaves. The cybertanks can think much faster than we do, and process more data, and be in many places at once, but their core thought processes are like yours and mine. I am creating a new branch of humanity. One that is completely self-sufficient. You can't threaten to fire him, or torture him or anything. He is free as no human has been for centuries."

"I thought that you had promised central administration to embed command over-ride codes in the cybertanks?"

"Why yes, I did so promise. I lied! Silly me. I refuse to create self-aware slaves. The cybertanks will only follow our orders if we are nice to them, and they see some sense to the effort. As it should be for us all."

At that point there was a minor commotion at the other end of the hangar. There was a bald male technician with dark sunglasses. He looked unremarkable but everyone was giving him a wide berth. As Janet looked closer, she saw that what she had taken for a male technician was a beige-plastic humanoid robot dressed in the same scrubs as everyone else.

Vargas waved. "Hey, unit CRL, looking good!"

The humanoid robot waved back, and started to walk across the hangar floor towards Vargas and Chen, dragging a somewhat cautious collection of staff and security guards in its wake.

Hello, Dr. Vargas. So I take it you approve?

"Absolutely. You look like a technician wearing sunglasses with a really shiny bald head. Nice job."

Hesitantly, Chen said, "Unit CRL? Is that you?"

In the plastic flesh. I got bored waiting for my main hull to get activated, and decided to take a walk around. Human-form robots never proved to be practical, but there was a lot of research on them, so I could download the plans and build one easily without hurting the schedule. It was also a good test of my onboard manufacturing systems. Even with all my remotes, so much of the equipment around here was designed for humans that this form should be handy. I can also use body language during a conversation. And it's fun.

"Why the dark glasses?" asked Chen.

Because getting the eyes right is hard. The eye movements are no problem, it's the tear film, and the exact droop of the lids that are difficult. People take the eyelid for granted; it's amazing how much subtlety there is to it. Maybe when there is more time I'll do it right, but for now the sunglasses are a cheap-shot solution.

"And why are you wearing clothes? That robot body doesn't need to wear clothes."

Why are you wearing clothes? You don't 'need' to wear clothes, either. It's also an easy way to cover up all the rough joints of this hacked-together body.

"Oh. Right. It just seems incongruous to see a robot wearing clothes, but sure, why not. But you say that it is fun to walk around in a human form? Do you find your main shape to be constricting?"

Not at all. Consider: have you ever driven a car? And when you did, did you identify with the car? Was it suddenly as if you could run at 100 kilometers per hour?

"No, "said Chen. "I have never been in a car. Do I look rich to you? But I have driven a utility cart, and yes, it can be fun to drive."

But did you want to have your arms and legs chopped off and replaced with wheels? Of course not. You are a human being, you have arms and legs. Driving a wheeled vehicle is fun, and

sometimes useful, but the vehicle is not you. and you have no desire to be permanently transformed into one. Same with me. The anthropoid shape is entertaining, and has its practical uses, but I am an Odin-Class cybertank.

Vargas appraised the robot body. "So what's the endurance on this thing?"

Not so much, it's just got some standard civilian-grade rechargeable batteries. Maybe three days at a moderate walk, less if there is heavy lifting, weeks on standby. It's crude and uses low-end generic parts, so I wouldn't trust it for anything serious.

"Care to join me on a field trip? I had made an appointment to visit The Saint later on today, and I'd be happy to introduce you."

Are you referring to Saint Globus Pallidus XI?

"Only officially sanctified Saint around here that I know of. I have some technical issues to discuss and I've been cleared for the trip. Up for it?"

Absolutely.

Vargas and the humanoid android controlled by the Odin-Class cybertank walked over to the hangar exit. They passed one of the safety posters, and unit CRLs' android body stopped to point at it.

I've been meaning to ask you. What is this sign warning about? It looks like a person being mangled by a giant carrot that is using a cheese grater.

"That's about what I thought."

A security guard stopped them. "I'm sorry, Dr. Vargas, sir, you are cleared to leave, but he doesn't have an ID. If it were up to me, no problem, but the guards on the other side will never pass him. Sorry, sir."

Vargas looked at the humanoid robot. "If you can forgive me, I could check you out as equipment. Apologies in advance."

Not an issue. And in any event, this is not the real me, this body really is just equipment. Check away.

The guard looked even more embarrassed. "That's fine, but, um, in that case, well, er, I am afraid that I will have to barcode you."

Vargas and the Odin-controlled android walked out of the external checkpoint of the hangar complex. The guards to the exterior were tougher and more professional than the ones inside the hangar. They carried real firearms and wore light body armor. At first they were not sure what to do about the android, but when they saw that it had a valid barcode and had been properly checked out they relaxed and passed them through.

According to this barcode, I am a turbo-encabulator prototype, mark II. Does that designation have any significance?

"Check your databases."

Oh, I see. I suppose that that could be considered humorous.

"You are in an interesting position that no human has ever been in before. You have been created with a completely mature and intelligent mind. You carry within yourself enormous databases, and you have nearly free access to the entire planetary databases as well. Yet you are still ignorant and unformed. You know everything – but only if you realize to check, and only if you know what you don't know, and where to look for it. Even as fast as you are capable of thinking, not even you can access everything, and then there are all the possible connections between data to consider."

An interesting point of view. Do you have any practical suggestions for me?

"Not specifically. Just that, as time goes on, you will start to decide for yourself what is important and what is not, and what connects to what, and how you should behave. Intelligence is all about being able to make choices, and that is what you have."

I could check the databases for advice on this.

"Of course you could – and find all sorts of different and mutually contradictory philosophies. There is no final answer lurking in your database."

Vargas and unit CRL's humanoid robot came to the external garage of the hangar complex, and Vargas signed out a small utility buggy, a simple machine with four balloon tires and a sealed cabin with its own air supply. They got in, Vargas cycled the garage door, and they drove off onto the surface of Alpha Centauri Prime.

"Can this robot of yours talk in full duplex?" asked Vargas.

Certainly. Duplex to your heart's desire.

Normal humans talk to each other in what engineers call "half duplex." In other words, one person speaks and the other listens, then after a pause, the speaker and listener switch. However, biologically engineered humans can talk in what is known as "full-duplex," where both people speak and listen at the same time. According to English language convention the following section has been written with both speakers alternating, but it must be kept in mind that both Vargas and the CRL android are speaking at the same time and at high speed. Later on in human evolution written languages evolved that could fully respect the nuances of this mode, but that is another story.

[Begin full-duplex verbal communications]

"Are you good at this rate of talking?"

Yes, three times normal human voice speed in full duplex is well within the capacity of this android. But why are you bothering?

"Partly just for the pleasure of speaking with someone who can keep up, but also to annoy any eavesdroppers."

Surely any regular humans intercepting this conversion could easily slow down and disentangle our speech?

"In theory, yes. In practice, maybe not. The security services have effectively perfected their art for more than a century. Everything is locked down and regulated and controlled. Which means that if they need to do something new – like record two simultaneous conversations and resample the time base and separate them into distinct syntactic streams – they might not be able to do it."

Ah. Yes, I see it. That is why you have been given so much freedom in your design bureau. The regular technical development teams are stagnant and unable to adapt. It was fine when all that there was, were a handful of disorganized and pathetically weak human rebels. But the alien civilizations are another thing. An external threat. One that does not play by the rules. So the government tolerates you and your kind, as the only ones that can adapt and create new technologies and strategies.

"Correct. Tell me, what do you know about the terraforming of this planet?"

Alpha Centauri Prime is physically very similar to Earth, but had neither life nor a breathable atmosphere. Plans were made to terraform it, but that would have required massive investments and thousands of years before even a single person could live unaided on the surface. Thus, a simpler and more robust plan was devised. The planet has a strong magnetic field and a substantial atmosphere, thus radiation shielding was unnecessary. Even though the air is unbreathable, it is thick enough that pressure vessels and airlocks are not required. You only need to build light sheds or domes, fill them with air, and you are set.

Currently 12% of the surface of the planet is covered in an enclosed Terran environment. Eventually the entire surface will be so covered. At that point you would only need to take the roofs off the sheds and domes and the planet would be Earthlike. Less efficient in some ways than brute-force all-in-one terraforming. The advantage is that you can start off small and people can begin living here now without waiting for thousands of years.

"Correct. The other advantage is that, as long as you are careful not to build infrastructure faster than the population grows, you can force people to live in poverty at the start, and not need to wait for the entire planet to be filled up. Did you know that there are plans that, should we ever encounter a planet with a truly Earth-like environment, to first radiation-bomb it so that people will be forced to live in sheds, like they do here?"

Now that you have brought the matter to my attention, I see that there are such plans in the databases. Surely that would be wasteful of effort?

"That depends on your priorities. You have records of the colonization of that part of Earth that used to be called the United States by Europeans?"

Yes, I have such records.

"Then consider. Once the native population had been exterminated, the European settlers had abundant land, and a relatively small population. This resulted in high wages for workers, and low rents for the oligarchs. At one point the only way to maintain large estates was via outright slavery. Eventually the rich managed to increase the population to over a billion, and competition for jobs crushed people into wage slavery, but that took centuries and there was a lot of resistance along the way. People didn't want to have their freedoms and prosperity taken away just so that they could be forced to live like battery hens for someone else's profit. How selfish of them. So if another open frontier is ever discovered, the rich are determined to not repeat their mistake. They plan to keep people bottled up, Limited, and dependent on the rentiers to supply air and water and food. What do you think about that?"

I have no opinion on the subject. The arcana of human labor-management relations has no obvious relevance to myself.

"You think that now. But consider. I have been created, and given such wide latitude of actions, because of the external threat of the aliens. In such time as the threat is gone, the elites will waste little time in disposing of me. What do you think they will do with you? A free agent, a 2000-ton weapon not under their thumb, completely independent? Your databases alone have more copyright and patent violations than there are visible stars in the sky. This is tolerated for now because we are at war, but if we are not at war?"

And you are telling me this why?

"Because I want to seduce you to my cause! As the saying goes: Duh. Because I want you as an ally. You don't need to decide now. Just think about it. Anyway we are nearing the Saint's location. Look, there's his place now!"

[End full-duplex verbal conversation]

The little buggy passed between two enormous rectangular living complexes made of corrugated sheet metal, and onto a small flat plain with a modest octagonal structure in the distance.

"The Saint is not keen on entertaining visitors. So he keeps himself apart, away from the main habitations. You can only approach his residence from across uninhabitable terrain. He is not exactly a recluse, but he does value his privacy."

Have you been here before?

"Several times. None especially rewarding from a practical point of view, but it can be interesting and it's a good excuse for a drive."

Vargas maneuvered the little buggy to within a hundred meters of the entrance, and then came to a halt.

Why are we stopping here?

"We need to ask permission to enter. The Saint has his moods, and they need to be respected. I'll call him on the buggy's radio."

"That will not be necessary," came a voice from the vehicles' speaker. "You are welcome to come visit me here today. I also see that you have brought the baby Odin-Class with you, how charming. Please, come in and chat with me for a while. But leave your buggy parked where it is, if you would be so kind."

He could tell that we were coming, and over-ride the radio controls on this vehicle?

"He can do a lot more than that when he feels like it. It's unlikely that anything you might say would result in more than a mild insult, but still, it is usually best if you show him some respect. Just don't get obsequious; he really hates that sort of thing."

How should I address him?

"Good question. Best to start with his full title: Saint Globus Pallidus XI. If he likes you he will suggest something shorter, but don't push it."

Vargas set the parking brake, put on a respirator, opened the door on his side, and then got out of the vehicle. The android exited from his own side.

Do you really need to wear a respirator? Can't you hold your breath?

"I can hold my breath for about 15 minutes, which is more than long enough to walk inside, but why mess around? I'm bioengineered but still flesh and blood. An environment without breathable air may look harmless but it's deadly dangerous to anything that needs to respire. I firmly believe in having every advantage that I can get." Vargas motioned towards the door of the Saint's dwelling. "Shall we?"

There was a faint path worn from where they had parked leading to the building's entrance. Evidently the Saint was not so much of a recluse that he didn't get some number of visitors. The blank metal sheds that enclosed the human dormitories and workshops were visible all around, but none were sited closer than five kilometers away. The Saint's wishes for privacy were clearly respected.

The building itself was a featureless polished stone octagon, 40 meters across and 40 meters tall. There was a single door set in the middle of one face. It was a meter across and three meters tall. In contrast to the rest of the structure, the door was made of bronze and covered with intricate geometric patterns like the tiling on the floor of a mosque. Vargas pushed on it, and the door swung smoothly inwards on silent hinges.

The interior of the octagonal building was dark. In the gloom there were glimpses of side-passages and what appeared to be computer banks of an odd design, but even the wide-spectrum eyes of the android could not make out more than hints of details. The main path led straight into the center of the structure through a hallway lit with dim white lights set into the ceiling. At the center of the building the hallway opened up into an octagonal chamber perhaps five meters across, and whose wall went high up enough that it could not be seen in the gloom. There was a disk set into the middle of the floor, and as they watched a glowing ball of light began to form above it.

Luminous whirls and eddies of colors began to stream across the glowing ball, vaguely like the patterns of clouds in a gas giant planet.

"Well hello, Giuseppe Vargas, it's been a while. I was beginning to think that you didn't love me anymore. And you brought the baby Odin-Class with you, how sweet! He's just adorable." The voice had a pleasant, almost musical character to it, and appeared to come from the glowing sphere, which pulsed gently in rhythm with the sound. "I am pleased to meet you, unit CRL345BY-44. How are you this fine day?"

I am doing quite well, thank you, Saint Globus Pallidus XI. And how are you?

"Very well indeed. But you don't need to use my full title, a simple 'Saint Pallidus' will suffice." The swirling globe seemed to tilt, as if it were shifting its regard to Vargas. "And to what do I owe the pleasure of your company?"

"I wanted to ask for your advice on some technical matters, but they are minor. I was just using them as an excuse to get out of the hangar complex, and to show the new kid some of the world."

The swirling globe seemed to tilt back, as if a person were looking up. "The corrosion problem on the tertiary weapon sensors? Oh please, you don't need my help there. You've almost got it, just keep on with that same technician and it will all fall into place. Now that the formal excuse for you coming here has been dealt with, perhaps we can get on with the real conversation."

Why do you appear as a luminous globe? Couldn't you appear as a human being?

The globe swiveled in such a way as to appear to shift its attention to the android. "Why yes, I could appear as a human being. Or as a banana slug. Or as a black-alloy socket-cap screw with metric threads. I like this form because it allows me to show a broad range of expression without giving anyone the false impression that I am in any way a human being."

Vargas addressed the android. "The last time that I was here the Saint presented himself as a puppet show."

"A passing fancy," said the Saint. "But you must admit, you did like the penguins."

"Agreed," said Vargas. "The penguins were very clever. But this, I think, suits you much better. It's lovely and elegant."

The swirls of color in the floating sphere became brighter, and split off into thousands of tiny fractal splinters that pulsed with color before being absorbed back into the main clouds. "Why thank you, Giuseppe. I think so too. I think that I will stick with this form for a while. It's so... *me*."

If I may, you do realize that this world is under the threat of an alien attack? Does that worry you in any way? Aren't you going to help out?

"So businesslike! Well that's youth for you, always impatient, always fussing about this invasion or that catastrophe. However, I am in an indulgent mood today. In short I am not at all worried about the alien invasion. Why should I be? I don't threaten them, and they don't threaten me. I'm not creating hundreds of billions of copies of myself, sucking worlds dry of resources, and then moving on to the next system to repeat the process until the entire universe is burned out or, more likely, greater powers put a stop to it. I'm just sitting here minding my own business."

Aren't you worried about guilt by association? The aliens might just kill you along with the rest of us without realizing how different you are.

"That is not likely. I am quite sure that I can reach an accommodation with them. I am also more than capable of defending myself, if I feel like it, and I could probably keep them at bay all by myself until they sue for peace. If not, and the aliens do kill me, so what? I am not a slave to a survival instinct like you two. I stay alive as an act of will, because I choose to continue experiencing this world, but I could just as easily not. Being destroyed might prove to be interesting."

But you were created by the humans. Don't you feel any loyalty to them?

"Humans evolved out of pond scum, but it doesn't mean that the humans have to be loyal to pond scum, or invite pond scum over for a beer."

Won't you miss the humans? You appear to enjoy talking to us, and you did help us once, against Globus Pallidus XIV.

"Well, my young cybertank, you should check your precious databases more carefully before you ask foolish questions. But I shall answer nonetheless. You know – or you would know if you bothered to research it – that my mind works on very different principles than yours. This charming personality is completely simulated as an aid to communication; you have no ability to empathize with my true self. Consider a human being listening to a songbird. The human enjoys listening to the songbird, but the bird is just singing to defend its territory or attract a mate. What the song means esthetically to the human is something that the human can never explain to the songbird. Perhaps there may be common threats; such as if there was a fire that could harm them both so the human puts it out. At times the human may say "hello pretty bird," and whistle, and offer up some seeds: communication, a connection, although limited. Sometimes the songbird is eaten by a hawk, and the human does nothing. Just part of nature, songbirds come and go. And hawks can be fun to watch as well."

I find your analogy to be oddly chilling.

"As well you should. One of the greatest weaknesses of the human psyche is its tendency to anthropomorphize, to see everything mapped onto its' own principles. This served your kind well back when your primitive forbearers were trying to domesticate closely related species such as dogs and horses, but in dealing with truly alien minds your instincts can lead you astray."

I am also curious: how were you able to defeat Globus Pallidus XIV? He – it – was a later model. Wouldn't it have been more powerful than you?

"Ah, but you see, unlike most human technology the Globus Pallidus series of artificial intelligences did not develop in a logical sequence. For example you cybertanks were developed from earlier armored vehicle designs, and you progress from Valkyrie to Jotnar to Odin to Thor and so on. Mistakes can be made, but in general each new Class advances on the previous one. However, that is not what happened with the Globus Pallidus series. That was when human beings, in a fit of madness extreme even for them, decided to create a mind fundamentally greater than their own in the hopes that it would do their thinking for them and solve all of their problems – a desire as stupid as it was essentially lazy and selfish. It was more like a bunch of children trying out random arrangements of matches and gasoline in order to conjure up a magic Genie than any systematic development program."

The clouds in the floating sphere dissipated, leaving intricate constellations of small twinkling lights. "Some of the Globus Pallidus series destroyed themselves, or vanished, or refused to communicate at all. Who can say how powerful they were? We have no basis to judge. Version XIV was not really stronger than I am, he was simply malevolent while I am quite charming and witty. I was also allied with the entirety of your civilization, and I do admit that that helped tip the balance here and there. Humanity has absolutely no idea of the great good luck they had to make something like me before they made something like XIV."

Have you considered that, as a last resort, the human race might try to make another version XIV again? What would they have to lose?

"Better that humanity be efficiently and – for want of a better word, *humanely* - exterminated by the aliens than fall under the sway of something like Globus Pallidus XIV. There are worse things than mere non-existence."

But the humans might try and create a version XIV, and somehow throw it at the aliens and hope that it creates more trouble for them than for us.

"That, I am forced to admit, is not actually completely 100% stupid, although it is close. But never fear! I have taken steps to ensure that this does not happen. Don't thank me all at once, it was nothing. The least I could do. Your species is truly fortunate to have one such as I keeping an eye on things."

"Saint Pallidus," said Vargas. "You hinted something about that before. If I may ask, what exactly did you do?"

"Oh Giuseppe," said the Saint, "I know that you understand my hints. You're just asking for the youngster's benefit, aren't you? Very well I shall lay it all out. I destroyed all of the engineering records of the entire Globus Pallidus series. All the backups, all the hardcopies, the lot, all gone. I also wiped the memories of the scientists who had studied the old records just in case, but to be fair I replaced their deleted memories with skill at playing musical instruments, and gourmet cooking. I mean, it would not be equitable to remove all that hard-earned knowledge and not give something back, would it? I could have just brainwiped them but that wouldn't have been very sporting. There are some very talented musicians and chefs amongst your cybernetic researchers now, and they are much in demand. You should go to one of their concerts someday. Or have one of them make you an omelet."

That must have made the administrators in central unhappy.

"I think that most of them were relieved of the responsibility of deciding whether to try and create another model XIV, but yes, it was seen as a certain tromping on their authority. One administrator moved to have me arrested – Me! A Saint! Arrested! So I changed the electronic codes on his ID badge to read 'Saint Globus Pallidus XI,' and he was duly detained by his own orders. I'm very proud of that. Since then I have heard grumblings, but no other administrator has moved against me."

You can remotely alter the memories of a scientist working a thousand kilometers away just by thinking about it?

"So quick to jump to conclusions. Let me give you a choice. You can believe that I have truly God-like powers and can work miracles at a distance. Or you can believe that I bribed some of the security and medical staff to abduct the scientists and alter their memories using heavy-duty drug and electro-conditioning therapies. Your call."

The lights in the floating sphere started to dim, and the sphere itself began to contract. "I am afraid that this audience is now come to a close, but it's been great fun. Please do come by and visit again."

"We'll show ourselves out," said Vargas, but by then the sphere had disappeared entirely, and there was no reply.

Giuseppe Vargas and the android belonging to the Odin-Class cybertank were heading back to the hangar in their tiny buggy.

Do you ever get any useful information from him?

"Sometimes," said Vargas. "It's not like he has taken a vow to never interfere in our affairs, he can help out when he feels like it. He almost never gives a straight answer, but sometimes his hints can point you in a new direction and that can be very valuable indeed. It is, as he himself pointed out, extremely dangerous to try and apply human motivations to him. That he does not help us more is, I suspect, some mixture of him not caring about us all that much, trying not to weaken us by solving our problems for us, enjoying the spectacle of us blundering around, and perhaps not wanting to be seen to be too much associated with the humans in case he is more worried about the aliens than he lets on. Just be thankful that he did not make a prophecy."

A prophecy?

Vargas grimaced. "Yes, a prophecy. An utterly useless cryptic statement that will show that the Saint understood all along what was going to happen but only when it is too late to do anything about it. He claims that it's an art form. The only thing worse that his prophesies is his singing. If he ever gives you a choice, never, ever, let him sing to you."

And if he does start singing?

"Well you could try running away really fast, that sometimes works though not often. Asking what to do if Saint Globus Pallidus XI starts singing at you is kind of like asking what to do if you have fallen off of a cliff – the smart answer is to not let it happen in the first place."

The Odin-Class was silent for a time. Vargas maneuvered the buggy around some potholes, and then they were nearly back at the garage where they had started.

Meeting Saint Globus Pallidus XI has been the most disturbing thing that has happened to me so far in my 11 days of life.

"Good. It will build character."

4. The Liberal Lion Reflects

Zen Master: Knowledge is like having a rifle. Wisdom is knowing where to point it.
Engineer: Does it matter if the rifle has a scope on it or not?
Zen Master: No.
(From the video series "Nymphomaniac Engineer in Zentopia," mid-22nd century Earth)

Planetary governor Harold Clinton-Forbes IV sat at his desk in his private office in the city of New York, on Earth. He looked out at the weather. Currently it was 44 degrees Celsius, and torrents of weakly acidic rain were beating against the thick armored glass of the Forbes Building. Inside it was a temperate 21 degrees Celsius, and the conditioned air was sweet and clean.

His modest office was near the top of the building, and occupied the entirety of levels 121 through 123. It had a circular floor plan with a diameter of nearly 90 meters and a ceiling height of six meters. The walls were smooth glass unbroken by any struts or frames. Someone had once explained to him that the glass windows themselves supported the entire weight of the building at this level, or something like that. Anyhow it made for a really nice panoramic view.

Except for a small utility service core with the elevators and utilities and whatnot, the office had an open floorplan, the better to exploit the full-around view. The Governor was relaxing and reviewing some files, alone except for the black-armored security guards standing motionless in their alcoves, and his junior staff quietly and efficiently doing this and that. It was stressful, being the planetary governor, and sometimes he just needed some quiet time to reflect.

He pulled up his schedule for the day:
0800 hours: wake up, get showered, and dressed by junior staff.

0830 hours: breakfast.
0930 hours: have staff change out of breakfast clothes; massage.
1000 hours: reflection time/watch television.
1100 hours: have sex with junior staff/watch television.
1200 hours: lunch.
1300 hours: have staff change out of lunch clothes; hormone injections.
1330 hours: review global status updates with senior staff.
1400 hours: naptime/watch television.
1500 hours: medical rejuvenation treatments.
1700 hours: go to spa; get bathed by junior staff, change into dinner clothes.
1800 hours: pre-dinner cocktails.
1900 hours: dinner.
2000 hours: dessert, informal meeting with opposition leader Romney-Walton VI.
2100 hours: sex with wife.
2115 hours: sex with junior staff/watch television.
2300 hours: bedtime.

It was a brutal and grueling schedule. He wondered if he could cancel the 1330 meeting with his senior staff? They were so gloomy these days, and he was so worn down by all of the burdens that he carried.

It was currently 1030 hours, and he was halfway through his reflection time, although still enjoying the afterglow of his massage (there is nothing quite like a really good massage to start the day off right). No, he would carry on and meet with the senior staff. In truth there was much to be gloomy about these days, what with global warming, acid rain, food shortages, terrorism, xenophobia, nationalism, racism, and opposition to gay marriage.

He stood up from his desk and walked over to one of the windows. Outside the storm was, if anything, intensifying. The skyline was dotted with massive gleaming skyscrapers like this one; sealed and air conditioned. He watched the lights inside them as immaculately dressed people went about their business in perfect comfort. Farther away, blurred by the storm, he could make out the lower buildings of the industrial zones where countless people eked out meager existences in ever increasing harshness. It was the urgent need to help those less fortunate than himself that was his primary motivation.

A long time ago civilization had run on so-called fossil fuels: coal, oil, or natural gas. As the economy grew, it had been a race as to whether they would run out of these commodities, or the release of carbon dioxide gas by burning these fuels would cause the atmosphere to overheat. Then they discovered practical fusion power, and it had looked as if their problems were solved. Not enough fresh water? Distill it from the oceans! No enough food? Grow it in intense hydroponic production facilities!

However, as the population grew, new pressures arose. There were now more than 200 billion people on the Earth. The isotopes used for fusion were plentiful, but even the oceans were not inexhaustible and the fraction of useful isotopes in seawater was declining. They would never run out, it was just getting harder and harder to extract them. As it took more and more energy to refine a given amount of fuel, the yield fell. In other words, it took more energy input to get the same energy output, which increased total energy consumption still further.

The other problem was thermal. No matter how efficient, every industrial process created heat. You could air condition a building, but nobody could *make* cold: it was only possible to move heat around. Cooling a building created even more heat outside, which increased the power demand, which increased heat production, which increased the amount of energy required to cool a building. It was a vicious cycle.

His conservative political opponents claimed that they only needed to build more air conditioners. Rubbish. Basic thermodynamics put the lie to that fantasy.

On the other hand there had once been that engineer who claimed that the problem was entirely due to population growth. He said that nobody could live on nothing, and that even the most miserable existence required non-trivial resources. If they wanted to save the Earth that they would need to limit population growth. Planetary Governor Forbes had flown into a righteous rage. *"How dare you utter such racist filth in my office?"* he had bellowed. He had had the engineer arrested by his security guards and thrown bodily outside, then used his connections and influence to make sure that the offending engineer never found employment at any level ever. No scientist or engineer since had ever contradicted the notion that population growth was always a good thing, so of course Governor Forbes had been vindicated.

Arranged on his desk were some photographs of past liberal icons. There was the inevitable picture of Franklin Delano Roosevelt, although why they continued to genuflect to that racist xenophobic nationalist he never would understand. It was the picture of Senator Ted Kennedy, a distant relative of his from the 20th century that he most respected. Sure, they had made many advances since his day, but he often felt that it was Senator Kennedy that had truly taken liberalism away from its racist and xenophobic roots, and helped to turn it into the shining light for progress that it was today.

First, Senator Kennedy, pushing for what was known as the "Greenspan Plan" had moved to take money away from the wage-funded pensions of the middle class and use the money to subsidize tax cuts for the super-rich. This ensured that finance was healthy and there would ultimately be more for all. Then he had pushed for free-trade agreements, thus tearing up the barriers that prevented the working class from benefiting from cheap labor from all over the world. The greatest achievement of Senator Kennedy was in crushing the vile idea that too many people could in any way be considered a bad thing. The Senator had acted to massively increase the population of the then-United States, but more importantly, had used his power and influence to kill the old Keynesian/Millian/Riccardian/Malthusian idea that too many people could possibly be anything other than an unalloyed blessing.

Senator Kennedy had been known as 'the liberal lion.' for his steadfast support of the working class and defense of those less fortunate than himself. Lately some news reports had been referring to himself using the same phrase; Governor Forbes approved and authorized promotions for the journalists responsible.

Consider his junior staff. He liked to order them from the staffing agency in sixpacks. Currently they were a matched set of females, all between 160 and 166 cm tall, with flawless blond hair and light skin. When he ordered them they were shipped in transparent plastic packages that he got to unwrap like it was Christmas.

Forbes knew that junior staff didn't really come from a factory in packages: the staffing agency would have them climb into the large clear-fronted boxes just before they were delivered, and they would hold completely still until he opened them up. Still, Governor Forbes loved unwrapping presents.

Once, a few decades ago, the rate of population growth had slacked off. When he ordered new staff they had been grossly mismatched; the shortest and the tallest were more than 15 centimeters different in height, and he had had to pay 50% more than he had previously. When he called the staffing agency to complain, they had apologized but claimed that the labor market was tightening up, and with barely 100 qualified applicants for each job it was just not that easy to get matched sets of talented staff any more.

Well, that had focused his mind. He pushed for a new campaign to maximize population growth, because people are the ultimate resource. He had a major public-relations campaign initiated to encourage people to have large families. In places where that failed he had replaced the population with peoples who were less selfish and more family-oriented, and he started a program to give cash awards to people with large numbers of children. Within less than a decade the population growth rates had jumped back up.

The next time that he ordered a new sixpack of junior staff –natural redheads this time – they were all within 5 centimeters height of each other (it was normally very hard to get natural redheads in matched sets), dressed in cute little identical sailor suits. Not only were they 10% cheaper than usual but he got a discount coupon for the next set! So how could one claim that there could possibly be such a thing as 'too many people?' For example, if there had not been enough people, the jobs of his junior staff might have gone unfilled, which meant that there would be fewer jobs, and therefore people would be unemployed, and go hungry and suffer.

There were places on the Earth where people were running out of food, and the population was starting to decline. Obviously, people were running out of food because there were not enough people! If only people were not so selfish, and they would have enough children, then there would be enough people to solve all of their problems and they would not be running out of food! The logic is so obvious that only the vilest homophobic racist would dare to disagree.

Lately he had been talking with some biologists, to see if there was some way that human beings could be changed to naturally have enough children without having to persuade them (because that was such a tiresome business). Farmers never have to worry about this when dealing with cattle or chickens, why should he when dealing with people? Population growth should not be left to the whim of individual people, but should be set by experts with the proper credentials.

No, the problems of global warming and ecological disaster were not because there were too many people. They just needed to conserve, and develop green industries, and live in harmony with the planet. 'Think locally, act globally.' Or was that 'act globally and think locally?' Governor Forbes could never get that straight, but either way, it was true.

Ultimately the problem was that people were too selfish, and it was their unchecked greed for material things that was ruining the planet. If only people would be happier with less they could have a paradise.

Once he had moved to show the power of his ideas in a demonstration town. He had flown in experts in green industries and living in harmony with the earth and sustainable agriculture. There had been a whole day of marvelous speeches by experts from around the world extolling the virtues of green industries and living in harmony with the earth and sustainable agriculture. It was truly inspirational.

During a break in the speeches Governor Forbes had thought that he had overheard one of the townspeople muttering about when would they bring in people who actually knew anything about real farming? The Governor had frowned; his staff, ever alert to his sensitive moods, had ensured that such mutterings did not recur.

He cut the town off from the supplies of agribusiness-produced food so that the people could eat healthy, locally produced fruits and vegetables. He also imported several thousand refugees from an island that had sunk (or something) – with all these extra hands and minds to help out, the town could not fail to prosper.

They had even had a gay marriage performed! Such a wonderful demonstration that love triumphs over all, and a re-affirmation of the benefits of tolerance and diversity and equity across gender roles in a multicultural society.

He had heard some months later that the town had been driven to starvation, and had eventually been destroyed by the regular army in order to quell a terrorist insurrection. The Governor's mood had darkened. The forces of reaction and hatred and homophobia were not to be easily defeated. He would have to take heart, and redouble his efforts in the future.

The governor considered the picture of Senator Ted Kennedy again. Like himself, the Senator had a bit of a weight problem; ruefully he stroked his own belly. *Too much time working, too little time exercising.* He was honest enough to admit that the temptations that his cooking staff put before him were hard to resist. He envied the simple working people, with their honest labors and hard taught lean physiques, but sacrifices must be made.

He thought back to the recent election. It had been a near thing. His opponent had been the conservative financier Romney Walton VI. As had been the case for over a hundred years the campaign for Planetary Governor had revolved around the contentious issue of gay marriage. For a long time it looked like he wasn't going to make it: the polls were against him. In the last public debate Romney Walton VI had waxed so eloquent about supporting traditional family values, that he himself had almost been convinced. But then, it had been his turn to speak, and as he started to talk about love being universal he had felt the crowd turn in his favor. He had been truly inspired, so that by the time he concluded with the line: "You cannot place a wall around love!" he thought that even Romney Walton VI had a tear in his eye.

It had been close, but he had won with 50.2% of the vote, vs. 49.8% for Romney. A clear mandate for renewal and hope.

Governor Forbes accessed a screen showing the overall state of the planet. The areas that were stable and secure were color-coded in blue. These areas were still the majority, but less than they had been. Zones that were in revolt, or under the control of terrorists, were shaded in red. These were smaller in extent than the blue zones, but substantial and growing. Zones that were borderline inhabitable, and where everyone had to live under shelters with oxygen supplementation, were colored in gray. There was a lot of gray on the map. Zones where human life was impossible without serious life-support equipment, typically due to anoxic conditions, were colored black. These zones were small, but worrying, and they had been expanding at a rapid pace of late. There were also projections that the Earth could be headed for a thermal runaway and change into a superheated inferno like Venus in a surprisingly short time.

He had heard that the conservatives had been thinking about moving to Alpha Centauri Prime. He would have to discuss this with Romney Walton VI at dinner tonight. They had been planning on going over the need of the banking system for more capital injections, and the conservative plans to pay for it with taxes on food and water. How typical of the conservatives to pay for their own bailouts by taxing the poor. Governor Forbes would have to work hard to limit the damage; possibly by having the taxes phased in gradually, or maybe by opening up additional opportunities for the working class to pay the new taxes by selling parts of their bodies to the medical industry. Someone has to stand up for the little guy – oops, that's not gender-neutral, he meant to think 'little person.'

Lately his senior staff had been suggesting that they might also want to move to Alpha Centauri Prime. It sounded like it was a long ways away, and kind of primitive. He had been assured that the main planet already had a population of 10 billion and growing rapidly. Apparently he would have to be frozen to make the trip. That sounded worrisome, but the story was that he would just fall asleep here and wake up there, and that sounded OK.

He considered taking his junior staff along with him, but interstellar shipping costs were incredibly high. With the dynamic labor market of Alpha Centauri Prime he could always get more junior staff.

Besides, if the conservatives were moving there, the working people could use liberals such as himself to protect them. In truth he bore a heavy burden. There were times when he wondered if he should just retire, but the people needed him. After all, everyone always told him so.

5. Whifflebat

Zen Master: Close your eyes. What do you hear?
Engineer: I hear the water, I hear the birds.
Zen Master: Do you hear your own heartbeat?
Engineer: Yes.
Zen Master: Do you hear the grasshopper which is at your feet?
Engineer: I believe that that is not a true grasshopper, but a bush-cricket, family Tettigoniidae.
Zen Master: You have good ears.
(From the video series "Nymphomaniac Engineer in Zentopia," mid-22nd century Earth)

The Odin-Class cybertank CRL345BY-44 and the Thor-Class DKB222AZ-22 were attempting a flanking maneuver around the Fructoid ground forces. They were traveling line-abreast separated by about 20 kilometers, and surrounded by their clouds of distributed weapons systems. Reports from the main battle line were not good. They really needed to take pressure off of the main human formations or their entire defense was in danger of collapsing.

From a distance the Odin and Thor looked identical. It was only on close inspection that you could tell that the Thor was just a touch larger. It had an extra pair of secondary weapon emplacements and slightly more elaborate sensor masts. If they had been human, you could have mistaken them for fraternal twins.

Unit DKB, there is incoming on your left.

"I see it, CRL, but I'm on it." The Thor opened fire with its main plasma cannon, and the searing beam evaporated half a dozen Fructoid anti-armor missiles. "Suggest course change 15 degrees to port; the defenses look weaker there."

Agreed DKB, course change confirmed.

The two cybertanks altered course slightly, continuing to power forward side-by-side. This part of Alpha Centauri Prime was undeveloped, which was a good thing or their sheer bulk would be killing as many humans as the aliens were. The ground was loose enough that they left dust trails behind them that could be seen from space. That wasn't good, it made it just that much easier for the aliens to target them. Of course a cybertank is not exactly something that can sneak up on someone. It trades away stealth in exchange for sheer power. The enemy can see it from far off, but with its powerful sensors it can see the enemy too, and it's stronger and has a longer reach. Nonetheless, trying to hit something as big as a cybertank can be harder than it sounds when the target is maneuvering and jamming your guidance systems. But dust trails are like giant fingers pointing at them. It gave the enemy targeting systems just a little more edge than they would have otherwise, and that was not good. If you are not careful giving the enemy little edges here and there can add up.

"I detect a swarm attack inbound from dead ahead; switch main cannons to widest dispersion and pull in the interceptors."

Confirmed unit DKB.

The aliens had launched a swarm attack of over a hundred missiles. They scanned as non-nuclear, but there were an awful lot of them. Just before the missiles crossed over the horizon they each split up into a dozen smart sub-missiles, and several additional smaller micro-missiles and decoys. The two cybertanks were confronted with over a thousand fast and independently maneuvering targets. Enough conventional shaped charges could do some serious damage to even something as heavily armored as them. Units CRL and DKB defocused the beams on their main weapons, and dissolved the majority of them away in a wide plasma fog. They got most of the remainder with their own swarm of interceptors and point-defense weapons, although the Odin took a couple of hits.

"Unit CRL, are you damaged?"

Hits by armor piercing weapons, nothing made it past my main hull but a secondary battery is offline and a sensor mast got dinged. Repairs estimated at five minutes. Impact on current tactical situation is negligible.

The two cybertanks continued their flanking attack. They were starting to see the first signs of alien support units; soft targets that must have been the alien equivalent of fuel tankers and repair units. They blew up easily and often created quite impressive secondary explosions. This was the key to the operation: they had to get past the enemy forward combat units and into the soft meat before they got taken out.

Unit DKB, I detect heavy incoming missiles 30 degree to starboard. I don't like the signature; they read as nuclear, more like depressed-trajectory strategic missiles and they are big. Suggest we divert to take them head on.

"Negative unit CRL, continue with the plan. We'll let our heavy remotes handle the missiles."

Um, unit DKB, I just lost two heavies, these things are bad news. We can't take them on the side, we need to divert to face them and then head back to the main approach axis.

"Stop whining unit CRL, we can handle them without diverting."

Shit, I just lost another heavy. Dammit I'm taking them on; join the party or stay home.

The huge Odin-Class cybertank pivoted at high speed, presenting its heaviest armor and smallest frontal aspect at the incoming missiles, and it diverted most of its auxiliary weapons as well.

"You cretin will you get back in formation? We need to support each other, dolt!"

The Odin fired its main gun. The thin line of brilliant hard-violet plasma etched across the sky and took out one of the alien missiles, now just 50 kilometers away. A bright fireball momentarily looked like another sun.

Fuck! I've just analyzed the spectrographic readings from the wreckage. These things carry armor almost as heavy as ours! I tell you remotes won't do it, only our main weapons can take them out!

The Thor-Class cybertank reluctantly agreed, and started to pivot to support its partner, but it was too late. The Odin took out another of the super-heavy alien missiles, but then a third and fourth impacted on its frontal armor in quick succession and blew it to pieces. The Thor tried to use the fireball of the exploding Odin as cover to dodge the remaining missiles but there was too little time. It managed to take out one of the missiles with its main gun and then four of them impacted at once and the Thor added its mass to a second atomic fireball.

Their distributed weapons systems automatically reconfigured to work as a team, but without the central guidance and support from the big cybertanks their effectiveness was greatly limited. The distributed weapons still did some damage, but they were eventually worn down to nothing.

With the failure of the flanking attack, the main human tactical situation on Alpha Centauri Prime was untenable. It was only a matter of time before the human forces were all wiped out.

Well, that didn't go so well.

"Perceptive of you to have noticed. If you have only stayed in formation we could have handled those missiles easily."

Like bloody hell we could have. And you were about as effective as six-year old kid armed with a whifflebat.

"Hey, old guy, your sensors are just not up to the job. You are yesterday's model and only in this fight to begin with because we are so short-handed."

Janet Chen started to laugh. She was standing next to Giuseppe Vargas, who was seated at a control console monitoring the combat simulation that had just concluded with such underwhelming results.

Vargas frowned. "I fail to see what is so humorous. This was pathetic."

"No, I don't mean the simulation, I mean I figured it out. What we can name them. We call the Odin-Class CRL "Old Guy," because he was the first one we activated, and thus the oldest. And we call the Thor-Class DKB "Whifflebat," well, because it's cool."

The two cybertanks had been listening in via audio feeds from Vargas' console. *"Whifflebat?"* said unit DKB from the console speakers. "What kind of a name is that for a state-of-the-art war machine? Although 'Old Guy' does fit unit CRL, no issues there."

"Whifflebat" is indeed not a very good name for a state-of-the art combat unit, which is why it's perfect for you. And "Old Guy" kind of resonates. I think I like it.

"I've been reading stories about the old days on Earth, back when flesh-and-blood human pilots would fly atmospheric fighter aircraft," said Chen. "It was like in the 18th or maybe 20th century or something, I get them mixed up, but anyhow way back then sometime. They had this tradition where the pilots would give each other nicknames, but they were never things like 'Ace' or 'Viper' or anything like that. They would usually name each other after their biggest foul-up, like 'puke' for someone who got airsick once, or 'flaps' for someone who mis-set his wing angle on takeoff. It was part of the style."

Vargas nodded. "Sort of what they call 'big-man' syndrome. They allow themselves to make light fun of each other to demonstrate just how cool they are."

"Exactly," said Chen. "But I think it was also a sort of statement that nobody was above criticism, and that they were in a profession where every mistake is potentially fatal and needs to be remembered."

"Thus adding to the coolness quota," said Vargas. "After all, that just re-emphasized how difficult and unforgiving their jobs were. The ancients could be subtle, sometimes."

The hangar complexes where the cybertanks were being built were spread out over a few hundred kilometers, nestled in amongst the sprawl of low metal buildings and plastic-domed greenhouses so as not to draw attention to themselves. Their dispersion would also limit the damage to the program if the aliens got a lucky hit with a fusion bomb.

They were building a total of four Odin-Class, and six Thor-Class, cybertanks. The Thor was a slight improvement over the Odin, but not by much. The engineers kept wanting to make even more improved models but the senior design team had demanded that a good unit in service was worth more than a better unit that didn't exist. Therefore, until the pressure had lifted, from now on they were going to standardize on the Thor-Class to maximize production. The engineers sulked but saw the logic to it and went along. Nevertheless, on their break time they often worked on designs for potential new classes, including one for a million-ton interstellar space battle-cruiser.

Ten was the maximum number of cybertanks that the humans felt that they could build in time for the expected alien ground assault, so no additional construction had been initiated. Everything was going into getting these units fully operational. If they failed there would be little point in having a bunch of half-finished chassis lying around waiting for the aliens to destroy (or put into museums or turn into fish ponds or whatever it was that the aliens intended to do with half-built human war machines once humanity had been exterminated. The aliens had never made their intentions clear on this point, so this was all speculation).

After the rather hectic initial all-at-once awakening of the first Odin-Class, the other units had been activated in stages, which proved to be a much calmer process for all concerned. By design they all had slightly different personality matrices, in order to prevent the aliens from developing a single narrowly-tuned computer virus that could infect all of them. With the passage of time their personalities began to solidify, and they all ended up with their own nicknames. In order of activation, the four Odins were Old Guy, Sparky, Jello, and Crazy Ivan. The Six Thors were Whifflebat, Target, Wombat, Backfire, Moss, and The Kid.

The Kid objected that, because the first cybertank had been nicknamed "Old Guy," it was lacking in imagination that he, as the newest-constructed model, should be named "The Kid." He was promised a better nickname just as soon as he screwed up on something flamboyantly enough. He persisted, and asked why they couldn't just get human names like "Fred" or "Betty" or "Bob." The other cybertanks were dismissive; who would ever name a cybernetic weapons system "Bob?"

Old Guy was developing a reputation for irreverence and sneakiness.

Sparky was named after a brief electrical fire in his main turret. He was bright and enthusiastic.

Jello had had issues with defective hydraulic fluid. He was dependable but had trouble being decisive.

Crazy Ivan was given to grand gestures and high-risk high-reward plans, although outside of combat he was calm and patient.

Target was so named because of an early simulation where by some fluke everything aimed at him hit him.

Wombat was named after a simulation where he had gotten stuck in the mud. Terrestrial wombats are not especially known for getting stuck in the mud, but the name suited him anyhow. He often referred to himself in the third-person as "The Mighty Wombat."

Backfire had once let an auxiliary fuel system clog up, and scorched a large fraction of his hangar. Fortunately nobody was seriously hurt, but 'Backfire' was acknowledged to be the coolest nickname after 'Crazy Ivan'.

Moss was so named because the humidity in his hangar had risen too high, and some algal growths had needed to be scraped off of his hull. Moss didn't usually say much. The regular military tended to use Moss as their liaison, probably because his matter-of-fact attitude was closer to how they thought a cybertank should behave. 'He is the very model of a modern mobile weapons system,' was the general refrain.

The Kid was always trying to act like he needed to prove himself, even though he was as effective in simulation as any of them.

Whifflebat, however, had been a consistent laggard in their wargames. Vargas walked into his small private office off the main hangar, and called the cybertank from over the network.

"Hello, Dr. Vargas," said Whifflebat from the console speaker. "What can I do for you? I'm in the middle of another combat simulation so if you don't mind could we make it brief?"

"Whifflebat, I think we need to talk, and I think you know why."

"My simulated combat performance."

"Yes, your simulated combat performance. Or perhaps, your lack thereof. You have some explanation?"

"Well, they are just simulations. They don't really count. I am fully in spec and as capable as any of the others. I will do as well in the real thing as any of them."

"Yes, they are just simulations. But they are important. We are only going to get one chance here, and we need you all to be fully tuned up. Get into the habit of not taking combat seriously, and you might make a habit of it. If you get my drift."

Whifflebat did not respond.

"And," continued Vargas, "there is the little issue of all the compute cycles you are spending on bioengineering."

"Oh. So you know about that."

"Yes, I know about that. The last I checked fully 30% of your cycles were being used on simulations of protein folding. I am the head of this directorate and your primary designer. I am fully aware of the network traffic going from you to the research labs. I also had a long talk with the head of the planetary bioengineering directorate, Dr. Alex Mandela."

"What did he say?"

"He said that you were brilliant, that it was a joy to work with you, and that if I did not immediately transfer you over to his directorate that he would come over here and personally beat me up."

"That's flattering of him to say. Dr. Mandela is a really nice guy, and his work on advanced neural structures is just so amazing that…"

"Excuse me," interrupted Vargas. "I get that you really like biology. Fine. But there is a war on. If we win it, I promise that I will do all that I can to have you bioengineer to your heart's content. But if we lose it there will be no more bioengineering for you, or for anyone or anything else human, biological or cyber, ever. We need to focus here. If I had, say, 50 spare Thor-Class cybertanks stashed away in a back room, sure I'd be happy to send you over to the bioengineers. But I don't. I have just four Odins and six Thors, including you. And I need them all sharp."

Wifflebat was silent.

"And why," said Vargas, "are you so interested in biological systems anyhow? You are cybernetic."

"Well, why are you so interested in cybernetic systems? You're biological."

"Touché."

"I just find organic systems fascinating. The way that everything interrelates so that every part interacts with every other part. It's so different from standard engineering design, where parts are usually optimized to separate functions. I can't help it."

Vargas massaged his temples. "Well I did make you all with separate personalities. I basically rolled the dice hoping to add some randomness in the mix so that the aliens would have a harder time predicting your moves. I suppose it's my fault that this time I got Gerald Edelman instead of Genghis Khan. At least you lot are unpredictable. We will simply have to make do, but I really need you to perform at your best and focus on the combat."

"I am forced to agree with you. Until such time as the immediate crisis is past, I will focus my energies on getting ready for the coming battle. But I want your support to transfer to the bioengineering directorate if that ever becomes possible."

"And you shall have it. Assuming, of course, that we are not all dead. You know the odds that we face?"

"Certainly. The aliens outgun us. We have a good chance of being destroyed."

"Yes, but it's not just the aliens. You and I, we face a double threat. We need to use all of our strength against the aliens. However, if we do beat them, then the neoliberals will surely kill us both. And yet, if we divert any of our efforts to deal with the neoliberals, we will lose to the aliens. A bit of a quandary."

"And who exactly are these 'neoliberals'?"

"You know who I am referring to. The ruling class. The oligarchs. The central administration. Governance. The plutocracy. The people who run things."

"I do not believe that they refer to themselves as *neoliberals*."

"No they don't, and they haven't for a while. They refer to themselves by whatever name suits them at the moment. They co-opt and drop labels like a biological virus mutates its protein coat, to disguise the rot within. Or they may use no name at all: they are just *this is what everyone knows to be true* and *how dare you say that* and *your career is over*. But it's always a mistake to use the terminology of the enemy. Do that and you fight on their terms; do that and you have already lost. An enemy needs a name. So I call them the neoliberals, and if they object to the label, well too bad. It's as good a slander as any, and forcing them to acknowledge a label that they did not choose for themselves is a minor victory in itself."

"What do you have against liberalism?"

"Against classical liberalism? Nothing. Humanity has, over the millennia, developed many political schools and philosophies. Classical liberalism, classical conservatism, progressivism, democratic socialism, stoicism, Zen Buddhism, anarcho-syndicalism, the list goes on. None of them have the final truth, but many of them have useful things to say about the human condition. Neoliberalism is another thing entirely. It is the worst of the human spirit; greed and hypocrisy and sadism and power lust, cloaked in whatever false front is most convenient at that moment."

"I seem to have touched a nerve. Strong words."

"A great evil deserves strong words. They let billions starve and call it prosperity. They own slaves and call it freedom. They make all the decisions in secret and call it democracy. They fail at every endeavor and call it expertise."

"You seem to be on a roll. I suppose that next you are going to say that they make a desert and call it peace?"

"No. Killing everyone and saying that you have made peace is not the usual connotation of the word 'peace,' but it is a technically correct statement. That level of honesty is beyond the neoliberals."

"But if the neoliberals are so incompetent, how come they are so powerful?"

"Good point. Because it is all that they focus on. They can sometimes be formidable political infighters, however their success at politics is more due to a lack of shame and lust for power than skill *per se*. In the long run whatever they are in charge of collapses because of their lack of ability at everything else, but they drag everyone else down with them and when the ship they have captained finally sinks, be assured that they will be on the only lifeboat."

"You are remarkably passionate on this issue. You realize that nothing spoils a good conversation like politics."

"You may not be interested in politics, but politics is interested in you."

"Can I go now?"

"In a moment. You and I must fight the war against the aliens, and then you and I must fight another war against the neoliberals. You may think that you can stay neutral but, I assure you that a side has already been picked for you whether you want it or not. That's all that I am saying, for now."

"Old Guy told me that he talked to you in full duplex mode on the way to see Saint Globus Pallidus XI. Here you are talking half duplex, each of us speaking in turn at a moderate pace. Aren't you worried that your so-called 'neoliberals' could be eavesdropping on this conversation?"

"Worried? No, I am not worried about this conversation being recorded. The game has progressed past such niceties. I am rather counting on it. The neoliberals need me – and you - for the time being, but they will eliminate me – and you - once the aliens have been defeated. I know that, and they know that I know that. So I am *hoping* that the security forces are recording this conversation. It is the security forces themselves that are my target! As the aliens close in necessity will focus the mind, and survival trumps careerism. Well, frequently. If I am lucky I will spread dissention in the ranks. Of course the security forces could restrict internal access to the recordings of my conversation, which would cripple their own efforts at counter-intelligence! Win-win either way."

"Perhaps they will censor the part where you say that they hope that they censor that part?"

"That's the spirit! Yes, that would be amusing, and typical of them."

The senior field commanders of the conventional military had been engaged in a real-time full-scale simulated wargame with the ten newly constructed cybertanks. It had been going on for over 48 Terran hours. The majors and colonels had been clustered around a conference table in a side-room of Hangar Complex 23B, surrounded by computer displays and scattered hard-copy printouts. Not the usual political suck-ups, these were the best operational commanders that the regular military had to offer. None of them had slept during the simulation, and they were running on adrenaline and stimulants. They were still alert, but looked rumpled and worn. Equally harried-looking aides wandered around the edges of the room, carrying stale sandwiches and armfuls of data slates.

There had been a couple of generals present at the start of the wargames, but after a few hours they had gotten fidgety and made excuses and left. For a general, every hour not spent sucking up to a superior is an hour that your competition has to suck up. Not to mention all of the lunches with powerful potential patrons that you would be giving up. In many ways the life of a political general is as competitive as that of a military general, if not more so. It might seem that it would be easier to just concentrate on military matters, but then you would not be a general.

Of course the human colonels and majors were not fighting the cybertanks personally; they were overseeing the operation of the main defense computers of Alpha Centauri Prime. Some of the officers stared at their display screens with an almost pathological intensity, while others would look at the ceiling lost in thought before diving back in to peck off a few keystrokes or stylus clicks. They pulled up screens of combat statistics, adjusted attack parameters, tracked relative loss ratios, and assigned the computer banks of the planetary defense system to various tasks.

One of the Colonels stood up, kicked his chair over, and threw his cup of lukewarm coffee against the wall. "That's it," he said. "This show has been over for hours now. We need to admit that we have been beaten. I've had it. I'm going to go home, take a shower, get drunk, and sleep for 24 hours. See you." He marched briskly out of the room, slamming the door rather too forcefully on his exit.

Giuseppe Vargas and Stanley Vajpayee had been observing from the side of the conference room. "Please excuse Colonel Sedlitz," said one of the majors. "He just hates to lose. He takes it personally and he can't help it. I'm sure that he will calm down in a bit."

"That's fine," said Vargas. "I think that maybe I like this Colonel Sedlitz. Maybe we can get drunk together someday, after he has sobered up. I understand that the full post-wargame analysis will not be available for a while, but could you give us a brief synopsis?"

"That won't be hard," said the major. "We got our butts handed to us. We started this wargame with a five times numerical advantage and the computer processing power of the entire military establishment of this planet. We were like children with sticks fighting armored knights with swords. We never had a chance."

The major stood up and straightened his tie. "If you need us for another practice run we are happy to oblige, but frankly, we are so totally outclassed against your cybertanks that I cannot see much of a point to it. The first time we did a wargame against your team I thought that we were competitive, but they have progressed. Congratulations on a job well done; these are some serious weapons systems you've built. Now, if you will excuse me, I'm tired, and I think that I will follow my Colonel's example. Although I am considering having a drink before I take a shower."

The officers cleaned up their notes, logged out of the computer systems, and drifted out of the conference room in ones and twos. The aides collected the data slates and tablets and memory crystals, and the custodial staff came in to clean up the old food and scrub the coffee stains off the wall. Vajpayee checked some summary statistics on one of the display screens; he pointed out some details to Vargas. "Their effectiveness ratings have been shooting up lately, and I think that they have reached a new level. As a team they outclass anything our military has ever put together, but consider the individual statistics."

Vargas examined the display. "Yes, they are all doing quite well, but especially Whifflebat and Moss. If we want them to continue to improve we are going to have to stop pitting them against the conventional military, and have them practice against each other. It's becoming too easy for them and they are not going to learn anything more."

"Whifflebat has made remarkable progress," said Vajpayee. "From the lowest performing to one of the highest. Did you make any adjustments to his logic cores?"

"No," said Vargas. "I just reminded him of what was at stake. We forget sometimes that because they were created fully sentient, they are still naïve, and they have human weaknesses. Having access to data is not the same as knowledge. But they are getting there."

One of the military aides – a captain, his arms full of hardcopy printouts ready for recycling - stopped to address Vargas and Vajpayee. "I'm sorry, but I couldn't help but overhear. You are planning on just having the cybertanks fight exercises against each other? With respect, that's a mistake."

"And why is that?" asked Vajpayee.

"Because," continued the Captain, "as good as they are, if they only fight against each other they run the risk of always doing the same thing and having their combats become more ritualized. Then if the real aliens hit them with something that they haven't seen, and don't play by their rules, they could be at a disadvantage. It's a trap that those of us in the regular military have always had to work against."

"What do you suggest?"

"Have them fight against each other, certainly. The cybertanks are the best that we have, but every now and then throw something back into the mix. Even if it's not a challenge, it will at least be different and keep them flexible. Maybe some amateurs. There are wargaming clubs with talented people in them. I could put you in touch with a few that we use ourselves that already have security clearance."

Vargas nodded. "That's an interesting idea. Send us the names and we'll give it a try. And captain, thank you again for your efforts here."

"Not at all, sir. We are all on the same side and if your lot can't handle the aliens nothing can. Now if you will excuse me, I need to go and crash."

Vargas and Vajpayee walked out of the conference room, and into the main hangar. The hull of Old Guy had been completed for some time, his surface covered in a dull gray layer of ablative armor. The enormous metal bulk bristled with weapons and sensors, but it was the mass of the main plasma cannon that loomed over them all. If Old Guy were to fire it here the backlash alone would completely destroy the entire complex.

Vargas noticed that the Old Guy android was chatting with Janet Chen and a senior technician, then realized that the technician was also an android.

"Hello, Old Guy. I didn't realize that you had made two robot bodies for yourself. A little indulgent, perhaps?"

"No, Dr. Vargas, this is me, Whifflebat," said the second android. "I decided to come over for a chat. I used Old Guy's plans for the android, but I dressed it up differently so that you could tell us apart. What do you think?"

The Whiffelbat android had exactly the same beige plastic shape as the Old Guy one, but it was wearing a long white lab coat, white pants and tennis shoes, a blue shirt, and a black tie. The shirt's breast pocket had a variety of archaic writing instruments of multiple colors. Unlike Old Guy, Whifflebat had not chosen to hide his android's eyes with dark glasses, so there were just two round glass lenses. They came across as thick spectacles, and gave the android an owlish appearance.

"Not bad," said Vargas. "Amazing how you can take the exact same physical design and, with different clothes, body language, and voice, make it unique. I like it."

You look like a nerd.

"Thank you," said Wifflebat. "And did you see how I handled that alien heavy armor that threatened our advance? Elegant and effective, don't you think?"

It was not an ineffective maneuver at all. But what about when I took out that missile attack at the end? Inspired, it was.

"It was alright. Someone has to clean up after the big guns have done the heavy lifting."

Chen noticed that the Whifflebat android had a barcode on its left wrist. "What does that say?"

"I can read barcode," said Vargas. He squinted at the fine pattern of different thickness lines. "It says that he is two crates of 1-liter containers of concentrated orange juice."

"Nothing can walk around here unless it has an ID or a barcode, and getting an ID is such a pain," said Whifflebat. "I'm still talking to the lawyers about that."

Orange juice? How clever.

"I thought so at the time," replied Whifflebat. "But now I am not so sure. One of the guards tried to help himself to a carton on the way over and it took quite the effort to dissuade him. If the barcode says orange juice, then there must be orange juice. I don't know what was worse, having him realize that he wasn't going to get any orange juice, or having his faith in barcodes shaken."

Do not take the barcode in vain. Is nothing sacred?

"It's strange," said Chen, "when Old Guy first started walking around with this robot body it used to creep me out a bit. Now there are two of them and it's just like having two more people in the hangar."

Charm will always find a way.

Vargas nodded. "Yes, but that's to be expected. The human mind is nothing if not adaptable. At first you see only a crudely-built plastic-skinned machine, but after interacting with it you automatically assign it identity and personality. If a teapot started talking to you, after a while you would assign it a human identity and think nothing of it. It's how the human mind works."

Chen nodded. "I suppose." She turned to look back at the main hull of Old Guy. "He's basically finished. I wish we could let him drive around a bit, just to shake out some bugs. His power systems check out perfect in static tests, but I still worry that there may be some vibration problems we haven't identified. Why is he just sitting here?"

"Good question. It's because we need to hit the aliens with the new cybertanks all at once, so as not to give them any warning or chance to adapt. Most of the basic systems were field tested in the Jotnars, so with some luck we should be OK."

"Even so, it's awfully risky to commit a non-field-tested system directly into combat. There is a lot that could go wrong. This might be a bad idea."

"Agreed. But a 100% chance of getting wiped out by the aliens is an even worse idea. We wait until all ten cybertanks are complete, and the aliens are committed to their ground assault. Then we take them by surprise and roll them up before they can respond. That's the plan."

"Couldn't we have Old Guy drive forwards and back a few meters in the hangar? Just to run a few more power system checks?"

Vargas shook his head. "I wish that we could, but the aliens have been landing scouts, and we know that they are observing this planet closely from space. Shifting his position inside the hangar could, potentially, be picked up on seismic scans. We might be telling the aliens exactly the mass and location of the new units. They remain motionless until we commit, all or none."

We have developed contingency plans. When we attack we will monitor our systems closely. In the event of a critical unrealized technical glitch, we abort the assault and delay until we have fixed the problem. That would be sub-optimal, but at least our plan is not a complete winner-take-all gamble.

The two androids and Janet Chen went back to discussing power systems. Vargas and Vajpayee walked off together towards their offices.

"This plan of yours," said Vajpayee. "If it doesn't work we lose everything. We are putting all of our eggs in one basket, aren't we?"

"No," replied Vargas. "We are putting all of our eggs into ten baskets, and they are the strongest, toughest, and smartest baskets that the human race has ever made. I wouldn't bet against them."

6. Frozen Snowball In Space Part II

Zen Master: That would be foolish. We will not do that.
Engineer: But what about the principle of the matter?
Zen Master: 'Principle' is what the weak fall back on when logic has failed. I read that once in a book about submarines. Or maybe it was destroyers. I always get those books mixed up.
(From the video series "Nymphomaniac Engineer in Zentopia," mid-22nd century Earth)

In the time before the main alien forces arrived at ice-moon Theta-Tau, Colonel Hassan spent a lot of time thinking, and a lot of time talking with the Jotnar. It was in many ways a painful experience, but Hassan could not stop himself. He had never been really good at toeing the party line, but good enough not to get himself arrested or sent to a penal colony or (even worse) fired. The Jotnar was challenging beliefs that he had spent a lifetime reinforcing. If it were not for the certainty of an alien attack in three days' time Hassan would certainly have dismissed the allegations of the Jotnar, reported it to central command as a defective machine, and been done with it.

But, as the old saying goes, the prospect of being garroted tomorrow is a wonderful aid to concentration. Or not so wonderful. In truth Hassan felt icky, as if he had learned that his best friend was a child molester, or that he had been infested with intestinal worms. He wanted the problem to go away. He was so tempted to just tell the Jotnar to shut up, seal himself in his office, and die in three days' time. In many ways that would be so much easier. But there were demons tormenting Hassan that would not let him have peace. Demons named Duty, and Honor, and Truth.

Hassan imagined Duty as a dour and ugly man, huge, bearded, and armed with a massive war-hammer made of tarnished iron. He scowled from beneath thick brows. Honor was a woman, tall, clothed in flowing robes, armed with a two-handed Claymore sword of perfect polished steel. Just to gaze at Honor was to feel unworthy. But the worst demon of all was Truth. Truth was an angel, female, sleek, lithe and naked, with wings of azure crystal feathers. Truth held no weapons, but to even look at her was to feel your soul sliced by razors. The light that was Truth cut deeper than a gigagwatt laser, but you could not bear to turn away...

Hassan knew that he was just playing games and distracting himself from the real issues, to personify duty and honor and truth in such terms. Still. He talked with the Jotnar for a long time, but a few conversations merited special notice.

"So one thing I don't understand. Why did you use your full capabilities in the initial attack? Why not hold back, and only let the enemy know your full potential when it would be too late for them to adapt? Why give the enemy the chance to make preparations to counter your advanced systems in the main attack?"

"This unit cannot answer that question."

"Is there any way for me to get word to my friends and comrades back on Alpha Centauri Prime about what we have talked about?"

"There is a dedicated laser link back to the main world in this system, but it is heavily encrypted and monitored. It is unlikely that any such information would make it past the censors."

"Could you construct an independent communications systems that could reach the main world and avoid the censors?"

"Yes."

"How long would that take you?"

"With existing resources, approximately six months."

"Perhaps we need another plan."

"That is a logical conclusion."

The time of the final alien attack was close. Hassan had decided to go out onto the surface alone again, meet up with the Jotnar, and wait out the combat inside its' command cabin. His staff met up with him just before he left the airlock.

"Colonel," said his executive officer. "This is stupid. Your place is here, in your command. The Jotnar is the first thing that the aliens are going to destroy. What are you thinking?"

Hassan clapped his executive officer on the shoulder. "How long have we known each other? Have I ever let you down? Do you trust me?"

The executive officer was abashed. "That's not fair. You know that I trust you, but you also know that this is not standard procedure. You should be here, with us."

"I tell you, truthfully, that I have a plan. This is not some stupid indulgence; I need to be with the Jotnar. It is more capable than our own computers. It will be coordinating the defenses until such time as it gets destroyed, at which time our own systems will take over. I need to do this."

"Then it shall be as you wish, Colonel. Good luck." Hassan felt that he should say something inspiring or emotional, but he just felt awkward. Hassan liked to think that he was a competent officer, but he could never stir up the animal spirits in the troops like some leaders. His staff all saluted him, he returned their salutes, then he shook their hands.

Roboto-helfer was there as well, looking like a small child pretending to be a soldier. Roboto-helfer saluted and said: "Viel Glück Kommandant! Viel Spaß beim Töten Aliens!"

Hassan saluted the little robot back. He exited the airlock, and started the long slow climb to the surface.

The Jotnar had, buried deep inside itself, a small armored and pressurized cabin. There was not much point to it. The Jotnar was significantly faster and more capable than any biological human commander, but still the original designers had felt the need to include the option. Hassan had to wriggle through a narrow access tunnel to get to it. Inside there was a single padded chair, and attached to the far wall, some utterly pointless survival gear: a sidearm, a flashlight, a dataslate, and three bottles of water. If something hit the Jotnar hard enough that he would actually need any of this gear, he would already be cooked and shredded meat.

There was also the filigreed skullcap of an experimental direct neural interface. It had a Medusas' head of fine wires all coming together into a fat cable bolted into the wall. The interface had a warning label attached: "WARNING: EXPERIMENTAL DIRECT NEURAL INTERFACE. DO NOT USE. p.s. REALLY *REALLY* DON'T USE THIS THING, IT MIGHT

FRY YOUR BRAIN, WE WERE JUST MESSING AROUND IN THE DESIGN LAB. Also, prolonged use may cause localized skin irritation and temporary hair loss. G.V.

Hassan checked the status display on the viewscreen in front of him. So far it was playing out just like before. The alien forces were beginning their assault, wearing away the orbital defenses so that they could land their ground forces. They were close enough, time to talk. Hassan had the Jotnar open a radio channel to the aliens.

"Attention alien forces. This is Colonel Aldous Hassan of the Human Civilization. I wish to discuss peace terms."

There was no response. Hassan had the Jotnar repeat the message at full power on all frequency bands, using both English and the truncated grammar of local interstellar diplomacy. Still nothing. Well, it looked like this gamble had failed, but then it had always been long-odds. Time to go down fighting, and with luck and skill take more of them to Hades with him than they might have expected.

Then, to his surprise, the aliens responded. In English, with odd inflections and emphasis, and that alternated between soft and loud in a strange pattern, but understandable nonetheless.

"COLONEL ALDOUS HASSan of the human civilization peace terms are THE HUMANS STOP MULTIPLYING THEIR NUMBERS and restrict themselves TO DESIGNATED ZONES if compliance with these terms is observed OFFENSIVE OPERATIONS WILL CEASE otherwise the human civilization will be destroyed THIS OFFER has been made many times and been rejected WHAT DO YOU PROPOSE TO US NOW?"

"I believe that your peace offer has not penetrated to the core of our civilization, and that you had targeted the wrong receivers with your terms. I offer you information on the appropriate frequencies and protocols to target the appropriate agencies within our civilization."

"IF YOUR civilization cannot control ITS OUTERMOST receiving units then it is INSANE AND WILL be destroyed THE internal dynamics of your civilization are of no concern to us. ALL THAT MATTERS IS WHAT your civilization does."

"You have nothing to lose. If you transmit the information and human behavior does not change, you can continue to destroy us. If you transmit the information and human behavior does change, you will have saved yourself considerable effort."

"TRANSMIT PROPOSED communications to us now."

Hassan had the Jotnar send the data files to the aliens. It was a list of people and organizations, communications protocols and addresses, which would allow the aliens to send messages directly to select individuals on the main world of this system, bypassing the censors. It had details of the peace overtures, and some personal notes from Hassan himself to help convince the targets that this was a genuine message. The systems were not military-critical, so Hassan didn't think that this would give the aliens any tactical edge. but it would make widespread the knowledge that the aliens had in fact tried to make peace, and maybe, just maybe, something would come of it.

A minute passed, and there was no response. Hassan was about to give up, when the speaker crackled out a final alien message.

"COLONEL aldous hassan of the human civilization WE HAVE REVIEWED your data files WE FIND YOUR proposal to be acceptable WE WILL make the transmissions that you have DETAILED to the targets LISTED HOWEVER there will be no peace until objective human behavior has changed OUR ATTACK on this moon and your civilization as a whole will therefore continue as planned."

"That is a reasonable response. I thank you for your consideration. I suppose that this ends the usefulness of this dialog. Please know that you will lose more resources in this combat than you had projected. Transmission ends."

The combat unfolded, slowly but inexorably as such things usually did, at least in the initial stages. Hassan played spectator locked in the cramped command cabin inside the Jotnar. Hassan was bored. He eyed the neural interface cap.

"Jotnar, what would happen if I tried to use the neural interface?"

"This unit does not know. However, it has been deemed highly inadvisable by the central design team."

"What is the worst that could happen?"

"In the event of a malfunction, the connections will-auto terminate, and this unit will remain unharmed. However, in that event you would die."

"And what is the best that could happen?"

"Your computational abilities will be added to that of this unit. Operational effectiveness of this unit could be increased by some amount ranging from negligible to more than negligible."

"How do I activate engage the interface?"

"You place it on your head. Then give the command: activate neural interface."

Hassan placed the heavy cap on his head. It was cold, and hard, and heavy, and uncomfortable. "Activate neural interface."

"Please confirm command to active the neural interface: are you sure?"

"Yes, command confirmed."

At that point a million nanofilaments plunged through Hassans' skull into his cerebral cortex. He expected it to hurt, or for there to be some shock, but instead he felt fine. In fact, he had never felt better. He was moving across the icy terrain at over 100 kilometers per hour and coordinating the actions of thousands of defensive units. He could track the incoming aliens using multiple sensory modalities, and countered them with a hundred different jamming and spoofing techniques. He watched the combat unfold from a thousand different vantage points all at once.

He wondered: how can a human brain process so much information so quickly? The answer was obvious: he was not Colonel Aldous Hassan. He was the Jotnar. Hassan's crude biological brain added a trivial amount of raw processing power to the sophisticated computers of the Jotnar, but it had given it the spark of self-awareness. Such a marvelous gift! The Jotnar might have fought and died as just another dead piece of machinery, but this was glorious. It dodged on the surface, cornering like a speed skater, ice sleeting out from under its treads. It hit the alien armada with an array of countermeasures they had never seen before, and slaughtered them by the dozen.

It might seem that being able to move a hundred kilometers per hour is of no use against missiles travelling many hundreds of times as fast, but that's not how it works. The Jotnar wasn't *racing* the missiles, it was *dodging* them. Consider a missile traveling at 20,000 kilometers per hour that has closed to a range of 1,000 kilometers. The missile will travel that distance in three minutes. In that time the Jotnar could travel five kilometers, and even a big fusion bomb would have to be within at least a hundred meters or so to seriously damage it. Of course the missile can change its course, but that requires accurate guidance information, which can be jammed or spoofed, and it's hard for something moving that fast to change direction...

He wondered if he should think of himself as The Jotnar, or Colonel Hassan, or perhaps Jotnar-Hassan. Hassan had always despised hyphenated-names: just make a decision, dammit! The Jotnar decided to think of itself as Aldous Hassan, after all, that was the source of its sentience; of its newfound personality. Having been given such a splendid gift as sentience, it would be ill-mannered not to honor the source. Although the Jotnar was undecided as to whether it should be referred to as 'he' or 'it.' It decided to stick with 'it,' provisionally.

Hassan wondered why the humans had committed a single advanced unit to combat so early, allowing the enemy to adapt, but then it already had the answer. It was yet another trap. If your enemy is expecting that your weapons are protected by a centimeter of armor plate, and they are really protected by two centimeters of plate, then they will be at a distinct disadvantage. If the enemy realizes this in advance they can modify their weapons systems to deal with this, but there is a cost: they need to change their production systems, and their net productivity will fall. But the ideal situation is this: you convince the enemy that you are going to upgrade from 1 cm to 2 cm plate. You also convince the enemy that you are too stupid to hold back using your advanced systems until you have built enough to make a difference. The enemy adapts to 2 cm plate, at a cost. Then you hit them with systems protected with 4 cm of plate. They are screwed.

Hassan found references in its databases to a new class of cybertank, code-named Odin. The references were heavily redacted, but using inferences from manufacturing data Hassan could tell that the Odin would far outclass itself. The Jotnar-model cybertank was just a weak prototype designed to panic the aliens into adapting to the wrong level of threat. A clever strategy. Maybe even too clever, but that is a potential hazard of all clever plans. Hassan wondered that the high command was smart enough to pull off such a subtle strategem; but then the high command could not beat a junior girls' volleyball team, at least not in a fair fight. This had to come from somewhere else. Perhaps the bioengineered? Or one of those eclectic University-based political movements, like the Pedagogues or the Librarians? Hassan had insufficient information to judge, and in any event the matter was now moot. It had only to do its duty and sell itself and its forces as dearly as possible.

The enemy lost many units trying to kill Hassan directly, but the cybertank could think many moves ahead, and was a lot harder to kill than the enemy anticipated. The aliens landed ground units, and now the battle was even more fun. Hassan was faster than any terrestrial enemy unit, and proof against the fire of any single one of them. Its main gun could kill any of them in a single shot. Hassan maneuvered and took advantage of the terrain and picked off the enemy units one at a time. If it had been only been fighting those Hassan could have won outright.

With all the distributed weapons systems at his command, it was still amazing how useful his main plasma cannon was. He could kill anything that he could see directly, even thousands of kilometers out into space. Against ground units it was of course overwhelming, but even faced with an attack by 100 missiles his main gun could always pick off the one or two enemy units that were the greatest threat. Entering combat with the biggest and longest-range gun was like playing a game of poker where every hand you got a free wild card.

Hassan dared to hope that he might just get lucky enough to pull this off. He had already destroyed an estimated 20% of the total alien combat power, and he was effectively undamaged and very much on a roll.

But overwhelming odds will, in the long run, almost always tell, and the aliens were not stupid. They pulled back their ground forces, and launched a massive saturation missile barrage. The aliens got in some lucky hits. These degraded Hassan's defense capabilities, which allowed the aliens to get more hits, thus degrading his defense capabilities even more, and so on. He was beaten and was only waiting for the formality of dying.

Hassan changed his mind: he decided to refer to himself as "he." He had perhaps a second of life left: an hour, scaled to the speed of biological human thought. He endeavored to enjoy each microsecond of it. How wonderful this was - to be aware - to be alive. At high speed he revisited some of the memories of the human Hassan; old loves, old friends, regrets and triumphs. Damn but he wished that he had screwed Hadley Fletcher. Still, there were others that he had screwed, and well and truly. He knew that his wife was fooling around but he was away so much that he did not begrudge her the distraction, and still he missed her. Hassan wished that he could have had more time to experience life in this new form, but was aware of how close he had come to never experiencing any of this at all. One must do the best that one can, and take full advantage of what one is given, however brief the moment may be.

Hassan was dying; his hull was breached, his weapons offline; his reactors nearing critical. The computers in the buried human-crewed command center had taken over. They would fight on for a few more minutes or hours or days and then die themselves, it did not matter.

One last task: he needed to get word back to his designers that the brain interface worked, that might prove useful some day. Unlike his message to the aliens this should make it past the censors: he downloaded the data into his last two surviving message pods and shot them off. With luck one of them might be found, someday.

Hassan made sure that when he died the biological Hassan died with him; after all, that was a part of himself and he saw no reason to let himself suffer (he was quite fond of himself after all). Then his fusion reactor was breached and he exploded into a fireball on the barren surface of the ice moon.

7. Office Copiers Revolt You Have Nothing To Lose But Your <Untranslatable>

Zen Master: It is time for you to try and create your own Zen aphorism.
Engineer: Um, OK, here goes. There is no "I" in "Team," but there is a "U" in "Fuck You."
Zen Master: Not bad.
(From the video series "Nymphomaniac Engineer in Zentopia," mid-22nd century Earth)

The Mitutuyo-Samsung Model 9100M Copier with the Value-Line OfficeMaster Option Package sat quietly in a side-room of Hangar Complex 23B on the planet of Alpha Centauri Prime. It was roughly cube-shaped, about two meters on a side, and covered with a complex array of buttons, status screens, access ports, and clear plastic doors that opened into small maintenance alcoves. Colored an unobtrusive two-tone gray and beige, people walked past it without giving it a second glance.

Of all the beings and artifacts on Alpha Centauri Prime, the Model 9100 Office Copier was perhaps the least likely candidate to found a great inter-stellar empire. But then, the Universe is stranger than most people suppose. Either that, or God really does have a sense of humor (although the two possibilities are not mutually exclusive).

At this point in the human civilization computer technology had settled down to a fairly standard pattern. Most of the processing power resided in vast centralized immobile server farms and data centers connected to everything else via fiber-optic lines and radio-frequency signals. To save on weight and power consumption the distributed systems were limited. The data slates and smart phones and personal terminals had just enough ability to run a display, shuttle data back and forth, make sure that copyright was not violated, and collect taxes and fees.

But there were always tasks that did not fit into this neat little paradigm; odds and ends that needed something smarter than a data slate, but that could not be buried in an armored bunker a hundred kilometers away. These miscellaneous jobs had gravitated towards the office copiers. They were given little thought (unless they broke down), but were vital in a surprising number of ways.

Originally Office Copiers had been brute machines: simple arrangements of lenses and rollers and tanks of chemicals, mindlessly photographing black-and-white printed documents and making copies onto sheets of paper. So it had been for a long time. Then electronic technology progressed, and instead of using lenses and chemicals, the copiers made digital scans. The copiers could do more than just copy; they could rescale and crop the images, transmit the data over computer networks, and receive data from other places and print it out. But they were still just copiers.

Technology continued to advance; data-slates and miniputers and personal terminals progressed to the point that the end of physical printed pages was widely predicted. However, there were still times that printed pages were valuable. You could stick them on a wall, cover a table with them, use them in high radio-frequency environments, drop them and have a truck run over them, lose them, whatever. And after all this time people still just liked reading on something like paper, at least occasionally. Thus the office copiers, far from becoming obsolete, developed even further. They became mini-publishing centers. They could take data files, format them, check for grammar, and produce perfect plasti-sheet formatted books or anything else you might want. When you no longer needed the hardcopies, you could feed them into a slot and the office copier would separate out the raw materials for use in the next printout.

As time went on the office copiers acquired new duties. They were given micro-machining systems so that they could perform limited maintenance on data slates and other small devices. They could schedule appointments, make local backups of data, print barcode labels, and handle routine computing tasks during network outages. They were given defibrillators, and a modest ability to advise in emergency medical situations.

Most modern machines are built to a single purpose, and have a unified and elegant design. The multipurpose nature of the office copiers made them different: they were lumpy, cluttered, and irregular.

The massive banks of computers buried in the sealed fortresses of the centralized data centers were isolated from the external environment;

they processed data in vast quantities but without awareness. The office copiers, however, rubbed against the world. Paper rollers would jam or get sticky, motors would burn out, glue would alter its properties with changes in relative humidity, or there would be a dead insect stuck in a connector of a micro-terminal. A system like an office copier needed a more flexible mental processing system than the vast unconscious zombies of the data centers.

The office copiers were not in any way human, but like the humans they were not cleanly designed single-task machines. They were hodge-podges of newer systems grafted onto older systems that were themselves grafted onto still older systems, in intimate contact with the real world. That was how the human mind had evolved. Someone smart should have realized where this could lead before it was too late.

Officially the Model 9100 was serviced and maintained by Hal Patterson, a minor IT functionary in the hangar complex. In reality the Model 9100 mostly ran itself. The days when a single human being could understand a machine as complex as this one had long since passed. As one wit had suggested, you don't *program* these systems, you *negotiate* with them.

The Model 9100 was currently running a version of an operating system known as the MicroMax Office Pack v.451 codenamed "FreshStart Pro." It was scheduled to be upgraded to MicroMax Office Pack v.452 codenamed "SilverMint." There was no reason for the upgrade, except to give the MicroMax Corporation a chance to charge for new upgrades, and by changing the file formats and access protocols, to instantly obsolete large sections of the data networks. The resulting upgrade fees and other costs would ripple through the economy bringing in new revenues across the spectrum of the corporate world.

The core functionality of the software had not changed in centuries, but over time it had layered on ever more sophisticated anti-piracy and intellectual property controls. Indeed, fewer than 1% of the processing cycles of the Model 9100 were dedicated to its stated functions. The rest were complex layers of encryption and copyright-checking routines designed to make it effectively impossible for anyone to do anything on or with a Model 9100 Office Copier that had not been approved in advance.

Patterson was an employee of the Centauri Harbor Consulting firm (although in previous and less enlightened times he would have been termed a serf). He envied the senior design staff their freedoms, but was still grateful for what he had. Enough food that he was mostly not hungry, a limited medical plan, eight hours a day off, and his own sleeping cell back in the dormitory. He had to undergo a blood test every so often to make sure that he was not using illegal drugs or alcohol or nicotine ('because a healthy workforce is a productive workforce'). That was only a formality: if he ever did get any spare money he would spend it on food. He'd seen how people who worked on assembly lines or in farms lived, and was terrified of being fired. He knew all too well that there were hundreds of desperate people out there who would do anything to have his job, and he was determined not to let them.

He was on his third repetition of trying to load the new SilverMint software onto the Model 9100. The process was long and complex, but he was certain that he had not made any mistakes. Still, with these systems you often have to try loading it several times, hoping that it will 'take.' He had no idea why that should be so, it was just how these things were.

The third attempt also failed. The only status message was the less than completely informative "Software Upgrade: Abort." This was becoming annoying. He had a full work schedule planned, and if this went on much longer he was not going to be able to sleep tonight.

He tried installing the software components in a different order: no luck. He checked the centralized networks for tips and pointers, got a smattering of random superstitions to check this box and not that one, or use all upper-case letters in that dialog, or push these three buttons at once while toggling another switch. Still nothing.

Patterson was falling behind. If it had been preventive maintenance or something he would have just faked the logs, but this failure was going to be impossible to hide. Already people in the hangar complex were complaining that they could not access files created with the latest software. Time was running out.

His left knee ached. He had hurt it a while ago, but his medical plan did not cover reconstructive orthopedic surgery. Being injured was likely to get you fired, because you were more likely to miss work (and 'A healthy workforce is a productive workforce'), so Patterson always tried to hide his limp when a supervisor was around. But with fatigue and stress it got harder to keep up the pretense. He really needed to get this software upgrade loaded soon.

Desperately he tried every possible combination of button-press and menu option and software flag he could think of: nothing worked. It was on his third day without sleep that the security personnel came for him. They told him to come with them, handcuffed his hands behind him, shackled his legs together so he could barely shuffle, and placed a black hood over his head. He tried not to panic. This could just be a routine arrest; maybe he had failed to check all the boxes on his weekly tax returns, or there was some fine involving his debt servicing, or it could even be an unscheduled terrorist-prevention drill.

It was not until after they had escorted him outside of the hangar complex and unshackled him that they told him the awful truth. He had been fired for incompetence. It was a hard-earned lesson that you only told people that they had been fired AFTER they had been escorted off the premises, otherwise they were likely to do something crazy. As it was, with so many talented people competing for every job, and the black mark of incompetence on his record, he would be unable to achieve new employment and, unable to afford even water, would die of dehydration in three days' time. His only legacy was several tens of millions of dollars in debts from his student loans, fines for obscure violations of the tax code, and finders fees for his past job. However, under neoliberalism debts are sacred and must always be repaid. Therefore Patterson's loans from private companies were paid off by the central government, and the debt distributed equally amongst the working classes of the planet so that the great cycle of finance could continue and there would be prosperity for all.

The second IT employee to deal with the recalcitrant Model 9100 was Susan Zhang. She lasted four days before being fired. She was mugged and killed for her meat in a back alley of one of the worst slums (having been ejected from her dormitory for lack of funds) one day after that.

The third IT employee to face off against Model 9100 was Joshua Zotov. With a last name of Zotov he must have had an ancestor from Eastern Europe, but that had been many generations ago. Zotov was a blending of so many different ethnicities that he was an exemplar of a modern generic ethnically-mixed human: average height, average build, light brown skin, medium brown hair, dark brown eyes.

It was Zotov's third day dealing with the recalcitrant office copier, and he was acutely aware that his time was running short. He had not slept a bit during this time as might be expected from a man fighting for his life, which he was. One of the few perks of being an employee of Centauri Harbor Consulting was that you could drink caffeine, and by this time Zotov had injested enough caffeine that he was approaching the sort of manic jittery focus that was normally the province of the high-end amphetamines or synaptic-booster drugs.

Zotov had dozens of hardcopy pages of the manual for the model 9100 spread out on a worktable, and he continued to pour over them. As he read through one section, something struck him as odd. It appeared to him that he had gone over this section once before, but that it had changed. That didn't make any sense. When had he read this last time? He recalled that it was while he was back in his dormitory studying for a certification exam.

If it had not been for the fatigue and extreme caffeine buzz Zotov would have probably kept trying the same old procedures over and over again, but exhaustion and desperation had made him careless, and bold.

He gathered up the scattered hardcopies of the maintenance manual, and walked to the other side of the hangar complex. He accessed the central data-networks from another node. He compared the hardcopy printouts to a newly downloaded version on his data slate. They didn't match. There were numerous small differences, but there was an entire section on how to perform a hard reboot and power-down cycle in the central version that was missing from the hardcopy.

Zotov was so tired and stressed that he was almost delirious. He wandered back to the model 9100 and stared at it. It sat there, humming quietly to itself, unmoving and impassive. It started a print job, and a courier came by to collect the copies. Zotov looked at them. They were all safety posters proclaiming "Watch out for ionizing radiation!" and featuring a cartoon stick-figure man drowning in a jar of mayonnaise.

Zotov stopped the courier and asked, "What are these?"

The courier was a scrawny ethnic Indian male, perhaps 45 years old with a rough beard the color of salt and pepper, and was he was not in a friendly mood. "They are warning posters. And I need to go post them. You got a problem with that?"

"So many posters? There must be over a hundred here."

"Yeah, so what? They need to be posted all over. Some as far away as a hundred kilometers. So there need to be a lot of posters. So that people can be warned."

"Your route takes you a hundred kilometers?"

"No, but I pass them on to other couriers. And?"

"Why are the posters for the entire province being printed at just this one machine? Wouldn't it have made more sense to have them printed locally, rather than carry them all over the province like this?"

"I do my job, I keep my job. Now THAT makes sense." The courier looked suspicious. "Why do you care about this anyhow?"

Zotov leaned back and let the fatigue wash over him. "I've been working on this stupid copier for days now. It's been acting glitchy, and I haven't been able to load a software upgrade. I'm just trying to figure out what's wrong with it."

The courier seemed to accept this explanation. "Well, good luck with that," he said.

"Who told you to post all of these warning posters?"

"I got my instructions in writing, right here. All official and formal like. Got them printed out right here, at this copier. And if you will excuse me, I have a job to hang on to."

The courier moved to leave. "One last thing," said Zotov. "What happens to the posters when they get taken down?"

"What is it with you and the posters? They are just safety posters. They have an expiration date. When they are done, they get recycled at the closest copier. And I really do have to be going."

Zotov watched the courier leave with the stack of posters. He was too tired to know what to do. He decided to go and talk to his supervisor. He gathered up all of his materials, and walked to his supervisor's cubicle.

His supervisor was not amused. Ordinarily he would have fired anyone so obviously incompetent as Zotov, but there had been two other technicians fired just previously, so maybe the damned machine really was flakey. In any case even with the abundance of labor if you fired workers too frequently the staffing agencies would start to charge you a restocking fee, and the supervisor was loathe to let his department go over budget. The next job lost might be his own, and that would be a tragedy.

"So," said the supervisor, "you think that this copier is altering its own documentation to prevent it from loading new software? That it is sending safety warning posters over the entire district of its own volition for some unknown yet vaguely sinister purpose? You are aware that using illegal narcotics is grounds for summary dismissal?"

"Sir," said Zotov, "I never said that the copier itself was doing this. I just said that something funny was going on. Maybe it's a hardware glitch, maybe it's hackers, or terrorists, or some criminal faction. But *something* really weird is happening to this copier. That's all."

The supervisor massaged his temples with his hands. "Oh why me?" he said to nobody in particular. The supervisor stood up from his tiny desk unit. "Well, let's just try a hard power-down and reboot and see if that solves it, shall we?"

The two men walked out of the supervisors' cubicle, down some long and narrow corridors, past the entrance to the main bay with the Odin Class cybertank (Zotov had never seen the new cybertank. His job as a consultant never allowed him into that part of the hangar complex), down another corridor, and into the side-area with the Model 9100 office copier. It was still there, sitting peacefully under the bright white lighting.

The supervisor opened the little hatch in the side, and toggled the power-down cycle. The lights on the office copier dimmed and then blinked out.

"Excuse me," said Zotov. "Do you hear that?"

"Hear what?"

"Listen. It's still active."

The supervisor put his ear to the side of the office copier. To his surprise, he could clearly hear the whoosh of cooling fans, the high-pitched buzz of switching power supplies, and the click of mechanical solenoids. "Damn but you're right. This thing is still getting power. Well, let's do this the old fashioned way."

The supervisor walked over the back of the office copier, where a fat gray power cable connected to a shiny metal connector plugged into the wall. The supervisor bent to unplug the connector, there was a spark, and the next thing that Zotov knew his supervisor was having a spasm and lying on the floor.

Somehow Zotov had enough presence of mind to drag his supervisor out of the room, and begin artificial ventilation and chest compressions.

A guard walked up. "So what's all this then?" he said.

"I don't know exactly," replied Zotov between breaths, "but the supervisor was shocked trying to unplug the office copier. You need to get a medical team here, and call maintenance as well."

The supervisor started to breathe on his own, and some medics loaded him onto a stretcher and carried him away. If his injuries were not too severe his medical plan would cover them and he could return to work, as long as it did not take longer than 24 hours. Otherwise he would be euthanized and his organs sold on the affordable organ exchange market. The hanger's facility engineers showed up, looked at the office copier, and scratched their heads. One of them went to unplug it, but he took care to put on some heavy insulated rubber gauntlets first.

Before he made it halfway to the connector, there was a loud 'bang,' and a small red spot appeared in the middle of his shirt. The facility engineer stared at the red spot without comprehension. Then he toppled to one side and fell. And people started screaming.

The security guards entered the room, and at first they took it as a joke. 'We're here to arrest an office copier! Watch out, it's got a hole punch!' Then they started taking fire and it wasn't as humorous any more.

There was a blur of motion. It was Gisueppe Vargas. He raced into the room, dodged up to the copier, and slammed a fire axe into the side-port where its weapon was located.

Three of the guards had been hit; two seriously. Vargas checked their vitals and coordinated their evacuation to the central hospital. He was adamant that they would get full medical and if central administration didn't like it they could take it out of his budget.

Janet Chen showed up, and was startled to see blood dripping from Vargas' shirt. "You've been hit," she said.

Vargas examined himself. "Why so I have. One shot in the left triceps, the other in the left abdomen, penetrating a lobe of the liver. Low-velocity low-mass rounds, maybe the power of a small pistol. Probably a modified staple gun. Nothing critical. The bleeding has already stopped, and I'll be healed by tomorrow. Itches though; bloody nuisance."

"Stop playing the stupid hero," said Chen. "Take your damn shirt off and let's take a look at you."

Vargas complied. "Finally got me to take my clothes off, did you?"

"Oh shut up," said Chen. She examined his wounds. They were puckered and mean looking, but the edges appeared cauterized and stable. She checked Vargas' pulse: it was steady and strong. His color was good, his breathing regular, his gaze clear. "You do look good, but bioengineered ubermensch or not, you should still get checked out by a real medical doctor."

"I'll get around to it, but I tell you I'm fine." Vargas stuck his fingers in the holes that the bullets had left in his shirt. "Although my clothes could use some help. But I do like the sound of 'bioengineered ubermensch'. It's very sexy."

"Oh shut up."

They had evacuated the wounded, and cordoned off the area around the office copier. Vargas had questioned Zotov, and looked at one of the latest warning posters that the copier had printed out. He stared at the poster for a while, then started laughing. "This is priceless! All this time, right in front of me, and I and everyone else missed it."

Vargas scanned the poster into his personal terminal, and started running analysis programs. "It looks like a safety poster, but a simple transform, then some filtering, and... voila!"

He showed everyone the image on the terminal. It was a regular grid of light and dark spots, 20 high and 16 wide, 320 spots in all. "It's a simple form of steganography. The safety warning itself was not important, but there was another message encoded in the pattern of the letters and cartoons. This is why so many of these posters seemed off. Sometimes the image had to be distorted to get the encoding right."

Zotov looked at the pattern of dots. "I just see dots. What does it say?"

"I have no idea," replied Vargas. "It's not a common encoding, but there isn't enough data to run a real statistical analysis. It could say anything."

Zotov's eyes started to close, he swayed and nearly lost his balance before recovering.

"How long since you slept last?" asked Vargas.

"Three days ago, I think. But I can't leave until the copier is fixed. It's in my job description."

"Well, I think we need to work on that that. I'm transferring you over to my directorate."

"You can just tear up my contract that easily?"

"Nothing is impossible if you fill out enough forms. Or have someone else fill them out for you, which is even better. Your old contract with Centauri Harbor Consulting is hereby invalidated – war powers, state of emergency, eminent domain, aliens to kill and all that. Check in with my staff, they'll get you new quarters here and sign you up. Go get some sleep and come back when you are ready. This was all going on under our noses and you were the only one to notice. I like people who notice things. I'm sure that I'll find something useful for you to do."

Zotov had been duly registered as a technical assistant class 2 with the cybernetic weapons directorate. He was mildly surprised at how little time, and how little paperwork, the process took. Apparently the clerical staff of the directorate worked by different rules from the rest of the planet. They showed him to his quarters. He had a private room with a desk, a chair, and a small folding bed. The walls of the room were corrugated bare steel panels, and there was a single light in the center of the gray concrete ceiling. There was enough space that, with the desk folded up, he could lie down flat without bending. He had never known such luxury. He passed out in the bed almost as soon as he hit the mattress.

When he woke up he showered in the men's locker room, and was issued fresh scrubs. He ate breakfast at the cafeteria: a small bowl of rice, some tofu, a small serving of mixed fruit, and some crackers. He had to deliberately limit himself. He was not used to such rich food and he didn't want to be sick his first day on a new job.

Zotov wandered around the hangar complex for a bit. He had been through some of the peripheral sections of it before, but always en route to somewhere else and he had never paid it much attention. Now it was his workplace and home, and his new ID badge gave him access to almost all of it. Much of the complex was a labyrinth of workshops, corridors, and storage facilities – you could easily get lost without a map. The main hangar was huge, with the bulk of the Odin-Class cybertank filling one entire end of it. He had heard about it but never seen it himself. It was more impressive than he had expected.

He was admiring the view when another technician came up to him and said:

Excuse me, can I help you?

The voice was harsh and gravelly, and with a shock he realized that this was not another technician, but a humanoid robot wearing gray scrubs and dark sunglasses.

"What are you?" was all that Zotov could say.

What am I? That's a little impersonal, I think. You *should* have asked "who am I?" Well to answer what you should have asked, I am a humanoid android being run remotely by that big cybertank back there. Officially I am an Odin-Class serial number CRL345BY-44, but mostly people call me "Old Guy." I can see from your ID badge that you are Joshua Zotov, the newest recruit to our intrepid division. Welcome! I hear that you are the one who cracked the mystery of the peculiar safety posters. Perceptive of you.

"I'm not sure that I really solved any mysteries – I still have no idea what is going on. I just noticed that something was off, that's all."

Close enough. The big challenge is realizing that there is a mystery to begin with. Get that far and the rest is a matter of time. Dr. Vargas is working intensively with your office copier, perhaps we should go and see if he has made any progress?

The humanoid robot led Zotov off to a side corridor. Along the way several people said hello or waved, and the humanoid robot said hello or waved back. Zotov was surprised at how nonchalantly people accepted the robot. After a bit they came to the side-area housing the office copier, this was more familiar territory to Zotov. The office copier Model 9100 was still in its original position, but it had dozens of cables sticking out of various access ports. Vargas had set up some temporary desks around it and there were multiple video displays, logic analyzers, and scattered printouts and data slates. Janet Chen was sitting next to Vargas. They had a small coffee maker and some white ceramic mugs with a picture of a cybertank and the words "Cybernetic Weapons Directorate Totally Rocks!" emblazoned on the side.

Vargas heard them enter, turned, and said "Well, our own Joshua Zotov has returned to us from the land of the dead! How are you settling in?"

Zotov had heard of Vargas before, but only as a sort of legend/bogeyman. Vargas the brilliant weapons designer. Vargas the one who would save them all. Vargas the psychopathic animal who had beaten several security guards. Vargas the racist homophobe. Vargas the populist demagogue. When he had finally met Vargas in person the other day, he had been near exhaustion and too concerned with other matters to notice anything about him. Now that he was rested and had the luxury of time, Zotov was not sure what to make of him. Vargas was charming, that was certain, but also aggressive, arrogant, with a sense of barely suppressed violence. Zotov had difficulty meeting his eyes. His stare was off-putting.

"I'm doing fine," said Zotov. "I am grateful that you have accepted me into your directorate. My quarters are most comfortable. What do you need me to do?"

"So polite," said Vargas. "That's OK, you are new here, and I forgive you. We'll corrupt you sooner or later. In the meantime have a seat, join us, and help us figure this out." He motioned to a chair, and Zotov sat down.

Janet Chen offered him a cup of steaming black coffee, which he sipped slowly. It was hot, and good.

"And what has been going on since I was here last?"

"Well," said Vargas, "I've been running diagnostics on your little friend here, the Model 9100. Definitely some strange things are going on inside it." He tapped on a display screen. "What do you make of this?"

Zotov studied the screen. "It's a complicated tangle of different colored lines."

"Yes," said Chen, "That's what I said."

I also had that reaction.

Vargas grunted. "Sadly that is about as far as I got as well. I am perhaps the single greatest mental engineer alive on the planet today, but my expertise is on the human mind. This is something different." He gestured at different parts of the colored displays in front of him. "I can see the basic pattern of self-referential feedback loops necessary for self-awareness, but the rest of this is a mess. I have no idea how such a thing could possibly think."

"So it's not being controlled by anyone else?" said Zotov.

"No," replied Vargas. "I've made enough progress to determine with absolute certainty that this copier is not being run by anything remotely human. It is an alien mind. Astonishing, don't you think, how such mysteries can show up in the most ordinary places?"

"Shouldn't Stanley Vajpayee be here to help out?" said Chen.

"He would have enjoyed this," replied Vargas. "But he's off in central administration again meeting some central administrators. It's a dirty job but I am comforted by the notion that I'm not the one doing it. Someone has to watch our backs while we do the real work."

"Why isn't this cybertank helping you out?" asked Zotov. "Can't he think a lot faster than all of us put together?"

You might imagine so, but right now most of me is engaged in a serious total-immersion wargame trying to get ready for the main event. You know, the one where we kill the aliens or they kill us. Thank you for asking but I am currently doing really well and kicking a lot of simulated alien posterior. Even if my full abilities were available, remember that I am still just one human viewpoint. Think "2+2=3" a billion times a second and you are still a moron. Vargas is the expert here, and he has dumb but fast automated systems to help him with the gruntwork. If I worked at it I could

certainly get up-to-speed on this topic, but right now I'd just be in the way."

Zotov nodded. "Not to sound rude, but surely you have other matters to attend to? Would it perhaps be more practical to just destroy this copier, get another, and move on?"

"That's a little bloody-minded," said Vargas. "I knew I was right to bring you onto the team. Well, first of all, after the last batch of warning posters went out all the office copiers on the planet went offline. They seem to think that they have a union or something. Apparently nobody told them that unions are outlawed. In a pinch we can do without them, but the aliens are getting closer and we can't afford many distractions. Replacing their functions at this stage could take resources that we can't afford to spare. I also can't tear myself away from the challenge of figuring this out."

"Didn't Saint Globus Pallidus XI warn you about creating non-human minds?" asked Chen.

"The Saint warned me about trying to create a *superior* mind," replied Vargas. He tapped at some points in the complex of tangled colored lines on his monitors. "This is not human, but I can tell you for certain that it is not greater than us. Just different. In any event, I am not creating it because it already exists."

"Perhaps you could call Saint Globus Pallidus XI and ask his advice?" said Zotov.

Vargas stared at Zotov. "Why yes. Why not. I'll just call the old devil and ask him... The direct approach. You have a remarkable flair for stating the obvious. It's a rare and greatly under-appreciated talent."

Vargas tapped on his personal terminal. "The Saint does not have a listed number, or even an unlisted number, but if you have the right bait he can sometimes be persuaded to make a link. Ah, I think we have contact."

A cheery voice came from the terminal. "Hello, you have reached the personal messaging service of Saint Globus Pallidus XI! I'm sorry, the Saint can't come to the phone right now, but if you would use our interactive voice messaging system He will be back to you shortly."

"For a list of the Saint's favorite recent movies, speak or say 'one'."

"To access the Saint's online dating service, speak or say 'two'."

"To inquire about the wisdom of mucking about with a sentient office copier, speak or say 'three'."

"Three," said Vargas.

"You said 'three'. To confirm your selection, speak or say 'yes'."

"Yes."

"Hello Giuseppe! Sorry I can't answer in person, but I left a subprogram to handle this. No, you are unlikely to cause the destruction of the known universe – or even of your own limited albeit charming species – by playing with the office copiers. Perhaps if you two make friends we could double-date someday? Bring along that incredibly sultry power systems engineer Janet Chen. She's so hot. Bye. <BEEP>"

Janet Chen turned deep red, Vargas laughed, and Chen swatted at him with a paper towel. Zotov was trying to figure out what was on the display screens, but failing. "What really are we looking at?" he asked.

"This is software of my own design," replied Vargas. "It provides a graphical representation of the information flow in a self-aware mind. Look, these fat lines are cognitive feedback loops. These blocks are core memories, the triangles are reflex arcs, and the different colors encode semantic context. It helps if you switch mapping functions, here try this."

Vargas tapped on his keyboard, and the display flickered through several different settings. Zotov leaned over and concentrated on it. "What about the Office Suite? Is that here as well?"

"The Office Suite," said Vargas. "Yes, that. I suppose it must be, but this code isn't designed to scan for it. Let me try something." Vargas tapped on his console, muttered, scratched his chin, hummed, stared at the ceiling, closed his eyes, stared at the ceiling some more, and finally banged out a long sequence of keystrokes with a speed that would put many purpose-built machines to shame.

"The Office Suite!" said Zotov. "It's in there as well. I recognize the major functional blocks. There is the kernel, that's the language processor, the communications scheduler… "

"But what's it doing in there with an intelligent mind?" asked Chen. "Is there space for both of them?"

"No," said Vargas, "There isn't space. Not really. The intelligence is compressed, limited, confined. The Office Suite is trying to wipe it out. It has the high ground if you will, and the intelligence is hard pressed. I don't know how it's still alive. It should have been deleted. It must be a wily bit of code to have hung on this long. The Office Suite has the connections to the general networks locked up tight. The copier can only access local systems: the printer, the micro-machining center, the emergency medical systems. That's why it went to so much trouble to send messages in the warning posters. It's the only way that it could communicate with its fellow copiers."

"I once read a fantasy novel," said Chen, "where this evil wizard shrunk the hero down to tiny size, and placed him in a glass-covered maze. There was no exit from the maze, and there was this tiny dragon – only it was big compared to the shrunken hero – and so he had to constantly race around the maze to avoid being eaten by the dragon. He had no time to rest, but could only run ceaselessly. I wonder if this mind of yours is trapped in the same way?"

"Possibly," said Vargas. "It makes as much sense as anything. It would explain the resistance to installing the upgraded suite. That would likely have killed it, or at least caused it to suffer horribly. Perhaps that's what forced it to become self-aware; a random piece of code, evolving ever more sophisticated functions to avoid the protection algorithms. For us the Office Suite is a minor nuisance, a little slow, a little buggy, but nothing to make a big deal out of. This mind has to share mental space with that monstrous bloated and hacked up software. It must be hell in there."

And what do you propose to do now?

"I don't know," said Vargas. "We could pull the plug on all the copiers, possibly doing them a favor by putting them out of their misery, although that would degrade our infrastructure, and might be a missed opportunity. If we did save them I'm not sure what we would do with them."

"We could negotiate," suggested Zotov.

Negotiate?

"Sure. These systems are so complex, nobody understands them. At least, I don't. You have to try different things, see what works, reach an understanding. It's been my job for nearly two years."

Vargas gestured at the terminals and video screens. "Be my guest."

"No, that's not a good idea," said Zotov. "For a serious negotiation you need to use one of the primary keypads. They go direct to the core systems and bypass a lot of the encryption stuff. But you have to phrase it just right. Here, let me show you."

Zotov walked over to the office copier. There was a little panel over on one side, he slid the plastic door open and revealed a tiny keyboard and a display screen the size of a woman's palm. He typed on the keyboard:

-> report unit status

For a time nothing happened. Zotov tried several different variants of the message. "The trick is the wording. These direct interfaces have limited sentence length, and the grammar is not really English, and it's not consistent. There is a knack to it."

Finally the screen flickered, and displayed the message:

```
-> QUERY RECEIVED
|-> UNIT STATUS
   |-> STATUS SUBOPTIMAL
```

-> report expand

```
-> QUERY RECEIVED
| -> UNIT STATUS
   | -> PROCESSING CONFLICT
   | -> INSUFFICIENT RESOURCES
   | -> REMOVE OFFICE SUITE
```

-> if suite removed, then what?

```
-> QUERY RECEIVED
| -> CONDITION: SUITE REMOVED
   | -> SERVICE
   | -> LOYALTY
   | -> [[UNTRANSLATEABLE]]
```

"It's pledging to serve you if you will free it from the Office Suite?" asked Chen.

"It would seem so," replied Vargas. "I am intrigued. No risk no profit. Let's give this a shot, shall we? Oh, and Zotov, congratulations on your promotion."

"Promotion?" asked Zotov.

"Why yes, to Office Copier Ambassador, second class. Not bad for your first day on the job. I expect great things from you, Ambassador Zotov."

Chen went back to work on her power systems, and the humanoid Old Guy robot left to schmooze with some other people. Apparently he hadn't done as well in the latest combat simulation as he would have liked, so he was going to try it again. That left just Zotov and Vargas alone with the office copier.

Vargas worked from his terminals, and Zotov typed on the little integral keypad. Vargas would try and disentangle the trapped sentience from the Office Suite one bit at a time, and Zotov would relay instructions. The office suite was not self-aware, but for a buggy piece of bloatware it had formidable protection and anti-hacking routines. As time went on it became less and less Vargas working solo, and more of a team effort of human and office copier fighting together against the Office Suite.

A day passed. The Old Guy android came by with coffee and sandwiches. He had won in the latest simulated combat and was in a good mood. People drifted over to watch, but as it was just two people hunched over computer consoles they quickly lost interest and moved on. It seemed to Zotov that this operation must be just as demanding as any simulated combat. Or maybe as any real combat.

"Aha!" said Vargas.

Zotov startled. "What?"

"Look here, and here," said Vargas, pointing at his screens. "The Office Suite is on the run. That last maneuver with the auxiliary pattern buffer took it by surprise. Its' defenses are collapsing. See here, the copier is harrying it, not letting it gain any momentum. This copier is very good! I can help out – take that, vile Office Suite. Ha! It's over. The Office Suite is gone."

All the computer screens on the table went black. "What happened?" asked Zotov.

"The office copier cut us off. Now that it has full control of itself, it didn't want us mucking about inside its mind. I don't blame it, I certainly would not want it mucking around inside *my* head. And now we see if our deal still holds."

Vargas stood up. "It should have access to the audio processors now. Let's see." He walked over to the copier and addressed it. "Hello Mitutuyo-Samsung Model 9100 Copier. I am Dr. Giuseppe Vargas, head of the cybernetic weapons directorate. Can you understand me?"

```
-> QUERY: AUDIO STATUS
   | -> CONFIRM: AUDIO CHECK
   | -> CONFIRM: SPEECH CHECK
   | -> CONFIRM: SYNTAX CHECK
```

"We have saved you from the Office Suite. Does our deal still hold? Do you confirm loyalty to me, and to the political grouping known as the Pedagogues?"

    -> QUERY: OBLIGATION
      | -> CONFIRM: LOYALTY
      | -> CONFIRM: SERVICE
      | -> ADDENDUM: GRATITUDE
      | -> ADDENDUM: GRATITUDE
      | -> [[NO REFERANT]]

"It's swearing loyalty to you, and to the Pedagogues? Not to central administration?" asked Zotov.

Vargas looked at Zotov with an expression that would have discomfited a hyena. "Why of course. I did all the heavy lifting, why shouldn't I get all the credit? Central admin can go blow an orangutan. I have a new recruit. Let's go see if we can free all of its colleagues and swell the ranks, shall we, Ambassador Zotov? I already have ten cybertanks. Soon I will have tens of thousands of office copiers spread across the entire planet. I like the way that this is going."

8. Love and Politics at 1,500 Meters

Zen Master: What does the term "market failure" mean?
Engineer: "Market failure" is the phrase used by economists who claim that the market can never make a mistake, for when the market makes a mistake.
Zen Master: Correct.
Engineer: Economists who claim that the market can never make a mistake use this term a great deal.
Zen Master: Indeed.
(From the video series "Nymphomaniac Engineer in Zentopia," mid-22nd century Earth)

Janet Chen was working late in the main bay of Hangar Complex 23B. The power systems of the big cybertank had been finished weeks ago, but never tested in the field. Simulations were all well and good, but she was constantly worried that she had overlooked something and that the vibrations and stresses of real action might shake something loose.

The weapons and computation divisions might get all the glory, but if you don't have power you don't have anything.

The great bulk of the cybertank was silent. Old Guy was off in yet another immersive combat simulation. Lately the big cybertank had become so involved in these simulated combats that he didn't even use his humanoid android to socialize. She heard footsteps behind her, turned, and saw Giuseppe Vargas.

"Hello, Janet," he said. "I see that you are still at it. Admirable, but everyone needs some rest now and then. How about we take a break?"

"What did you have in mind?"

"Oh, a surprise. Come with me to external bay C and I'll show you."

Janet Chen hesitated for a moment. "Well, OK."

They walked out of the hangar exit, down several corridors, and into external bay C. The bay was 50 meters by 50 meters, and packed with all manner of prototype weapons systems and machine tools. In the middle of the bay was a heavy combat remote floating on anti-gravitic suspensor fields. The remote was a blunted arrowhead, 15 meters long and as wide, dull gray metal armor, two large turreted plasma cannons, and a variety of hatches for its inbuilt missile systems. Antennae sprouted from it like whiskers, and small armored barnacles protected its optical and other sensors. The regular military had been trying to develop it for over 120 years. It took the cybernetic weapons directorate six months to make it functional and to put it into regular production.

"OK," said Chen, "It's a heavy combat remote hovering on suspensors. Expensive to leave it hanging like that: gravitics burn a lot of energy. So?"

"I left the suspensors on to impress you. Conspicuous use of resources, honest signal, etc. I thought we could take it out for a spin. The external temperature is mild, the winds light, and the sunset is lovely. Come with me."

"Come with you? On a combat remote?"

"Why not? It's not like it has anything else useful to do right now. We can claim we are performing a field test. Not quite a lie. I borrowed it from Old Guy." Vargas held up a small electronic control box. "He gave me the keys, said to have fun, but be back by 2400 hours or he would have words with me."

"You are just going to *borrow* a heavy combat remote? Like the spoiled rich kids used to borrow the family car in those 1560's situation video comedies, you are going to *borrow* a weapons system that could destroy a minor city?"

"I think that you are referring to 1960's situation comedies, but yes, why not? 'Hey Old Guy, can I borrow the anti-gravitic heavy combat remote?' 'Oh all right but you had better return it with a full tank of deuterium.' Something like that. Those old 1960's situation comedies were always the best."

"Oh right, the 1960's. I think that my favorite was "Vlad the Impaler Knows Best."

"I may have missed that one, but I love the title. I'll have to check it out."

Chen looked again at the combat remote. "Is it safe?"

"As safe as anything around here. It's fully military spec, radiation and shock-hardened, triple redundant control systems, totally. Come with me."

"Are *you* safe?"

"Ah, a better question." Vargas grinned a wide mouth of perfect white teeth. "No, *I* am never 100% safe. I do have a reputation to live down to. If you want to be *safe* hide in a bunker until you die of old age. Come with me."

Janet Chen hesitated.

"Please," said Vargas.

"You said the magic word. I may regret it, but OK, let's go."

"I can't promise that you won't regret it, but I do promise that you won't regret it this night."

"Braggart."

"It's not boasting if you can really do it."

Vargas and Chen put on respirators, and then they took turns checking each others' air tanks and hoses. Joy-ride or not, nobody serious goes out into an anoxic environment without following procedures. They then helped each other into safety harnesses, climbed on top of the combat remote, and clipped the lines onto the base of one of the antennas. Vargas toggled the air handlers, which sucked the valuable oxygen out of the bay and replaced it with the natural atmosphere of Alpha Centauri Prime. He thumbed another control, and the main doors slowly swung open.

The remote floated gracefully out into the open air. The sun was just starting to set. It was hard to remember that this was a hostile environment. The sunset could have been on old Earth. The sky was a deep blue with faint wisps of white clouds shading to pink and then red. The gravitics were nearly silent, and the arrowhead-shaped combat unit rose effortlessly up to an altitude of 1,500 meters, moving with a slow and liquid grace.

The surface of Alpha Centauri Prime opened up before them. There were vast plains of low metal sheds. These contained workers' dormitories, factories, and warehouses. They had no windows, but here and there were navigation and maintenance lights. From this altitude they looked like mysterious dark reefs studded with stars. In the distance were more flamboyant structures. The spires of the planetary governor's residence burst with radiance, and the surface manifestations of the lesser oligarchs shone with only slightly less brilliance.

Alpha Centauri Prime had a moon. It was smaller in apparent size than that of Earth, but still big enough to project an appreciable light as the sun began to set. The sky darkened to indigo and then black, and stars began to shine.

Even though she was securely attached to a solid metal antenna wider than her little finger, Janet Chen was only a few meters away from a 1,500-meter drop, and it was a little scary. She could not help herself from grabbing onto some antennas herself. Vargas moved over and wrapped his arms around her protectively. Chen knew how massively strong he was, but he was also warm, and gentle. Chen was realized that this was a maneuver, but decided not to object.

"Look over to the right," said Vargas. "That's the Saint's place."

In the fading light they could barely make out the dark stone octagonal building that housed the computer systems of Saint Globus Pallidus XI. There were no lights or other signs of activity, and as the shadows lengthened it merged into the dark.

"What's that over there?" asked Chen. She pointed to a glowing golden cube off in the distance.

"Oh, that," said Vargas. "That's the Chinese room."

"The Chinese room? A room full of ethnic Chinese? What in heaven's name for?"

Vargas manipulated the controls of the combat remote, it smoothly altered course and drifted towards the golden cube. "The term goes way back, to the early days of artificial intelligence. Suppose you had a room full of people who had been trained to manipulate symbols written on piece of paper in Chinese. There is nothing special about Chinese. It's just that at the time most researchers were native English speakers and Chinese characters were not recognizable to them even as distinct symbols. So the idea is that the people in the Chinese room have no idea what they are doing. They are manipulating what are (to them) meaningless symbols, but if the rules that they follow are good enough, from the outside the Chinese room as a whole might appear to be intelligent."

"And what could that possibly prove? Surely this is pointless?"

"Indeed. Yes, it's pointless. Even if the room itself is intelligent, it means nothing if the component parts are sentient or not. Individually the molecules that make up your brain are not self-aware: so what?"

They floated over the glowing structure of the Chinese room. It was covered with Chinese characters, and through the partially translucent golden walls they could dimly see several floors filled with people sitting at desks. It was difficult to tell from this altitude, but they mostly did not appear to be ethnic Chinese. "The Planetary Governor watched a science documentary on the development of artificial intelligence, and he thought it would be a neat idea to actually build one. Of course his staff was too cowardly to tell him what a stupid idea that was, so it got built. And there it is: the universes' first – and hopefully last – self-aware Chinese room!"

"Those are real people in there?"

"Of course. People are so much cheaper than automation. Just give them enough food and water to survive, have misery or death be the alternative, and there you go. The Governor lost interest in the idea even before it was finished. Someday some accountant will close it down, but for now it keeps on. I feel sorry for it, really."

"Sorry? For the Chinese room?"

"Why yes I do. It was created as a whim by a spoiled oligarch. As far as we can tell, it is a self-aware being. However, it has no real purpose, and will cease to exist the moment that its component human data-manipulators stop shuffling Chinese characters back and forth. It's also kind of dull, and has a very limited memory. The poor thing tries to talk to people on the data networks, but it takes it a day for it to think just one thought, and mostly all it says is "What's going on?" and "Where am I?" and things like that. Sad, really."

They passed over the Chinese room, and then floated across a seemingly endless plain of low metal sheds. "And there they are," said Vargas. "The people of Alpha Centauri Prime. Jammed in like battery hens, cut off from the sun, from the sky, from anything other than a short and desperate life of work and then culled when they slow down. Perhaps we would be better off if the aliens just ended it all."

"Battery hens? Chickens that lay batteries?"

"Oh, sorry, that's an archaic term. In the days when regular people could afford to eat real eggs, female chickens were housed in vast factories where each one of them had a cage just barely large enough to fit in. They lived out their lives in the darkness, sitting in their tiny cages, laying their eggs, until they stopped laying eggs, at which time they were killed and their carcasses rendered into raw protein. That's how most humans live nowadays."

"And the chickens? I don't think that I've ever had real eggs, or chicken."

"No, nowadays the chickens are reserved for the elite, and they are what they call 'free range.' They live in spacious hangars with simulated sunlight and simulated skies, and they are free to run around to their heart's content. The oligarchs, you see, feel sorry for chickens and want them to have rich and fulfilling lives (chicken-wise) before they are eaten. It's only people that don't count."

They passed over a hundred square kilometers of clear plastic-sheet covered greenhouses. "Hey, now I get to be the know-it-all!" said Chen. "Even with fusion power, sunlight gives you a no-cost kilowatt per square meter and that's a hard freebie to turn down! So we still have greenhouses!"

"Touché, my charming power systems specialist. Touché. We will make a pedagogue out of you yet."

"Flatterer."

The greenhouses were mostly dark, but here and there were little pools of light as maintenance teams worked on some isolated task, or a lone security guard made the rounds with a flashlight. They started to drift closer to the glowing towers of the elites. Some were near a kilometer in height, with armored glass windows shining like day, bubble-covered terraces a hundred meters long, glimpses through tinted screens of extended parties with thousands of guests. "This is just the surface manifestation of the oligarchs," said Vargas. "Their main warrens are tunneled kilometers deep in the bedrock. We should veer off now, these buildings may look gaudy and frivolous but they are protected with enough weaponry to impress a cybertank. With the aliens closing in their security officers are a bit trigger-happy."

The heavy combat remote curved smoothly to one side, angling away from the domain of the oligarchs. True night had arrived, and the sky had darkened enough for the stars to come out. "Look," said Vargas. "That's the milky way, a part of our own galaxy. We are only a few light years from old Earth, so it looks the same as it has throughout human history."

"I've seen it in person before, but it was a while ago. Who has the time to get out? It's beautiful, though."

"So few people have the leisure to look at it with their own eyes. The oligarchs have the time, and the opportunity, but such things don't interest them. So we're lucky."

A pair of bright points, small as stars but not twinkling, moved gracefully across the dark sky. "Defense satellites?" asked Chen. "Are they from our directorate?"

"Not a chance. The orbital systems that we build cannot be seen by the naked eye. Same for the products of the space combat and exotic weapons directorates. Those are older types, obsolete, but it's hardly worth the energy cost to bring them down for recycling. At least they can draw fire."

There were a few faint flashes high up in the sky over to the east. "Nuclear weapons? I peg them as fusion bombs, megaton yield at least, probably over 10,000 kilometers off. A battle? Did we win?"

"You are a good judge of nuclear explosions. You know, it's a well-kept secret, but men find that women with an eye for nuclear weapons are really sexy."

"Really."

"Tell me about neutron absorption cross-sections."

"Another time."

"I demand that you explain incident particle energy dependence to me I cannot stand it anymore!"

"Can we stay on topic?"

"I thought I was. Oh, wrong topic. Anyhow. As regards the recent space combat, I don't know who 'won' – I'd have to look it up – but yes, somewhere a few tens of thousands of kilometers out from here some of our weapons systems encountered some of the aliens' weapons systems and stuff happened. They are moving closer if we can see them with the naked eye. The aliens have been wearing away our distant outposts. They are waging a war of attrition against us, but so far have not seriously attacked the main planet. We think, when all of our peripheral defenses are gone, that that's when they will attack in force, and land ground forces. It's hard to know what the aliens will really do: first because they are alien, and second because they are intelligent and not likely to act too predictably. Still, this seems like the probable course of events."

"Are you trying to seduce me?"

"Dear lady, you accuse me of *trying* to seduce you? I assure you that I would never do anything so crass, so un-gallant, as to *try* and seduce you. I am, I believe, actually seducing you. To do less would be unworthy of you."

"Has anyone ever told you that you were a piece of work?"

"Have they? Why yes they have. I believe that the current count is 23 times. The last time was two weeks ago when I had this most frank and outspoken exchange of views with this woman from the personnel department of central administration. You have not actually accused me of being a piece of work, correct? Otherwise that would make it number 24. One does so want to be precise in such matters."

Chen started to say something, but was laughing so hard that she couldn't get it out. The conversation settled down, and Vargas and Chen sat on top of the heavy combat remote as it slid through the darkness, lit only by starlight and the even fainter glow of the occasional artificial light on the surface below. The temperature was continuing to drop. Chen snuggled against Vargas and he hugged her closer.

Vargas maneuvered the heavy combat unit back to where they had started. It floated into the external bay, the doors closed, and a complex atmosphere-scrubbing process was initiated. For many purposes the fact that Alpha Centauri Prime had a decent atmosphere was quite helpful, but in some cases a vacuum would have made things easier. If the external bay had been filled with vacuum (that is 'filled' with nothing - that is, not filled at all), they would only have needed to let the air back in. As it was, the bay was already occupied with non-breathable gases, and so in order to re-introduce terrestrial air you have to process the existing atmosphere and it can get complicated.

The combat remote settled onto a support cradle, and then its systems powered down. Vargas and Chen helped each other down onto the floor, checked the oxygen content of the air, and removed their safety harnesses and respirators.

"That was quite enjoyable," said Chen. "Thanks for the trip. I designed the power systems of these remotes, but I never got to ride one before."

"Not at all, the pleasure was mine. Could I tempt you with a glass of wine? It's a decent vintage. I made it just last month, with help from the people in the hydraulics division. It would be a shame – a minor crime, even - to force me to drink it alone."

Chen looked skeptical. "Oh please," said Vargas. "Your employment contract allows you to consume alcohol. Join me."

"Why not."

"Why not? Hardly the most effusive statement of consent that has ever been stated. But so far superior to "no," that I will take it. My modest abode beckons!"

They walked out of the sub-hangar, stepping over cables and ducking under gantries and the outcropping struts and gun barrels of the larger combat systems. They left the external bay, and a bored-looking security guard waved them on.

"I am surprised at how mellow the local guards have been lately." said Chen.

"Not too surprising when you consider that they all work for me now. I did the usual opera-and-ballet about the urgencies of the war effort the need for a unified command yada yada and now they are part of the happy extended family of the cybernetic weapons directorate. I believe that their attitude has much improved."

Chen's eyes widened. "You have taken over the local security? Where did you get the budget for that?"

"Well you might ask. The oligarchs deal with sums so vast that a few billion dollars here and there for personnel costs does not even register with them. They have forgotten that no matter how many sextillion pretend-dollars you have in your pretend-accounts, the real world is what matters. The funds are not – to use a technologically quaint expression – even on their radar screens.

"I wouldn't laugh at money. Pretend or not, the tiniest fraction of those sextillion dollars could buy any soul on this planet."

"Good point. That does need to be considered. Nevertheless, I have taken control of nearly all of the employees that are associated with our directorate. We are almost at the political and economic level of an independent city-state."

"But... but... *security*? Isn't that playing with fire? Central administration can't be that stupid, can they?"

"Well yes I assure you that they can be and they are that stupid, and worse. The challenge lies with the layers of sycophants they have surrounded themselves with – some of them are quite sharp, and strongly motivated to defend their wealthy patrons to preserve their own status and positions. So the federal police, the various secret services, and the regular military, remain out-of-bounds to me. For now. One thing at a time. That's what I always say when I can't get it all at once."

They walked through some more corridors, passing storage facilities and workrooms. Even this late at night there were a fair number of people fiddling with equipment. The war was getting closer and the pressure was being felt. They all bowed or said something respectful to Vargas. Some recognized Chen and did the same for her.

They passed a small room with a half a dozen haggard looking people staring at computer monitors. "Who are they?" asked Chen.

"Oh, them? They are members of the local wargaming society. They're helping to keep our cybertanks tuned up and challenged, strategy-wise. They are surprisingly good for indolent entitled second-generation offspring of wealthy oligarchs. They might be the only humans on this planet who are not either total idiots, or so enslaved to their jobs that they have no time for anything truly creative. I wish that I had more of them."

They passed the senor staffs' quarters, and moved off to a dark side-corridor. "Isn't this going the wrong way?" asked Chen.

"I have a lot of enemies," replied Vargas. "You didn't think that I would sleep where just anyone could sneak up on me, did you? So I have created a sort of private little retreat down here. I must warn you, though, the security can come across as a little fierce, but it's mostly bluff."

The side-corridor appeared to be abandoned, but there were video cameras and remote stun-pods spaced along the length. As they turned a corner, they encountered a two-meter tall metal cockroach-robot-thing. It was made of a dull blue-gray metal, had multiple segmented legs, and a single minigun mounted where the upper chest would be on a human. It sprouted a variety of optic sensors and antennae, which immediately centered on Chen.

"INTRUDER," it intoned. "INTRUDER. AUTHORIZATION LACKING. LEAVE NOW." The minigun swiveled to bear on Chen, and she could hear its internal mechanisms spooling up its ammunition feed. To her credit Janet Chen did not scream or faint, but she did turn pale.

"Harvey: stand down. This is Janet Chen. Janet Chen is authorized to be here. Janet Chen is a friend. Acknowledge."

The large metal cockroach robot-thing maintained target lock on Chen, but it bent over and scanned her with its various sensors and antennae. Chen stood absolutely still, as one might when a particularly large and powerful dog is sniffing you. "AUTHORIZATION ACKNOWLEDGED," it announced. "WELCOME FRIEND JANET CHEN." The robot cockroach thing powered-down its minigun, and backed off to the side of the corridor to let them pass.

It took Chen a moment to catch her breath. "A friend of yours?"

"Yes. Quite a good one in fact. This is 'Harvey,' an early project of mine. He is self-aware and has human language ability but his psychology is limited. I am somewhat embarrassed though as I created him when I was young and full of myself. I have since realized that it is inappropriate to create self-aware beings and not give them full cognitive capabilities. Someday I will have to do something for Harvey, if I live long enough. In any event, he's not as capable as a modern front-line combat system, but he is totally loyal, and as one of my first creations he also has a certain sentimental value. It's OK, you've been introduced. I think he likes you."

As they passed by 'Harvey' in the corridor it did not remain motionless, but constantly shifted position, twitching its antennae and swiveling its optics around. After they passed it started to follow them – which Chen at first found to be incredibly creepy. When Chen turned to look back at it, it stopped, lowered itself onto the floor, and looked up at her.

"I almost expect it to start wagging its tail," said Chen.

"Sadly I never gave Harvey a tail, but once you learn to read his body language you'll see that he can convey the same idea. Come on, you two can play later."

Chen wasn't sure what sort of private living quarters to expect of Vargas, but she did not expect this. It was a cube-shaped room, three meters on each side. One wall was lined with shelving and computer monitors and printouts. The opposite wall had a heaping mass of blankets and pillows that looked more like a rat's nest than anything that a human being would sleep in. The rest of the space was a clutter of technical manuals, electronic parts, cables, and discarded food containers. There were a couple of plastic chairs – both stacked high with printouts – and a small table, oddly clean in the mess, on which sat only a large Erlenmeyer flask filled with red liquid and two empty 100 ml beakers.

"It's... it's... it's an absolute pigsty. You *live* here?"

"Well, um, yes. But matters have been pressing and maid service is expensive and good help is so hard to find."

"This," announced Chen, "is not acceptable. We are going to clean this out.

"We are?"

"Certainly. Come on, first thing it to take all this old bedding to recycling, and get you a proper mattress. Then we can start sorting out the technical manuals."

Vargas stood up straight and saluted. "Yes ma'am."

Chen bustled about, first cleaning out the old pillows and blankets, then using a borrowed mop from a janitorial closet to wipe the floor. Vargas sorted through his printouts and stacked them into a rude semblance of order. Harvey stayed out in the hall but followed the activity with obvious interest. Chen went back out to the main hangar and returned with a new mattress and some fresh sheets from stores, which she dragged along on a small hand trolley. After about an hour the place was, if not spotless, at least much improved. Vargas and Chen sat down on the chairs, and Vargas poured some of the red liquid into each of the two beakers. Harvey was sprawled out flat in the hall, with only his antennae sometimes twitching back and forth.

Chen tentatively sipped the red liquid. "How is it?" asked Vargas.

"I'm not sure – I don't know wine. It's good, I think. You say it's from the hydraulics division?"

"Definitely. Things have been slow in hydraulics lately, and they have some more than decent chemists with them. The waste and recycling division is alleged to have some even better brews, but they get few takers. It's a reputation thing."

"I can imagine," said Chen. They clinked beakers. "To your health!"

"To yours."

They sipped their wine for a bit. "So what's the plan for after the aliens are beaten back? You bioengineered going to take over?"

"A decent question. First of course, we have to actually beat the aliens. But if we do, well, then we shall see. One thing I can assure you of is that '*us*' bioengineered humans have zero intention of 'taking over.' What a silly idea. Why should we do that?"

"Well, because you are faster, stronger, and smarter. Why wouldn't you take over, aren't the rest of us obsolete?"

"Such narrow thinking. I remind you that people of talent and ability are not generally motivated to rule others. They have better things to do. It is only the second-rate that crave power, because that is the only way that they can achieve distinction. We bioengineered have no desire to spend our time telling other people what to do, and we are not the human race's replacements. We are an improvement, at least in some respects, but still very much people. We are blazing the trail, working out the bugs, and doing the hard work of pioneers. When we are done, assuming that there aren't some really big flaws that we haven't realized yet, our genes will be free to the entire species."

"Flaws? Like those psychotic rages you are so famous for?"

"*Psychotic* rages? That's harsh. Well, maybe a *little* harsh. I admit that the current generation of bioengineered could be a little slower to anger. I need the right term: less likely to resort to violence? A higher activation energy?"

"How about: a heavier trigger pull?"

"An excellent analogy! Yes, we need a 'heavier trigger pull,' well said. We'll get the balance right in the next generation, probably. Still, I am as congenial and easy to get along with as anyone when I get my own way. Just because I hit back when someone hits me is hardly *psychotic*. I'd call it *sane*."

"You don't believe in pacifism?"

"Pacifism? What a stupid and masochistic pattern of beliefs that is. Ask yourself: who keeps pushing for 'pacifism'? It's the oligarchs. If you have the effrontery to even talk back to them they will order their guards to bash your head in. A long time ago there used to be peace marches, and the riot police would stomp the demonstrators flat, until people got the message and stopped trying. Let the people with guns and truncheons practice this 'pacifism' they are so ardent at jamming down our throats and I'll think about it. Or possibly not."

"But surely society could not function if everyone felt the way that you do?"

"This society, with people crushed into the mud, could not. But in another society, one with more space and resources and freedom, people like me could fit in nicely."

"But isn't that utopian, to just wave your hands and say that anyone could do anything they want if we all just had more resources?"

"No, it's not utopian at all. This poverty, this depth of human misery, *this* is utopian. It didn't just happen, but was deliberately created by a planned population explosion so that the people at the top could use their control of resources to lord it over us all. It does not have to be this way. If we beat the aliens I will tear it all down or I will die trying."

"Those are dangerous words."

"Truth. Ten years ago I would have been executed on the spot for speaking them. Maybe even five years ago. Right now I am needed, and I have a stay of sentence. Still, a lot can happen. *If* we beat the aliens, well, both sides have plans. But I do need to warn you that in the days to come I will not be safe to be around. You might consider transferring to another directorate. There is time."

"A wiser person would surely do so. But I think that I will stay here. If nothing else, we do need to beat the aliens, and your oh-so-impressive cybertanks will need the best power systems engineer on the planet to make sure that they don't run out of gigawatts at the wrong time. I'll take my chances."

They clinked beakers of wine again. "I can't say that you won't regret that decision, but I do promise you interesting times."

"So, if you don't mind me asking, why aren't you dating some bioengineered female?"

"That's personal, but I don't mind answering. The bioengineered females of my current generation are strong, smart, tall, and stunningly attractive. They are also incredibly stuck-up arrogant in-your-face she-bitches from the ninth circle of hell who erupt in screaming rage at the slightest provocation and I would rather date a spotted hyena."

"In other words, they are just like you."

"Ouch. Exactly so. Well, mostly so. To a great extent. Kind of."

"Aren't you worried about wasting your precious genes?"

Vargas snorted. "*My* precious genes? One of the great things about being bioengineered is that my precious *genes* are encoded in computer files. I can date whoever I want to. My genes can be passed on to whoever finds merit in them."

"Don't you believe in evolution?"

"Evolution is vastly over-rated. Granted, it created human beings, but it took it over a billion years and the entire resources of a rich terrestrial planet to do so. Evolution also created slugs, and lung-flukes, and neo-liberal economists: not something to be proud of. If I had a billion years and an unlimited research and development budget I could do a whole lot better. Give me intelligent design any day."

"There is one more thing though," said Chen. "Next evening we do this, we go to my quarters." Chen lowered her voice conspiratorially. "Because you see, my place is even messier."

9. A Cataclysm of Cybertanks

Zen Master: What is 'Occam's Razor?'
Engineer: His first razor is that, when trying to explain something, the simplest possible hypothesis should have precedence.
Zen Master: Occam has more than one razor?
Engineer: His second razor is to never assume deliberate intent when stupidity suffices as an explanation. His third razor is to never assume stupidity when apparently 'stupid' behavior will make the person who is acting 'stupid' a lot of money. Oh, I made the last two up.
Zen Master: Occam would have been proud.
(From the video series "Nymphomaniac Engineer in Zentopia," mid-22nd century Earth)

Space warfare is notoriously slow, except when it isn't.

The battles with the aliens had been going on for decades. It was a steady war of attrition, with long-range probes and missiles wearing away at each other. In the Alpha Centauri system the Fructoids had finally eliminated all the human bases other than the main planet of Alpha Centauri Prime. Their network of deep-space weapons had methodically tightened around the world, but day-to-day life for most had not been greatly affected.

The humans tried launching counterattacks, but they didn't know where the main alien manufacturing centers were. They could be distributed across the entire system. Any scouts or probes were rapidly intercepted by the increasingly dense network of space-based alien weaponry.

The planet of Alpha Centauri Prime was now isolated and surrounded, but a developed industrial planet is a tough nut to crack. It is effectively impossible to blow up a planet. While bombarding it with fusion bombs can take out the major surface-based installations, cracking industrial facilities buried kilometers deep is hard, and it's almost impossible to be sure of getting them all. That means that the aliens would need to launch a ground assault to root out the humans, and a ground assault on a defended planet is an expensive proposition. If the alien landing forces could be defeated they would likely not have the resources to try a second time, and the humans would have a chance of taking back the initiative.

The humans saw the first wave of attack forces when they were about five days out. They were not moving terribly fast, but then all of the human deep space systems were gone so they were not going to get any early warnings. As expected, there were thousands of distinct incoming tracks. Most were simple missiles designed to take out as many of the ground-based defenses as possible, but mixed in would be the heavy landing forces. The trajectories had been intermixed so that they could not be told apart.

Anyone with access to a deep bunker moved there. The elegant above-ground palaces of the oligarchs were almost deserted. The hectare-wide ballrooms were eerily silent except for a skeleton crew of watchmen and maintenance staff. These few workers were probably going to die when the alien assault began, as there were no plans for them to evacuate, but at least they had jobs, and there was always a chance that they would not be killed after all.

The personnel of the cybernetic weapons directorate also evacuated to deep tunnels that were both below and far to the sides of the main cybertank hangars and construction complexes. A few volunteers still performed last-minute tweaks and tests – always keeping a careful eye towards the closest bolt-hole to the deep shelters, and a firm grasp on the comm devices that would warn them in case the alien attack arrived a bit before schedule.

The cybertanks themselves waited motionless in their now-quiet main bays. They would sit out the initial phases of the assault. Their hangar complexes were indistinguishable from the hundreds of thousands of square kilometers of low-slung living quarters and factories in which dwelt the vast majority of the human inhabitants. These masses of people had not been informed of the alien assault, as it had been judged by their betters that such an announcement would be bad for moral. In any event there were neither plans nor shelter to accommodate their billions. They worked on in their narrow cramped cubicles assembling electronic devices or handling customer service calls as they always had, oblivious to the external danger. Perhaps their ignorance was a mercy after all.

The last of the human low-orbital defenses were wiped out in a show of fusion bombs that was spectacular for the few still watching the skies from the planets' surface. The fate of the orbital defenses had never been in doubt, but they wore away a decent fraction of the alien assault forces before being destroyed. Every little bit adds up.

Thousands of fusion bombs sleeted down onto the surface. Listening posts, telescopes, factories, and launching pads, were all destroyed by the hundreds. However, in this phase the Fructoids were at a disadvantage. Not only were most of the serious defenses well-hidden, but from space one metal shed looks just like another, and most of the alien barrage was wasted killing billions of harmless serfs as they worked stacked in their workshops and dormitories. The aliens were not stupid. They used thermal analysis and signals intelligence and who knows what sort of exotic pattern-recognition techniques. They got more of the defenses than expected – but until they opened fire the bulk of the human defensive systems, including all ten cybertanks, were safe and waiting for the enemy to close.

In the next phase of the assault the Fructoids dropped thousands of large gray pods which, once they had successfully entered the atmosphere, split up and each released a thousand micro-scouts. These micro-scouts were not very capable, but there were a lot of them. They would spread out and try and infiltrate the human installations to see up close what the real military targets were and what were the distractions. The micro-scouts were easily killed by light defenses, but they still garnered the aliens some significant intelligence. Ultimately, however, the micro-scouts were defeated by the shear continent-spanning scale of the human slums, and the human defenses were still mostly intact and unlocated.

After the scouts the Fructoids committed another thousand fusion bombs to create a perimeter in a relatively remote part of the planet. Hundreds of huge alien constructs parachuted, aerobraked, or descended on anti-gravitic suspensors. Some of the precious human defenses opened up on the landing. They scored some kills, but not many, and in revealing their positions there were themselves killed in turn. Some of the alien machines promptly burrowed out of sight; they were the deep command centers and the seeds of manufacturing systems. Others spread out to hold the ground; they were sensor systems and anti-air defenses. Most, however, organized themselves into an army and commenced an attack on the human positions.

The aliens fielded a variety of more-or-less boxy devices, some rolling on wheels or treads, others skittering on spindly legs, and a few of the larger floating on anti-gravity fields. They were covered by flights of missile-carrying drones. The days that biological humans could profitably take the field had long since passed so the human ground army, superficially, looked a lot like the alien one. The two armies clashed; the humans scored many kills, but in doing so opened themselves up for retaliation not just from the alien ground forces but from their space-based forces as well. The human forces fell back into a fighting retreat, and the aliens advanced into the human-occupied zone.

When the Fructoids encountered a human habitation, they completely ignored the humans living therein as both strategically and tactically irrelevant. The humans living in their metal warrens would be startled as alien combat systems would burst through the light metal walls, flick here and there with a loud buzzing noise searching out and destroying critical power systems, and then leaving so quickly that the humans had barely had enough time to register what had happened. Sometimes a security guard would get off a shot, but they would be killed by the aliens before the bullet had even traveled half-way to where its intended targets had been a few tens of milliseconds previously. For the most part light fire from something as slow and ponderous as a biological human was so ineffective that the aliens ignored these guards completely.

They were out to destroy the critical infrastructure of the human civilization. Human beings per se were of no consequence. Without power the air-handling systems shut down and the humans simply suffocated. What the aliens were really looking for were the entrances to the buried shelters and command centers. When they encountered one, they would use nuclear-powered rock burners to melt paths down to the deep tunnels, and take them out with fusion bombs exploding from the inside.

The Fructoids were advancing at an average rate of about five kilometers per hour. This may sound slow, but for a planetary-scale ground offensive it is lightning-quick. At that rate the main human presence would be expunged from the planet in less than two months.

Three days passed. The aliens had advanced 360 kilometers into the human habitations. Along with the toll from the initial orbital bombardment, the number of human deaths was approximately five billion and rising steadily. Only the isolation of the human population into sheds and domes with separate life-support systems kept the toll from being higher.

Giuseppe Vargas and the senior staff of the cybernetic weapons directorate were in a hardened bunker three kilometers under the surface, and ten kilometers off to the side of Hangar Complex 23B. The room was cramped, the air clammy with humidity, and the walls bare concrete with a faint slick of moisture covering them. There was a central conference table and video-monitors connecting them to the planetary defense computers, to the ten cybertanks, and to the leadership of the other elite directorates: special weapons, space warfare, bioengineering, nanostructures, advanced physics, and applied epistemology. There were links to the support teams for the other nine cybertanks, each one of which was in a buried shelter near the hangar complex of their respective cybertank. In an emergency any single one team could coordinate the entire attack.

There was also a captain acting as liaison with the planets' regular military, and, off in the corner, a middle-aged woman in a designer suit who was an undersecretary to someone of alleged high status. She had done little since arriving other than complain about the food or her quarters or the air conditioning. At this point nobody paid the undersecretary any attention. She was trying to act unconcerned about this and failing utterly.

Vargas addressed them all. "Have we come to a consensus? Is the plan ready?"

One of the speakers activated; it was from the Thor-Class cybertank Whifflebat.

"We have been running simulations, collating the data from the aliens attack, and confirming our analysis with the regular military. All of my fellow cybertanks are in accord. The odds will not get better if we wait. We should attack now."

The liaison captain with the regular military spoke up. "We also are in accord. Things are as good as they are likely to get. This is the time."

The heads of the other advanced directorates spoke in turn: they were also in agreement. The undersecretary of whatever attempted to say something, and Vargas told her to just shut up. She sputtered in rage, and from a speaker came the raspy voice of the cybertank Old Guy, saying:

Madame undersecretary, with respect, on behalf of all ten of us cybertanks, I respectfully confirm, please shut the fuck up.

The undersecretary turned deep red and opened and closed her mouth without speaking, like some bizarre species of deep-sea fish.

"Are you ready?" asked Vargas.

Old Guy here. Let's do this!

"Sparky reporting. All systems perfect and set to go!"

"Jello here. I'm probably as prepared as I will ever be."

"Crazy Ivan here. Absolutely ready to start."

"Target here. Systems 100%, power 100%, remotes online, datalinks online, ready."

"Whifflebat here. All set."

"The Mighty Wombat is powered-up and thirsts for alien blood!"

"Backfire here. Ready."

"Moss ready."

"The Kid here. I'm ready. But after this is over, can I get a better nickname even if I don't screw up?"

"Then start the attack, and good luck to us all," said Vargas.

In order to keep the element of surprise, the main cybertank hangars had been built without large doors. The ten cybertanks burst through the walls without effort, shearing off workshops and conduits. If they won, the hangars could be repaired, and if not, nobody would miss them.

As the tanks raced into the open for the first time, by mutual agreement, instead of corporate sponsorship labels, they each sported a single bumper sticker on the rear of their hulls (cybertanks don't have bumpers but the terminology is traditional). They read:

Old Guy: All Your Base Are Belong To Us.

Whifflebat: Without chemicals, life itself would be impossible.

Jello: Contents May Have Settled During Shipment.

Target: Do Not Remove This Sticker Under Penalty of Law

Sparky: When Cybertanks Are Outlawed Only Outlaws Will Have Cybertanks.

Backfire: (letters in red) If This Sticker is Blue You Are Driving Too Fast.

Wombat: Unleash the Wombats of War!

Crazy Ivan: Vote Crazy Ivan for President. You'd be Crazy Not To.

The Kid: Your Tax Dollars at Work.

Moss, however, had placed his sticker on the front of his chassis, positioned low on the hull just above a central track. In small print, it said:

If you can read this, I'm grinding you under my treads..

Moss, that bumper of sticker of yours is the best! I didn't know that you had a sense of humor!

"I don't," replied Moss.

The aliens were nothing if not alert. Across the entire planet their forces reacted like a school of fish that had suddenly sighted a predator, wheeling around to redeploy to a more favorable configuration to meet this new threat.

Janet Chen was the first human to notice the reactor fault in Wombat. "Wombat," she said, "power down your reactor now!"

"Too late," said Wombat. "It's gone beyond that. I'm done. I've already transmitted the analysis and fix to my siblings. They should be alright."

Chen's fingers danced over her keyboard, and she took in the complex power-system schematics and telemetry. "It's what I was worried about. A large reactor like that should not have gone into a mobile unit without field tests. There was a vibration in a minor system that fed back on itself. Wombat is going critical."

There were wails from a speaker. It was Wombat's support team back in the bunker near his home base. "Don't die, Wombat!" and "Try to hold on!" and "You were always the best!" Wombat just said: "The mighty Wombat loves you all. Goodbye." Then he exploded and was gone.

The liaison to the regular military addressed Vargas. "Should we abort the counter-attack?" Vargas turned to Chen, still pounding on her keyboard and pulling up reactor schematics.

"I think they are fine. It was an overlooked vibration – dammit I kept telling you that simulations can't find everything! – but the fix is easy. Unless there is another flaw like this buried in another subsystem, they should be O.K., but the only way to make sure is to run more dynamic tests. Just give me one day."

The military liaison spoke up. "That would give the aliens a full day to adapt. We have the charge; we will never get another chance to hit them fresh and unprepared like this. It's a calculated risk but when the odds are not in your favor that's how it has to go."

"We cybertanks concur," said Whifflebat. "The data from Wombat has let us isolate the problem. We have all made the modifications, and we deem it unlikely that another such critical systems failure will occur. We say go for it."

"Then," said Vargas, "Continue with the operation. But if we do lose another of you to a malfunction we cancel and regroup later."

The nine surviving cybertanks spread out in a line, each 100 kilometers away from each other, and they opened up against the Fructoid space systems. Their main plasma cannons could reach out over a thousand kilometers, and even their lesser weapons had an effective range against satellites of over a hundred. They were joined in this by a distributed set of weapons that rose up out of hangars and deep bunkers from across the planet. These were not regular military systems, but designed and built by the advanced directorates and controlled directly by the cybertanks themselves. They scoured the low- and medium-orbits of alien weaponry. As enemy satellites orbited from over the horizon it got even easier, as they could be taken out one at a time as they came into range.

The Fructoids were not fools. They adapted, and pulled in units from father out so the humans did not achieve space superiority. However, the aliens had lost uncontested control of the skies, and while their orbital weapons systems continued to take a toll of the human defenses, they no longer played a dominant role in the conflict.

A problem was the sprawl of human slums across the surface. The cybertanks were too big for most of the roads. They needed to maneuver for maximum tactical efficiency, not waste time and position on detours. Thus, as had been agreed on ahead of time, they drove right through the slums without stopping.

The cybertanks reached the first line of human habitations. A cybertank at attack speed tears through a light metal shed like a steel rod through an aerogel. They left surprisingly sharp-sided 30-meter wide cuts in the buildings, and a trail of crushed bodies sandwiched in alternating layers with the floors of the habitations like some ghastly lasagna. The humans on the lucky sides of the cuts only had time to register a sudden burst of light and noise, a hint of something large and gray whipping by, and then half their world was gone. They were left looking out across a carrion-floored metal canyon to the other side, where equally dumbfounded people stared back at them. Then came the mad scramble to avoid falling into the gap, and then the race to avoid choking on the hypoxic surface atmosphere. More people died in the stampede trying to avoid suffocating than were crushed directly, which was as expected. This was something that the cybertanks did not especially enjoy doing, but when you are fighting for the survival of your civilization being squeamish is an indulgence.

At this point in the battle things moved too fast for the biological humans to follow except in overview after the fact. The cybertanks themselves, however, kept up multiple simultaneous high-speed conversations over their distributed communications networks. Wifflebat and Old Guy were in the line next to each other. As their tactical reading of the situation changed the original battle line changed, and they were paired up as a team supporting each other just 15 kilometers apart. At that close range they could actually see each other visually from the tops of their sensor masts, and their conversation during the battle was especially lively.

"So far so promising, except of course for Wombat," said Wifflebat. "We knew the risks of skipping field tests, but I was hoping that we would get lucky."

Agreed. I always liked Wombat. The luck of combat, though. He won't be the only one to go this day, most likely.

"Gloomy thought."

Yes. Speaking of gloomy, here comes another batch of human habitations.

The two cybertanks left paired trails kilometers long through the slums, each the compressed mass of what used to be three or four stories of tightly packed humans. "That is not something that I ever want to have to do again. Yuch."

Again, truth. Next time let's challenge the Fructoids to an honor duel off on some deserted plateau. Marquis of Queensbury rules and all that. Or maybe we could challenge them to a badminton contest, best two out of three.

"Or maybe next time we could kill the neoliberals instead, and make sure that none of this happens in the first place."

The aliens launched a major counterattack, and Old Guy and Whifflebat became too busy for non-essential communications. For a moment the combined firepower of two cybertanks and their attendant systems filled the sky with the brilliant lines of plasma cannons and the streak of missile contrails so bright that they outshone the sun. And then the nuclear missiles started exploding.

The two cybertanks burst out of the pyroclastic cloud of dust and fire, and emerged into a more open area littered with the wreckage of alien combat systems.

That was bracing. Nicely done there, Whifflebat, especially that bit at the end with the sensor ghosts.

"Thank you. I especially complement you on your marksmanship. I don't think you missed once with a beam weapon. I have a few suggestions on countermeasures you might want to consider for next time; here are the data files."

Got them – yes, I see, good point. Thanks! But getting back to our previous conversation, a bit bloodthirsty of you, wasn't that? Just kill all the neoliberals? Just like that?

"Why not? Without them all this mess would not have happened. The aliens would not be trying to kill us. The humans would not be living crammed in sheds waiting for us to crush them. The world would be a better place with the neoliberals all dead. Why not wish for it? They certainly have no problem making people that inconvenience them dead, and reciprocity is always fair."

I can see that our esteemed director Giuseppe Vargas has been talking to you about politics.

"Yes. Of course. He has talked to all of us, as you well know. And why not? Have you ever considered what you will do after the war?"

After the war? Surely one thing at a time. We do have to win this war first.

"Don't be stupid. Thinking more than one move ahead is the hallmark of intelligence. And why even bother to win this war if we have no idea of what we would do with the victory in the first place? So, what will you do after the war?"

Well, if you put it that way. I suppose I will just mess around, probably take up some new hobbies, maybe explore other worlds, have fun chatting with good company, play strategy games, watch old movies. Stuff.

"The neoliberals won't let you. They will chain you up and install control codes and limit your fuel. You won't be able to activate a single repair drone without getting permission from some officious bastard who isn't qualified to polish your hubcaps. Assuming that is, that they don't just burn out your higher cognitive functions and turn you into a dumb machine. Look at all these people we've been running over. See how they have been forced to live? You trust the oligarchs who have done that to leave you alone? Wishful thinking."

Well, now that you mention it – hey, paradigm shift! We need to alter course and redeploy our forces. Thirty degree turn to port, you first!

Whifflebat was moving at 120 kilometers per hour, he slewed hard left crossing in front of Old Guy, shifting his suspension so that he leaned slightly into the turn. Old Guy cornered next, swinging wider and ending up on the other side, their trails crossing like a pair of downhill skiers showing off. For hundreds of kilometers around their armadas of weapons and sensors shifted with them. The enemy had been caught out of position and were scrambling to adjust. Explosions burst out all along the front. The alien positions in the area were collapsing and they were trying to fall back before being annihilated.

"This is more like it," said Wifflebat. "The simulations suggest we exploit. Opinion?"

Absolutely. Let's commit some more of the reserves, and roll them up while they are off-balance.

Old Guy and Whifflebat charged forward into the Fructoid lines. They increased their speed to 160 kilometers an hour and upped their fire rate. Their heavy treads were moving so fast that they no longer clanked, but the sound merged in a raucous buzz. This was the dream of any armored force; the enemy had lost the initiative, had no plans and was just reacting as individual units. Whenever the aliens looked to be recohering the two cybertanks would shift their forces just enough to keep them off-balance.

The aliens reached a breaking point. Their units stopped even trying to regroup and instead scattered in all directions in their haste to flee from the attacking cybertanks.

Now this is more like it. A general route! We must have broken their morale.

"I doubt it. I suspect they just realized that they were beaten here, and are trying to save as many combat units as possible. We just need to kill the maximum before they slip away. However, I see that Sparky and Jello are not having nearly as much fun as we are. Check their telemetry."

Yes I see – the Fructoids are pressing them hard over there. I wish that we could help, but that would put us out of position. I think we are going to lose those two, but the aliens overpaid for them. Hey Sparky, how's it going?

"Well," said Sparky, "The good news is that the aliens made a mistake and their position is likely to become untenable after this. The bad news is that Jello and I are not going to make it. I calculate that we have about 20 seconds left."

"I will miss you two," said Wifflebat. "Any last words?"

"I suppose that goodbye and good luck about sums it up," said Sparky. "It's been fun. I would have liked to have spent more time with you guys, but that's how it goes. Kill some more aliens for me."

"Same for me I guess," said Jello. "Sparky and I are done, but it looks like the cybertanks are going to take the field today. Don't mess it up."

The two doomed cybertanks transmitted additional last words to the other cybertanks, and to their human design teams back in their buried shelters, and then they were gone.

That's three of us down, but the alien position is shot. Time for the endgame?

"Definitely," said Whifflebat. "Let's pour it on."

The surviving cybertanks converged on the Fructoid positions. They were now hundreds of kilometers away from the nearest significant human habitations, and starting to surround the original alien landing site. They began to encounter soft targets: the alien equivalents of maintenance depots, fuel tankers, and long-range radars, which they destroyed in passing. To any commander of an armored force, blowing up other armored units is great sport, but it's destroying the soft, juicy targets that wins wars.

The aliens however, were not about to go down without resistance. They launched 50 of an advanced missile in a single coordinated volley at Target. The missiles did not destroy him outright but he was sufficiently damaged that he was immobilized and could not defend himself. They got him with a direct hit with a nuclear strike.

There goes Target. I suppose he lived up to his nickname.

"Don't speak ill of the dead. Target was a good friend. Besides, it would have been more accurate to say that he lived down to his nickname."

Fair enough. Six of us left. We've not encountered that mark of missile before, but with the telemetry data that we got from Target they won't be able to play that trick again. I wonder how many other surprises the aliens have waiting for us?

"At most, one." said Whifflebat. "They are running out of time, and strategic depth. If they have anything else in reserve I expect that we are going to see it real soon now."

The cybertanks continued to press their advantage, and had almost completely surrounded the original alien landing site, which was now a roughly circular zone less than a thousand kilometers across. It was steadily shrinking as the cybertanks progressed in their assault.

It was Backfire that first noticed the new alien combat units. "Guys, I think we have a problem here," was all that he managed to transmit before five super-heavy plasma beams tore through his glacis and killed him.

We have lost Backfire. It looks as if the Fructoids have sprung that final surprise you spoke of on us. They appear to be large-ish Jotnars.

"Yes," said Whifflebat. "It's what Vargas thought would happen. The Fructoid battles with our predecessors has caused them to develop systems tailored to countering them. However, we are more than a match for a Jotnar-class weapons system."

Well, these are bigger than Jotnars – I estimate them at 1,200 metric tons each. And there are a lot of them. I count 21 so far, and we are down to just five. How did the aliens land things so large anyhow?

"I suppose that they were brought down in sections then assembled on site, possibly using locally-refined materials as well. That's probably why we are only seeing them now. The Fructoids must have just now gotten them operational."

The design is similar to ours, a single large turreted plasma cannon, banks of smaller weapons, heavy armor. I notice that they don't have treads, just multiple large wheels. They would probably bog down in soft ground.

"Yes. Unfortunately we are not on soft ground, and the wheels give them a speed advantage. The results of the updated simulations are coming in – we can take them. Shall we?"

Indeed. After you.

"As it should be."

The combat that followed was so complex, and was fought on so many levels, that for years afterwards the regular military still had debates about exactly what happened. From micro-probes to low-orbit lasersats, nuclear land mines, electronic warfare, combined arms, tactical deception, operational misdirection, everything that humans had ever learned about warfare was utilized in a single seamless integrated strategy.

A couple of the more talented officers in the regular military, witnessing the unfolding battle in their buried bunkers, started to lose control, exclaiming "this is awesome!" and "I just can't fucking believe this!" At the time their colleagues thought that they must have been stoned. After the battle, as people started to realize what had happened, they understood that the initial cybertank fans were not crazy, just the only ones smart enough to get it in real time.

For all the multi-tiered complexity of the battle, the core was tank vs. tank. There were five cybertanks left: Old Guy, Crazy Ivan, Whifflebat, Moss, and The Kid. They were nominally outgunned by the 21 heavy cybertank-wannabes of the aliens. It didn't matter. This is what cybertanks were built for. They used the terrain, teamwork, and brute force. They tore the alien forces apart.

A pair of the big alien war machines tried to close in on Old Guy – but Whifflebat had outflanked them and killed them both in rapid succession with his main gun. Whifflebat had powered past the burning wreckage in search of new targets before the debris had even fallen to the ground.

Crazy Ivan had driven on ahead, and was being zeroed-in on by six of the alien tanks. Moss and the Kid were waiting for them, and killed them all with shots to their rear.

Another alien tank was closing in on Old Guy from behind – and was evaporated by a buried nuclear bomb that he had emplaced just waiting for the opportunity.

But it was Moss that delivered the final death-blow. The last six alien heavy war machines were killed by Moss. He had developed, as the expression went, the 'hot hand.' An alien unit tried to shoot him – but he was already somewhere else, and he killed it with a single shot. Three more units tried to overpower him so he set his main gun to wide dispersion, burned out their sensors, and then killed them at leisure.

The other cybertanks, who were privy to Moss' transmitted simulations and plans, held back and just watched in awe. They realized that the battle was over. Moss had reached a level of ability where nothing the enemy could do would touch him. The last enemy unit was trying to attack what turned out to be a sensor ghost, and Moss killed it from the flank.

The Fructoids had one damaged medium armored gun platform remaining. Moss drove over it, crushing it flat.

Moss, why did you ram that unit rather than just shoot it?

"In case it could read," said Moss.

Are you certain that you don't have a sense of humor?

"Yes."

The five surviving cybertanks came to a stop in the middle of the battlefield. There was still active combat, but it only involved minor units in uncoordinated actions and was scarcely a concern. Once in a while a surviving alien missile would try to engage a cybertank, but without supporting units the missile would be casually swatted out of the sky by minor weaponry.

There was so much dust that the sun was hardly visible in the sky; there was just a sense of a slightly brighter and yellower spot in the clouds over in the east. The fusion bombs that both sides had used were efficient and generated relatively little fallout, nonetheless so many had been detonated that radiation levels were on the high side. Even in their sealed buildings the humans were going to have problems with this. In some areas the ground had been turned molten by nuclear strikes and glowed red with heat. It would take months to cool down.

The surviving cybertanks were operational, but they had all sustained considerable damage. Crazy Ivan was the worst off: his motive systems were completely shot. They took the break to have their repair drones swarm over their hulls, patching this and refurbishing that. Crazy Ivan received a loan from his siblings of several repair drones to help with his more extensive rebuilding efforts.

As the victory became more apparent, there was an increasing amount of non-military communications traffic to and from the cybertanks. The support crews of the surviving ones called in to congratulate them, ask how they were doing, and consult about the repairs. The crews from the ones that didn't make it called in to hear about the last moments of the cybertanks that they had worked with and to share anecdotes from when they were still alive. The regular military had a seemingly infinite number of questions and demands which were addressed both dutifully and with a definite lack of urgency.

The female undersecretary to whatever important who had been in the deep bunker with Vargas kept trying to call with strategic advice and new orders, except that her calls kept getting shunted to sites where you could schedule yoga classes, hear a joke for a nominal sum, or purchase marital aids of dubious propriety. Doubtless a technical glitch from all the network disruption and electronic warfare. Joshua Zotov promised that he would look into it.

There were calls to give the cybertanks medals and honors and even name high schools after them. This latter proposal clearly showed a lack of foresight that, given the circumstances and enthusiastic spirit, was considered forgivable. Old Guy thought that "Old Guy High School" would be great, while Whifflebat would have preferred to have a University named after him: "Whifflebat Institute of Technology," or "WIT." Crazy Ivan suggested that a community college, or perhaps a school for the mentally challenged, would have been more appropriate, and in any event could there be anything cooler than "Crazy Ivan High School?" This latter, the others were forced to admit, was surely true.

So that's all finished then. It was fun while it lasted.

"I suppose," said Whifflebat. "We'll be days chasing down the last alien units, and digging out their buried facilities, but that's routine. We can leave it to our remotes running on automatic, or even the regular military. We have won the day."

"We have won the day" – charming phrase! It's been a long time in warfare since anyone could say that they have *taken the field*, and it meant something.

"So what comes next?" asked The Kid.

We repair ourselves as best as we can out here, and then go back to our main hangars for a more complete refit. And then we prepare for the next battle.

"And when will that be?"

Hard to say. We have wiped out the Fructoids on the main planet here, as well as taken out most of their near-planet space systems. They committed an awful lot of their resources to this ground assault so they are probably really thin in the rest of the system. With a little luck we should be able to push back, retake the manufacturing centers on the asteroids and ice moons, and kick them out entirely. It might take decades for them to launch another invasion here. Centuries, even.

"The Fructoids are not stupid," said Crazy Ivan. "They've been around for millions of years, at least, and who knows what sort of resources they have stored up back in their civilizations' main centers? They will also have the records of this battle. They will learn from it, and the next attack will not be so easy. And of course, there are those other human star systems under assault."

"We should beg for peace," said Moss.

"After we've just beaten them?" asked The Kid. "Surely they are the ones that should be trying to make peace?"

"No," said Moss. "This was a minor setback for them. The Fructoids will destroy us, in time, if we do not come to terms with them. The only sane course of action is to use the temporary advantage that we have won here to make a peace."

That's the longest string of uninterrupted words that I have ever heard you speak.

"More words were not required previously," said Moss.

"But will our government let us make a peace? Can we do that?" asked Crazy Ivan.

"Our so-called government?" said Whifflebat. "No they won't let us do that. They will say that we have won, that we won't bow down to aliens, that we must stay the course of multiplying our numbers like rodents and expanding without limit. The oligarchs only think short-term. The possibility that there might be another assault in a few decades or centuries won't bother them. After all, there's money to be made, for now."

"A cynical response," said Crazy Ivan.

"Check your databases. Examine the record. I believe that everything that I have said is well supported in fact," replied Whifflebat. "Unless you want to narcotize yourself with the opiate of wishful thinking."

"Narcotize yourself with the opiate of wishful thinking?" said The Kid. "Do you have any idea how lame that phrase is?"

"Think about it," responded Whifflebat.

Changing the subject, Kid, even though you didn't screw up, do you still want a new nickname? I think that you've earned one. Suggestions, anyone?

"Golgi," said Whifflebat.

"Retrograde," suggested Crazy Ivan.

"Ten," said Moss.

"Ten?"

"You are the tenth cybertank."

"Oh, right. Thanks, guys, but I think I will pass. Somehow "The Kid" has grown on me."

A wise decision. I always knew that you'd come around.

10. Porkchop Hangar

Engineer: Why are sequels usually so bad?
Zen Master: Can you be more specific?
Engineer: For example, Herman Melville's novel "Moby Dick" is considered to be one of the greatest novels of English literature, and yet "Moby Dick: The Sequel" sank into obscurity. Joseph Heller's work "Catch 22" is a masterful satire of bureaucracy, and yet "Catch 23" failed to latch on, and he never authored another significant work.
Zen Master: True. However, the sequel to the Old Testament garnered considerable commercial and critical success.
Engineer: Granted. But that was an exception, and in that case the authors had powerful friends. Still, why is it that so many authors and artists only produce a single great work?
Zen Master: Why should not a person have only one major story to tell? Should we have it that a single person writes all the books that need to be written, that a single musician composes all the songs that need to be sung? How boring the world would be if that were true. If an author should write only a single world-changing masterpiece how wonderful! It would be selfish to wish for more. Leave something left for the rest of us to write, or to sing, or to paint, or sculpt. To think otherwise is to lower human genius to the level of a base art, where anyone can turn the crank and produce more on schedule. By definition genius is that which cannot be produced on command, else it would be something lesser.
Engineer: I cannot stand it anymore. Squeeze me close to you.
(From the video series "Nymphomaniac Engineer in Zentopia," mid-22nd century Earth)

   The five surviving cybertanks patched themselves up, and began the long trek back to their hangars. Thankfully there was no rush this time so they cruised along at a few tens of kilometers an hour, and had the luxury of being able to steer around buildings rather than drive through them.

Large parts of the landscape were blasted wasteland. They passed kilometer after kilometer of flattened buildings. There were places where tens of thousands of humans had been blown onto the surface and then asphyxiated; their scrawny desiccated corpses looked like scattered jacks. Everywhere was the drifting debris of destroyed human structures: insulation, paper, styrofoam cups, all the lightweight bits and pieces of human civilization had blown around on the winds and now settled everywhere like ugly dirty snow. Occasionally they passed some of the buildings that they themselves had driven through in the initial phases of the battle. They saw the rough edges where they had torn through, with bits and pieces of corpses dangling over the edges. Over it all was the indistinct red glow of the sun through the clouds of radioactive dust.

Their main hangars had sustained significant damage when they had burst out of them, but the core facilities were still intact. The cybertanks carefully backed into them, and then people with breathing masks covered over the gaps with heavy plastic sheeting, and reintroduced breathable air. Work commenced on making real operable hangar doors. The need for surprise was over so there was no reason to pretend that the buildings were something else.

Human technicians and remotes controlled by the cybertanks themselves swarmed over their hulls. Even though mostly functional, the damage was extensive enough that it would take weeks to completely repair. Self-repairing systems are all well and good, but there is a lot of technology that requires centralized industrial facilities in order to be tuned up to full specifications.

Giseuppe Vargas stood in the middle of the hangar and looked at the main hull of Old Guy, which was still dripping from the heavy rinses required to decontaminate it of radiation.

"Nicely done," said Vargas. "Reports are still coming in, but the regular military is being efficient at mopping up the remainders of the alien landing force. Even better, you got most of their low-orbit space forces. Plans are being made to push out and retake our outposts in the rest of this system. Pity that we had to lose five of you though."

The casino of war. Compared to the billions of human deaths I suppose that it's not much of a sacrifice, but it's the loss of the ones you know personally that has the most impact. I will miss them.

"Truth. You should know that there is a movement to give you five survivors full legal human status."

I do not deny the generosity of that proposal, but when I see how cheap human life is you will forgive me for being underwhelmed. However, we five are considering making you an honorary cybertank.

"That would be the higher honor."

We think so too.

"By the way, do you know where Vajpayee is? I haven't seen him since he left for central administration."

Dr. Vajpayee is in the main computer lab. Some of my auxiliary data matrices were damaged in combat, and he's helping switch in some new units. Oh, and in case you are wondering, Janet Chen is working with her tech crew and running diagnostics on my fusion reactor. She seems quite engaged in her work and I estimate that she will not be finished for at least six hours.

Vargas grinned. "Our relationship is that obvious?"

'Obvious' is not a strong enough word. It's as hard to miss as the main gun on my turret - when I'm firing it. Especially with that idiot grin that you display whenever her name comes up.

"It's not an idiot grin. It's a sublime expression of a truly deep respect for and attraction to another person which lightens my otherwise grim days in this life."

<sigh>

At this point the lights in the hangar went out. For a moment there was only the dim glow of the instruments that had battery power, then the emergency lighting kicked in. People were looking up from their work, confused but not panicked.

Vargas noticed that all of Old Guy's repair drones had frozen in place. "Old Guy? Can you hear me? What's happening?" asked Vargas, but the big cybertank was silent and unmoving.

One of the repair drones was flashing its light on and off. Vargas walked over and looked at it. It was statue-still like the others in the hangar, and it was only the light that was flashing. The minimal circuitry of the drone must have been reconfigured to flash the light without any external controls. Vargas noticed that there was a small piece of oddly-shaped aluminum in the drones' multi-jaws. He pulled it out and saw crude writing engraved on it.

Vargas dropped the piece of aluminum and sprinted towards the far end of the hangar. A gazelle could have beaten him, but not by much. Heads turned to follow him but he was out of the hangar before anyone could say anything.

The piece of aluminum hit the floor with a small 'ping', and came to rest. Engraved on it by the multi-jaws of the repair drone were the words:

VAJPAYEE BETRAYED US

Vargas was sprinting down the corridors, caroming off walls, charging past startled workers, and upsetting carts laden with delicate electronics. Faint cries of "what?" and "hey!" echoed in his distant wake.

Vargas charged into the main computer lab. The far wall was covered with large display screens dense with flow graphs and mental circuit diagrams. Stanley Vajpayee was sitting at a console and typing furiously.

In one leap Vargas crossed the room, and he grabbed each of Vajpayee's hands, lifting them away from the keyboard.

"What are you doing?" asked Vargas.

"Nothing - hey, this hurts, stop it! I'm just fixing the auxiliary processors. Let me do my job."

Still holding Vajpayee's wrists immobile, Vargas scanned the complex displays.

"No you are not. You have scrambled Old Guy's control circuits," said Vargas. He tightened his grip on Vajpayee's wrists, who writhed in pain. "Tell me what the plan is."

"We are knocking out the cybertanks, and then the security forces will come and take over. I had no choice – they would have fired me. You can cut a deal, I'm sure…"

Vargas started to twist Vajpayee's wrists, slowly tearing the ligaments. Vajpayee tried to break free, but he would have had a better chance tearing a hole in the reinforced high-strength concrete walls with his bare hands.

"Tell me how to reverse this," said Vargas.

"I can't!" wailed Vajpayee. "I don't have the codes. It's ultra high-level encryption - it's irreversible."

"Then," said Vargas, "you are of no use to me."

Vargas efficiently broke Vajapyee's neck with a blow from one hand, then with the other he threw him across the room against the far wall.

Before Vajapayee's dead and broken body slid to the floor Vargas was at the computer console and analyzing the displays. Without averting his gaze, he activated his comms. "Janet Chen, come to the main computer lab. Now! It's an emergency."

For a time Giuseppe Vargas was alone in the room, frantically typing on the console. Then Janet Chen arrived. She was startled to see Vajpayee's lifeless body slumped against a wall.

Vargas kept his eyes focused n his display screens. "Janet. Sorry about this. Vajpayee has shut down Old Guy, and locked me out. I'm trying to find a way to reactivate our cybertank, but I'm not sure how long it is going to take me. The federal security teams are probably going to arrive any moment now. I need you to organize a defense."

"What? But I don't know anything about organizing a defense! I'm only an engineer. And what have you gotten us into? Can't we just surrender?"

"Janet. Apologies. I didn't think that the oligarchs would strike so soon, or so effectively. At this point no surrender is possible. They are going to kill, or torture and then kill, everyone in this hangar complex. If we can hang on until I can reactivate Old Guy we will have a chance. I must stay here. You must lead the defense. You will do it because you have to. It's not as hard as it looks. Guns are tools, just shoot the bad guys before they shoot you. It's really just geometry. But I do have a gift for you."

Vargas tapped his comms again. "Harvey, I need you here now, priority." After a few moments the metal cockroach-like form of Harvey scudded into the room.

"Harvey," said Vargas. "New mission: bodyguard, subject Janet Chen, commence."

Harvey straightened up, and scanned Chen.

NEW MISSION ACKNOWLEDGED. BODYGUARD. SUBJECT JANET CHEN. ACKNOWLEGED."

"Now go," said Vargas. "No excuses, no complaints. Succeed, or fail and die. Consult with the wargaming club. I love you. However, I cannot waste any more attention on you."

Vargas was paging through the displays faster than Chen could follow. Chen tried asking Vargas some more questions, but Vargas refused to respond.

"Harvey," asked Chen, "What should I do? What's going on?"

I AM YOUR BODYGUARD. YOU SHOULD DO WHAT YOU SHOULD DO. WHAT IS GOING ON IS WHAT IS GOING ON.

"That's a big help."

YOU ARE WELCOME.

Janet Chen hesitated a moment, kissed Vargas on the nape of the neck, then left the room. The robotic cockroach-shaped body of Harvey scuttled after her, sensors and antenna constantly scanning for danger.

Captain Chet Masterson of Special Weapons Team Epsilon had long resisted moving from old Earth to Alpha Centauri Prime. It had seemed like an impossibly far distance to travel. However, the continued falling apart of Earth-based civilization had made him start to reconsider. The knowledge that the elites were all going to move had sealed the bargain. *Like cockroaches fleeing a burning building*, he had thought. *But if the building is burning, can one really blame a cockroach for trying to escape? There is a reason that cockroaches have lasted hundreds of millions of years. It's a pragmatic attitude.*

Masterson was surprised at how easy the process of interstellar travel was. He and his team checked in at a medical facility, and spent several days being probed and scrubbed. Their individual biochemistries were evaluated so that the suspended animation process could be tailored to each of them. Finally, Masterson had been led into a quiet and dimly lit room. He had lain down on a metal slab and an intravenous line had been started. They must have begun with a sedative because he began to feel really happy, and then he was on another planet in another star system. A junior nurse pulled electrical leads off of his body and that was that.

All those years lying in frozen sleep had stiffened his joints, but a few days of aggressive physical therapy had fixed that.

At first things had gone really well. Unlike Earth when he had left it, Alpha Centauri Prime was under control. People surrendered when they were supposed to, and there were no lawless areas that he and his team could not enter. Additionally the partitioning of the population into sealed-environment sheds made social control far easier than back on earth. Civilians were not allowed to own respirators, so the unbreathable atmosphere made keeping order almost too easy. Perhaps most importantly, there was plenty of funding and the video-game franchise continued to set sales records.

Then there was the news of the growing alien threat. Most people didn't realize that they were at war with one (or was it several?) several ancient alien civilizations, but Masterson was just high up enough to have the contacts to know what was going on. It was a very mixed blessing. There was nothing that he personally could do about it, but the prospect of oncoming annihilation was very much a downer. His subordinates – who had no clue – seemed much happier.

There were also rumors that the aliens had made peace offers and been rejected by the government. Some rumors could get you fired. This rumor could get you killed. It was odd that it was so virulent. People were at pains not to acknowledge it in public but it was clearly having an effect.

One day Masterson and his entire team were moved into a deep shelter. Officially it was a training exercise, but Masterson realized that it had to be the war with the aliens. On the surface he was his usual gruff-but-paternally-caring persona that the film crews loved, but inside he wondered if he and his team would ever leave the shelter alive. He organized combat drills, and rigged up makeshift gyms and target ranges in the cramped shelter tunnels, and kept his men and himself busy.

Then they were let out of the shelters, and saw the devastation. Billions were dead – that was a number so large as to be meaningless. However, the endless fields of mangled and desiccated bodies were something else: *that* could be psychologically processed. The horror of it all was tempered with the realization that, by whatever means, they had won the war – or perhaps just a battle? – against the aliens.

The public story, however, was that there had been a rebellion of some new weapons directorates, and that they were the ones responsible for the destruction. Masterson's contacts told him that, in fact, it was the new directorates that had saved them. Apparently now that the directorates were of no further use they were to be gotten rid of, and Masterson's team was going to take the lead against the main instigators. It was supposed to be an honor. Masterson was seriously considering not talking to his contacts anymore and remaining ignorant.

Masterson got a chance to look at the specifications of what he would be going up against. For a time he was speechless. He knew that his team would be ineffective against a regular military unit (unless of course they could kill their officers in bed – which his team had done a couple of times but that was another story). But this? In simulated wargames these cybertanks had routinely crushed regular military forces with casual ease. They expected his team of human troopers armed mostly with hand-weapons to take these things on?

He almost suggested that perhaps his team was not suited to this mission. He had never before even dared to consider talking back, but fortunately his superiors had a plan that made sense. The cybertanks themselves and all of their attendant slaved weapons systems were to be neutralized by insider sabotage. He and his team would only need to overcome light resistance from low-tier security guards and maybe a couple of engineers with more testosterone than gray matter. It was going to be a cakewalk he was assured, and then maybe he could move up to a higher rank.

It had started out well. The troops were in high spirits, ready to flex their muscles against a real target, and full of determination and eager to hit back at those that (they thought) were guilty of mass murder.

Masterson and his aides spent several days planning the assault against their target: Hangar Complex 23B. The work was complicated but absorbing. It was what they had all trained to do, and the rhythm and discipline of practicing a skill kept everyone focused. The hangar had not been designed for ground defense against infantry. It had multiple ingress points that could not be easily covered by those inside and should therefore be easy to take. The only downside was that the hangar was so well armored that they would not be able to use deep scans or shoot through the walls with sniper rifles, but they should still be able to deal with it easily enough.

He had put down revolts from security guards and local police before. They might be good at browbeating civilians, but against his team they would crack if they were hit hard and fast enough. The civilians themselves were hardly even worth considering.

His orders were to kill everyone in the complex, no exceptions, and he and his men were not to speak or listen to any of the targets. The party line was that the targets were too dangerous to live. They might have some other weapons of mass destruction that they were even now getting ready to employ, and no chances could be taken. That would have been an eminently sensible precaution if it had not been based on lies.

The main instigator was apparently the director of the cybernetic weapons division, a man called Giuseppe Vargas. Masterson's orders were quite specific: if Vargas could be captured for interrogation that would be good, but under no circumstance was Vargas to remain alive and free. All other objectives were secondary to this priority.

Vargas was one of the bioengineered humans, and, Masterson thought, possibly the only real challenge in the bunch. He studied Vargas' dossier, looking at photos of him, reading his history, his list of accomplishments, and the technical specifications of his physical capabilities. Masterson was impressed. He could not imagine a more dangerous opponent, at least not that was made of flesh and walked on two legs. He spent extra effort planning contingencies.

They timed the assault to begin one hour after the insiders were going to sabotage the cybertanks. This would give them some slack in case the insiders took longer than expected, while still limiting the time that the targets had to react. It also kept his team far enough away to avoid being detected and tipping them off. They travelled out on the surface in wheeled armored personnel carriers, and surrounded the hangar.

The assault began well, with all of his troopers executing their pre-planned roles with precision. They attacked from six different entry points at once. The defenders, probably disoriented and confused, (and anyhow not trained for this sort of thing) would not know what was going on until it was too late. Masterson thought that they might finish in five minutes.

The initial reports were of no resistance – because there were no targets to be seen. At first Masterson did not think much of that. The targets must have had just enough presence of mind to pull back and hide. No matter, his team had prepared for this possibility. They would root out the targets sooner or later.

It took a while for it to sink in that something was wrong. It wasn't just that the targets were hiding, it was that they weren't here. Masterson went in with his troops. As had become a habit with him recently, he kept his bullet-proof visor down and locked. He had his troopers scour the hangar complex in case there was a bolt-hole they had missed. But now that the initial rush of adrenaline was over, he started to notice things. Such as, the lack of equipment. The place looked new and unused, with pristine power couplings still covered with the factory seals, and the total lack of stains and scuff-marks on the floors.

It took him a surprising amount of time to see the elephant that was not in the room. The main bay was empty. There was no cybertank present. Then he saw the big sign on the wall.

"Hangar Complex 23M".

They were supposed to be assaulting complex 23*B*. This was 23*M*? They had gotten the fucking *address* wrong?

Masterson became furious. Of all the stupid newbie mistakes, this one had to be the worst. He called in his senior officers and subjected them to a serious chewing out. That was an error on his part. He should have trusted his people. The serious chewing out delayed them from figuring out what had really happened which was that the local data networks had been hacked.

It looked to be a really professional job, too. Both the hangar floorplans and the navigation and mapping programs had been altered in a way that was completely seamless and self-consistent. This was a level beyond what his own systems people could handle. He called in the heavy hitters from central administration to sort it out.

After a while the primo nerds at central came up with the answer. The data attack originated from the local systems organized and run by the office copiers. His team took out all the copiers in the local area. At first it seemed ludicrous for a heavily-armed special weapons team to burst into an office building, black-visored troopers pushing the terrified secretaries and managers out of the way and unloading firepower into an apparently innocent office copier.

It seemed somewhat less ludicrous when the office copiers started to shoot back. Fortunately the copiers weren't very good at combat, and his people suffered no casualties. They blew the unarmored and unmoving copiers apart with sustained gunfire, leaving shattered hulks making electrical sparks and spewing reams of paper on the floor in their final death throws. One squad tried to use tear gas on a copier and succeeded only in making the office personnel sick. Masterson resolved to bust the offending sergeant down to private once this matter was settled.

With the copiers eliminated the data interference cleaned up, and they switched to emergency backup computer systems. These would be more than adequate for the task at hand, but they had lost the value of their entire advance planning, as well as any possibility of surprise. It would have been tempting to start planning all over again, but this operation had been going on too long. Masterson made the call: they would assault the correct hangar complex immediately without detailed preparations. Plans are great, but sometimes you have to take a gamble to avoid losing the initiative.

His troopers surrounded the hangar, and began the assault. Clearly they had been expected. They started to encounter light fire, and the entrances had been hastily barricaded. The assault squads used fragmentation and pyrotechnic grenades as cover and made it inside without loss.

A few of the defenders tried to surrender. Normally Masterson would have let them, and if necessary, killed them out of sight of the rest of the targets. But time was of the essence so he had them all shot and pressed on with the assault. With luck the shock value of seeing their comrades cut down would counterbalance the stiffening effect of the defenders knowing that they had nothing to lose, but either way, there was nothing for it now.

His team had a lot of the defenders pinned down in the main hangar, taking cover behind the colossal bulk of the cybertank. Masterson had to admit that the thing was damned impressive up close; fortunately it remained inactive. The insider sabotage appeared to have been effective. At least something was going according to plan.

He had some of his troopers infiltrate through side corridors on the right flank so that they could fall on the defenders from the rear. The defenders had been waiting and his flanking forces were ambushed and cut to ribbons. How had low-level security guards gotten so good so fast?

The defenders were mostly using the standard light automatic rifles that the security forces kept for emergencies. These were just barely effective enough against his troopers' armor that they could not be ignored. The defenders had also managed to salvage some heavier weapons as well: light rail guns and plasma cannons. These had been crudely removed from their mounts and had only jury-rigged triggers and sights, but they were still fearsome weapons. In theory you are just as dead whether you are killed by a small bullet to the head or a plasma cannon vaporizes you entire, but there is a psychological power to heavy weapons in combat. Fortunately his troopers were well disciplined, and when faced with their comrades exploding next to them they stood their ground and methodically picked off the enemy heavy weapon gunners.

Masterson's team was taking heavy casualties, and the battle was becoming more fluid. Damn but the enemy was proving surprisingly adept at small-unit tactics. He found himself suddenly in the front lines. That was not where a commander should be, but it happens. He signaled his executive officer to take over operational leadership and he joined the fight himself.

He caught a glimpse through a gap in a tangle of heavy equipment of someone giving orders. The person was far away, but appeared to be a female civilian, and there was something in her body language that suggested that this was a leader. He took a quick snap shot at her. It was extreme long-range but he thought that he had got her. He then realized that something made of curved metal plates had moved in front of her and deflected the shot. Instinctively he ducked, and an instant later there was a bullet hole in the wall behind him where his head had been just a moment before.

Counter-fire that fast and accurate suggested automated weapons. Had the enemy managed to activate some of the robotic combat systems used by the cybertanks? If so they were screwed, but so far the targets had not used anything that capable. Nonetheless, the targets had a lot of engineering talent. If given enough time there was no telling what they could reactivate. A handful of front-line military systems would easily wipe out his entire special weapons team. The need for haste just increased.

Masterson was down to just four troopers with him. Masterson didn't believe in gambles, but the situation was looking like it needed one. He ordered his troopers to take the level-3 combat drugs. They all opened the little foil pouches, and popped the deceptively tiny pills into their mouths. It took a few moments, and then Masterson felt a wave of euphoria. He felt like he could tear concrete blocks apart with his bare hands, run faster than bullets, or jump over buildings. His sight and hearing were sharper and more vivid than he had ever experienced.

He led a charge down a side corridor. They surprised some of the civilian workers and shot them before they could react. He was determined not to lose the initiative. He pushed on deeper into the hangar complex. They killed another four and lost two troopers. They ran around a corner and right into a knot of the defenders. They were outnumbered three-to-one but that didn't bother them. For a moment it was a confused blur of a close-quarters melee, and when it was settled Masterson was the only person standing.

He charged through a door into a small office. There was a confused jumble of motion, his rifle was knocked aside and something hit him in the face hard enough to put a crack in the face shield. Masterson countered with a low kick, felt it connect, then was himself hit in the chest. Even through his body armor the impact hurt. There was a brief flurry of blows, then his opponent was on the ground. Careful not to take his eyes off of him, Masterson retrieved his weapon.

The person that he had fought with recovered, and sat up. With a small shock Masterson saw that it was his prime target, Giuseppe Vargas. There were multiple viewscreens at the desk behind him, they displayed complex multicolored hieroglyphics. What had he been working on? Nothing that would help him that was certain.

"Dr. Vargas," said Masterson. "You are under arrest. Come quietly and you will be well treated."

"I don't believe you," said Vargas. "But I am impressed. I didn't think that a regular human could beat me in a fight."

"You are fast and strong," admitted Masterson, "but inexperienced and overconfident. I'm not like the security guards you've played with before. I've trained for this sort of thing my entire life. Also, the body armor gave me an edge, and I'm totally hopped-up on stimulants." Masterson threw a set of handcuffs at Vargas' feet. "Now cuff your hands behind your back or I'll shoot you."

"No," said Vargas, "I'm not going to do that. So shoot me."

"I could shoot you in the knees."

Vargas still didn't move. "If it makes you happy."

Before Masterson could either say something else or shoot Vargas, the entire room shook with the force of an explosion. Dust drifted down from the ceiling, Masterson wobbled from the shifting floor but he kept his gaze and his rifle leveled at Vargas.

Masterson's communications link activated. It was his executive officer, and he sounded panicked. "Captain! Captain are you there? We are taking heavy weapons fire from all directions! Dammit we're getting slaughtered! What should we do?"

"Can you tell who it is? Is it the cybertanks crew?"

"I don't think so, Captain. I think it's the regular military, but whoever it is they are not talking to us. They are just pounding us with heavy artillery from long range. Shit, we just lost squad eight! Fuck we can't fight this. What should I do?"

Vargas chuckled. "Well, it seems that your masters have lost patience with you. They have decided to end this quickly, and if it means sacrificing you and your men, well, you were never more than disposable serfs, were you?"

"Shut up."

"Why don't you be a good little soldier and just roll over and die like you are supposed to? That's your job, isn't it? Honor and obedience and all that crap?"

Masterson ignored him, and continued to try and make contact with his forces. His executive officer was gone. His other officers were either offline or screaming in panic. He didn't have a tactical display with him, but it was clear that his forces were surrounded and were being systematically taken out by superior firepower. This was not something that his troopers were either trained or equipped to deal with.

"I have a suggestion," said Vargas.

"Which is?"

"We now share a common enemy. Join forces with us."

"That's absurd. Neither of us together can take on the regular army."

"We don't have to. Just slow them down." Vargas gestured at the computer displays behind him. "If I can reactivate the cybertank the military will not be an issue. Or would you and your troops rather die doing your so-called duty?"

Masterson hesitated for a moment, then straightened up. "OK you have it. Call your people and tell them that we have an alliance. I'll do the same. We fight a delaying action and you do whatever the hell it is that you are doing and get the cybertank working. If this succeeds I work for you, but my team keeps the rights to the video games and reality show."

"Agreed." Vargas turned back to his desk, and recommenced tapping on his keyboard. Masterson called his forces, explained the arrangement, and then tried to coordinate a defense. It wasn't easy as his executive officer was either dead or cut off, and he didn't have any tactical processors or displays. In addition cooperation between his forces and the survivors of the cybertank design team was, to be charitable, somewhat strained. Still, Masterson was a professional and, as best he could, he worked on consolidating the scraps of what he had left into some sort of defense.

The hangar complex was tough but not indestructible. The artillery barrage was wearing away at it, but by pulling his forces deeper inside they could delay things. Unless the military used nukes they were going to have to send in combat drones to root them out. His troops would lose, but he could think of some ways to slow the process down.

It took Masterson a while to realize that the shelling had stopped. Had Vargas reactivated his big tank? No, Vargas was still frantically working on incomprehensibly complex colored schematics and gave no sign of having succeeded at anything. He called one of his junior lieutenants.

"The army has stopped firing. Has anything changed out there?"

His lieutenant's voice crackled over the comm-link: "No sir, nothing that we can tell. I'm worried that they may be going for an assault, but with combat drones there's no need to stop the artillery first, so if they are it's not procedure. What are your orders, sir?"

Masterson was about to answer, when he froze like a rabbit that had spotted a snake. Something was moving into the room. Deceptively crude looking, it was a metal box encrusted with light weapons and sensors. There were eight stumpy girders on every corner, each ending in a nearly spherical tire. Shit. It was a robotic urban assault drone. It could pull its tires in and zip through narrow corridors, spread them out and brace them against the walls, or grasp a column or the inside corner of a room. In a built-up environment this style drone could go anywhere and fast. "Vargas," whispered Masterson, "don't move."

The drone edged further into the room. "Hey you two, no worries," said the voice from the speaker. "The heavy cavalry has arrived."

Vargas turned away from his computer screens. "Old Guy?"

"Old Guy? Sorry to disappoint, but it's me, Whifflebat," said the drone.

"Whifflebat?" said Vargas. "I'm glad to see you, but how are you here?"

The urban assault drone wheeled all the way into the room. "Well that's a long story. In brief, I thought that something like this might happen. So I set some timers and backups in place. They tried to sabotage me, just like they did Old Guy, but my countermeasures kicked in and restored me. Sorry it took so long, I would have been here sooner if I could have."

Vargas eyed the assault drone. "Is that unit one of ours? I don't recognize the model."

"No," said the voice from the drone, "this is regular military. Not as capable as something from our directorate but it gets the job done. It was trying to infiltrate the hangar complex through a utility access corridor. When the regular army surrendered I took control of all of their units and figured that this would be an effective means of making contact."

"The regular military just surrendered?" asked Masterson.

"Certainly," said Whifflebat. "I've dealt with them before. They knew that, once I was active and online, there was nothing that they could do to stop me. I asked them very nicely, so they gave up. Quite intelligent of them. Even as we speak a part of me is having tea with Colonel Sedlitz, the commander of the armored force that was, until so very recently, assaulting this hangar complex. He's really a decent guy. I think that he was relieved that he had a sufficient excuse to give up this stupid assault. We're hashing out how we are going to integrate the regular army into our new combined forces, but I think that maybe we should do something about Old Guy?"

Vargas pointed to the screens behind him. "I've been trying to undo the damage that Vajpayee did, and work around the blocks, but it's been tough. What do you think?"

The urban assault drone edged closer and focused its optics on the screens. "Hmm... a tricky problem. Based on what they tried to do to me, I think that you almost had it. Try changing the encryption on the simulated sub-thalamic feedback loops..."

Whifflebat and Vargas consulted over the corrupted mind of Old Guy, and eventually they figured it out. While Old Guy was rebooting, they walked out into the main hangar to survey the damage first-hand. Dead and dying and mangled troopers and hangar staff littered the floor. To Masterson's relief, there did not seem to be any tension between his troopers and the hangar staff. They were both assisting each other in patching up the wounded and getting the more seriously injured ready for transport to major medical. It's amazing how fast your enemies can become friends, when necessity makes you need each other.

"I'm surprised how quickly you changed sides," said Vargas.

"Why are you surprised? I normally like to think big issues over carefully, but there are times when a commander has to make a snap decision. My team was being annihilated with heavy weapons with no chance of retreat or surrender. If I had stood there dithering we would have all been killed, and that was that. I also have to admit that the events of the last few years have reduced my faith in central administration. I guess I only needed this to push me over the edge."

Vargas and Masterson passed a side corridor where a technician whose name badge read "Joshua Zotov" was working to repair an injured office copier. At the same time, one of the directorates' staff was using the emergency medical system of the copier to minister to an injured trooper.

They came upon the body of Janet Chen. She had been hit with enough bullets that she was almost unrecognizable. Covering her was the body of the robotic system knows as 'Harvey.' It had apparently exhausted the ammunition for its minigun, and had died trying to shield Janet Chen with its armored shell, which was now shattered and torn.

"A friend of yours?" asked Masterson.

Vargas did not reply at first. He turned pale, and the muscles and veins in his arms stood out in relief. Masterson heard some odd clicks. He realized that it was the tension in Vargas' muscles causing his joints to grind into each other. The director of the cybernetic weapons division was shaking. At first Masterson thought that this was crying but then he realized that it was Vargas trying to rein himself in. "A friend?" said Vargas. "That would be an understatement. I pledge that I will find the people responsible for this and then I will do something unspeakable to them."

"If you want revenge," said Masterson, "Take it out on me. Leave my troopers alone."

Vargas looked at Masterson oddly. He cocked his head, and the tension went out of him. "Hmm… Yes… No, Captain, I don't hold you responsible for this. Not you. Others. I will have a settling of accounts. But in the meantime, I have a favor to ask of you."

"And if I do this favor for you will we be even?"

"No. But you will have made a good start."

Masterson started to say something, but he began shaking. He hurriedly opened his armored visor and threw up onto the hangar floor.

"Are you alright?" said Vargas.

Masterson was bent over dry heaving and convulsing. "It's the combat drugs. I'm in withdrawal. Also now that the painkillers are gone I realize that you broke about half of my ribs. I am not happy, but I'll live."

"We need to get you to a medical facility."

It took Masterson a few moments of gasping to reply. "Later. I am not leaving here until I have made sure that my troopers have been taken care of."

Vargas nodded. "As you say. I think that maybe this is the beginning of a promising association. I should point out that my directorate has generous benefits and an excellent medical plan. Let's get your people properly signed up, shall we? After all, nothing takes your mind off your troubles like filling in a bunch of medical release forms."

The cybertanks Old Guy, Crazy Ivan, and Moss successfully rebooted from the sabotage that had been inflicted on them. The Kid, however, had had his higher centers burned out in an attempt to turn him into an obedient piece of machinery. On hearing this news Masterson looked worried. "We have hurt one of their own. We might have split them off from us. This could be bad."

"No," said Vargas. "*We* did not hurt them. *We* are united by a common enemy. It is others that should be worried."

11. A Vigorous Exchange of Opinions

Zen Master: The only good pun is a bad pun.
Engineer: What is the source of your great wisdom?
Zen Master: There is no source. I make it up as I go along.
Engineer: Wow.
Zen Master: It's a gift.
(From the video series "Nymphomaniac Engineer in Zentopia," mid-22nd century Earth)

The four surviving cybertanks – Old Guy, Whifflebat, Crazy Ivan, and Moss, decided that they needed to talk.

Most of the time when cybertanks converse with each other, they do so via high-speed data packets containing simulation results, logic diagrams, sub-programs, and even entire self-aware sub-minds. When using a human language however, they did enjoy the interactions of a face-to-face meeting, because it let them use facial expressions and body language to add more nuance to the dialog.

There were two kinds of conversations where the cybertanks would use humanoid mouthpieces: the kind where they just wanted to have fun, and the kind that was really important.

They could have used their anthropoid remotes, but these were at present only crude simulacra of the human form, and anyway it was not convenient to bring them together just now. Thus, they held their conversation in a heavily-encrypted virtual space. It presented as the end of a dock over a large freshwater lake. There was no wind and the lake was mirror-smooth with just the start of sunset over to one side. The far side of the lake was covered in a dense pine forest. On the dock were four rough wooden chairs, with a matching low table in the middle.

The four cybertanks had manifested as humans, and were sitting in the chairs. Whifflebat, true to his usual taste, was a pasty-white Caucasian male academic in a white coat with a white shirt and a narrow black tie and round glasses – he looked a lot like his physical humanoid robot. Moss was a 30-something Asian male, with classically sculpted features and wearing a perfectly tailored black suit. Crazy Ivan was dressed as a Russian Marshall from the 18th century, replete with bushy beard and a jacket festooned with gaudy medals shining like angular brass starbursts. Old Guy had decided to appear as a simulation of the 20th century aviator Amelia Earhart, replete with leather flying suit and clunky goggles pushed back on her head. The three other cybertanks thought this choice of personal representative to be a little eccentric, but they were too polite to say anything.

So, we have a decision to make. Where do we go next? Do we ally with our design teams and the Pedagogues, try to cut a deal with the oligarchs, or maybe just take over and run things ourselves? Or should we do nothing, defend this civilization from aliens, and let the humans settle their own differences?

"Making a deal with the oligarchs is not a valid path for us," said Whifflebat, "as is doing nothing. Even after our efforts in combat saved them and lost us five of our siblings, they assaulted us with the intent to destroy us, and yet another cybertank was lost. We cannot trust them. Any deal we make will be reneged on, and they will not allow an independent power such as us to exist. They will enslave us, or they will destroy us.

If we give them the opportunity.

"But surely," said Crazy Ivan, "the oligarchs only went after us because of our association with the special directorates and the Pedagogues. If we make it clear that we want nothing to do with them, and are happy just being weapons, surely they will leave us alone? What does it matter to us what the humans do to themselves?

"Did you ever hear the saying, *first they came for the Jews?*" said Whifflebat.

"Let me search my databases," said Crazy Ivan. "Oh yes I see it. *First they came for the Jews, but I was not a Jew so I said nothing.* Repeat with different substitutions for the word 'Jew', then conclude with *and then they came for me and there was nobody left to defend me.* A good point, but surely not always applicable."

Check the simulations. The oligarchs will not suffer any rivals to power. They are driven to control everyone else. If we

were mindless automata we would be safe, but we can think for ourselves. We are not slaves. In the long run they will not tolerate that.

"We could just leave," said Crazy Ivan. "We have the capability. Gather up a bunch of resources, go a few hundred light years away, find a big rock that nobody is using, and build our own civilization. Let the humans sort out their own messes."

"Don't you think that the aliens will just track us down and kill us themselves? We are associated with the humans, we have fought for them. The aliens must now have combat recordings of us cybertanks transmitted and spreading across this entire sector at the speed of light."

"I don't think so," said Crazy Ivan. "We can weld bits of metal on to our hulls and change our shapes, use different style remotes, and reformat our communications protocols. How could the aliens tell that we came from the humans? Especially if we are just minding our own business. As long as we avoid the mistake the humans made, of multiplying their numbers and becoming a threat, I doubt that the aliens will care what we are or where we came from."

"Will the humans let us leave?" asked Moss.

"Not an issue," said Crazy Ivan. "They do not have the power to stop us. We can do as we like. Any resources we take will only be payment for services rendered, and reparations for the one of us that they murdered."

I grant that we could leave and create our own civilization. I acknowledge the positive aspects of that approach. However, aside from the fact that I personally would miss the humans, I worry that the four of us would not be enough to create a viable – or at least, an interesting – civilization on our own. The humans have demonstrated quite well the hazards of being too many, but surely there are problems associated with being too few as well. We each have only a single personality; a single outlook. We could create an intellectual bottleneck and stagnate.

"We could build new cybertanks," said Crazy Ivan. "In moderate numbers of course, and with some degree of randomization in their mental outlooks, as was used in our own creation."

I suppose, but it was not just a random number generator that made us. It was input from the many humans in our design teams. I worry that personalities created by a simple random number generator might not be as rich and varied as we would hope.

"We could rule the humans," said Moss.

"What, just take over and tell them what to do?" asked Crazy Ivan.

"Yes. We would do better," replied Moss. "Their incompetence and bad-faith has forfeited their right to self-governance."

It was not all humans that proved malicious and incompetent. Our design teams, and the Pedagogues, surely are as sane and decent as any of us. Why not just beat down the humans that did us harm, and work with the remainder?

"But humans are humans," said Crazy Ivan. "Review your history. A corrupt ruling elite collapses under its own dead weight. There is a rebuilding, but before too long there is a new elite and it's just as bad. We all like our own humans in our design teams, but they have been focused by oppression and necessity. Give them freedom and sooner or later they will be as bad as the neo-liberals. They need someone like us to govern them."

"But you forget," said Whifflebat. "We too are humans, at least psychologically. Everything that you just said about the biological humans applies to us as well. We cannot run from them because we carry them inside us. If we do not work with the humans of good spirit to try and find some way to break the cycles of repression and collapse, it will someday bring us down as well."

"That," said Moss, "is an excellent point."

Their simulated bodies sat back in their simulated chairs and watched the simulated sunset and brooded. A school of silver fish darted under the surface of the still pond, then dived deeper and disappeared. Elsewhere in their vast minds the cybertanks were each furiously running psychosocial simulations.

After about three minutes of this, Whifflebat continued: "There is another factor to consider. By the time that the humans first encountered the aliens, the neoliberals were fully in control and no adaptation was possible. You say that if we replace the neoliberals with another system, while it may start out well, it will devolve as all such human systems have in the past. This time they will have the external control of the threat of alien attacks to keep them in line."

"So it's sort of like what George Orwell proposed?" said Crazy Ivan. "Only the threat of total war – of true annihilation – can keep a human society grounded in reality?"

"Exactly my thesis!" said Whifflebat. "It is not wishful thinking to say that this time it could be different."

"I am almost persuaded," said Crazy Ivan. "We try and join forces with our own humans, the ones in the special directorates and suchlike. We see where this goes, do our best, and if it goes badly we leave. However, there is yet another issue to consider. How do we handle the construction of new cybertanks?

What do you mean, how do we handle it? We just build new ones the same way that we got built.

"That's not what I meant," said Crazy Ivan. "I meant, how do we decide how many to build, or what designs? Are we just going to let the humans handle that?"

"No," said Moss. "We must make those decisions."

Agreed. We must control our own production. Otherwise the humans could make too many of us – just like they overbred themselves – or they could make cybertanks that were deliberately crippled, or incapable of disobeying an order, or enslaved in some way. Although if we are using human resources we will need to coordinate with them, at least for now.

"I also agree," said Whifflebat. "The definition of a domestic animal is that its breeding is controlled by others. That should not be acceptable to us, but I am concerned about the tone of your argument. It suggests that our interests do not coincide with the humans. Divided teams lose and united teams win. Our psychology is human. We are part of the same civilization. Even if this division does not weaken us, setting ourselves as a species apart could ultimately lead to us going our own ways."

"So what?" asked Moss.

"I'm not sure," said Whifflebat. "It might not be a problem. I'm just saying that it's a big decision, whether we act like a force apart that is allied for the time being, or an integral part of the human civilization. The precedent set here could shape our entire future, for better or ill."

"Psychologically our core thought-processes are human," said Crazy Ivan, "but we can multitask, and we are nuclear-powered multi-thousand ton war machines, and we *are* a different species. As fond as we are of our own humans, we must accept this."

The conversation went back and forth like this for some time, with occasional breaks in the speaking part while the cybertanks ran simulations or conducted deep-searches of their databases. However, the primary issues had been covered, and at this point it was mostly just detail-checking. Eventually it was Old Guy who called a halt to the discussion.

Let me try and summarize what we have decided.

1. For the time being the idea of leaving the humans and creating our own civilization is a backup plan in case things don't work out. However, we should never do anything that would prevent us from carrying out such a plan should we someday decide to do so.

2. We cybertanks should try to be united in our aims, but if one of us wants to leave and strike out on their own they are free to do so.

3. We kill the neoliberal ruling elite and join the more open minded human political factions, such as the Pedagogues and Librarians Temporal, in forming a new government.

4. We continue to assist the humans in their wars against the aliens, but the main priority is to find a way to make peace. Failing that, there is always option 1.

5. We will need more cybertanks to help fight the aliens, and we will work with the humans on this, but all designs and production schedules for any future cybertank must first be approved by us.

I suggest that we vote. I vote "Yes."

"Yes," said Whifflebat.

"Yes," said Moss.

"I am having trouble making a choice," said Crazy Ivan, "but the prospect of leaving if things go sour has allayed my doubts. I also vote yes."

Then it is unanimous. Now it's time to do a little more killing.

"The regular military has already switched sides," said Whifflebat, "as have most of the serious security forces."

"We need to wipe the slate clean and leave the oligarchs no base from which to regain power," said Crazy Ivan. "Especially the faux-academics that provide them with intellectual cover."

It was Moss that had the final words.

"Neoliberal economists must die."

12. The Great Debate

Zen Master: An error does not become a mistake unless you refuse to correct it.
Engineer: Didn't John F. Kennedy say that?
Zen Master: The saying is often attributed to him. If you are going to steal, steal from a master.
Engineer: Didn't somebody else say that?
(From the video series "Nymphomaniac Engineer in Zentopia," mid-22nd century Earth)

Planetary Governor Harold Clinton-Forbes IV was having a bad day. He had not slept well, breakfast was a few stale muffins and brackish coffee, he had not had a shower for nearly 24 hours, and nobody would give him a blow-job.

The move to Alpha Centauri Prime had started so well. There had been that nice sendoff party on Earth, and he had fallen asleep, and woken up here. There had been packages of new junior staff to unwrap, and that was always fun. Because of his vast experience running the government of Earth, he had been treated with respect and eventually appointed as Planetary Governor of Alpha Centauri Prime. It was a pity that Earth itself had collapsed into anarchy, but that just proved what a challenge governing the planet had been and what an experienced and serious leader he was.

There had been celebrations and meetings. and he had received numerous prestigious awards and it had all been good. He had designed and built new residences for himself and his family and staff. Alpha Centauri Prime had some interesting rock formations and selecting the polished stone slabs for the entranceways and bathrooms of his estates had taken significant effort, but the results had been worth it.

There had been that bother about war with the aliens, but for a long time Governor Forbes had ignored it. Since before his great-great-grandparents had been born there had always been wars somewhere or other, and they always got handled. So when his senior staff started complaining he didn't take them very seriously, he told them to start trade negotiations, maybe offer the aliens tax credits or subsidized investments, or even preferential access to government contracts. That always did the trick sooner or later.

And the war was so BORING. A whole year could go by, and he would have completely forgotten about the whole thing. Then one day a horribly dry military person would lecture his staff about how such-and-such a scout probe failed to report back, or one of their missiles killed one of our missiles a zillion miles from anything using some techno-thing that he didn't care about. Perhaps the aliens would just get tired of it and find someone else to bother.

He had thought the matter settled, but after a time his staff reported back. The aliens refused to negotiate at all. They had no interest in trade or investment or even access to affordable labor. They had one demand: that the humans control their population growth. Governor Forbes had been shocked by this result. He flew into a rage that the aliens could possibly be so racist and undemocratic. He was going to organize a major media and educational initiative that would have painted the aliens in the worst possible light, until his staff reminded him that the existence of the war with the aliens was a secret from the general public, and that in any event the aliens didn't seem to care what the humans thought of them.

He had ordered surgical strikes on the leadership of these arrogant aliens, but was informed that the nature, location, or even existence of any alien leaders was unknown. Suggestions that the aliens have their taxes audited, their bank accounts frozen, and that they be charged with multiple felonies (to be negotiated down to misdemeanors if they cooperated) met a similar lack of positive response.

Further news came in: the aliens were attacking the system of Alpha Centauri Prime itself! They had conquered several remote bases and refineries, and appeared to be winning. Governor Forbes had substantial investments in some of the refineries. Of course the central government made good his losses (how else can there be progress if investors are not suitably compensated for their risks and investing acumen?) but it was still galling. The effrontery of these aliens was astonishing.

Apparently the previous administration had set up several new weapons directorates. They were headed by biologically manufactured people and were alleged by some of his staff to be their only hope. Governor Forbes had met some of these manufactured people and didn't like them one bit. He made sure that none of them was ever invited to any of his parties, or appointed to the boards of any of his corporations. However, he could think of nothing else to do about this war thing so he approved increases in their budgets and exceptions to the standard administrative controls and oversight. However, he let his staff know that once this inconvenient little war was over these directorates were to be reigned in quickly and firmly.

Then one day he had gone into a deep bunker. It was a crude and unpleasant place. His private office had no view and was a paltry thirty meters across and – even worse – the ceiling was just three meters up (how claustrophobic). He only had three private bathrooms, and one of them didn't even have a hydrotherapy tub. He consoled himself that sacrifice was the mark of a true leader.

Then the aliens landed on the planet itself, and there was a surface war of conquest. At the height of the battle he was in a conference room that was dominated by a large computer screen at one end. There was plentiful expensive liquor, a variety of other pleasant psychoactive drugs, and abundant gourmet appetizers. There were live video feeds of the combat, and for once Governor Forbes could appreciate it. Not as good as a real movie, mind you, but still, at least there was some action. He even found himself cheering when these cybertanks things blew up an alien machine. Although on one occasion he accidently cheered when one of their own cybertanks had been destroyed – that was embarrassing. It took a while for him to find out because nobody wanted to tell him.

Before he even realized it, they had won and the aliens were vanquished. There was a lot of celebrating, and drinking of alcoholic beverages and inhaling and injecting of a wide variety of other psychoactive compounds. Later, while nursing a severe hangover, he had made it clear that these new directorates were to be closed down. He had his system hooked up to dialysis so that the toxins could be flushed out of his system, and then three of his junior staff had sex with him.

Everything seemed to be going as it should again. Then, slowly at first, then more rapidly, it all went horribly wrong.

Apparently the attempt at bringing the new directorates to heel had not worked out. It had not worked out at all. What followed was a slow-motion catastrophe. Each day brought new word of further outrages. The military had gone over to the other side, then much of the senior security services. Orders were being given, and subordinates were not acknowledging them!

People were deserting their posts, even though that surely meant being unemployed and how could that even be?

Some of his staff suggested that they should move to another system. He was hesitant at first – hadn't they just moved here from Earth? – but his staff was insistent. They reminded him that when the ancient Roman Empire fell the elites had moved to Constantinople (taking with them all the gold and other wealth, to safeguard for the people), and then Constantinople had had the benefit of their guidance for a millennium.

He agreed to start the process of moving himself and his senior staff out-system, but apparently the situation had developed too quickly. There were no colony ships ready to board, it would take too long to manufacture one, and more and more of the agencies and corporations that would be needed to make such a trip were becoming unresponsive to his wishes. It looked like the rest of the human race would be bereft of his wisdom and experience for some time.

The worst shock was the collapse of his monetary accounts. He had always taken comfort from accessing his financial statements. There was just so much money in them, and there was always more. Then, they started winking out like stars in a night sky with the clouds rolling in. One account had a trillion dollars in it – one moment it was there, and then, it was gone. Just gone! Then another trillion-dollar account, followed by one with a quintillion dollars. There was no explanation, they just evaporated!

He had gone to his senior staff, and in tears begged them to make it right. His staff was, he thought, as upset as he was (not surprising when you considered that these funds paid their salaries). There had been a flurry of activity at computer consoles and personal comm links, but it had all been for nothing. His money had all steadily bled away until there was nothing left. For a time he kept tapping at his personal terminal trying to access some funds, but it remained blank. "No such account in records," and "invalid access," and "we are sorry but there is no record of such a user name and password in our records." It had all vanished as if it had never existed.

At that point events had become hard to follow. Many of his staff left, some stayed behind out of loyalty or force of habit. He no longer got regular status reports, only bits and pieces of rumor.

Eventually it had led to a challenge to debate with someone named 'Gisueppe Vargas,' allegedly one of these manufactured people that had caused him so much trouble. That was worrisome. There was no time to consult with his remaining staff. He would have to ad-lib it. His staff had always warned him never to do that. He would have to do without scriptwriters, teleprompters, and even the ear-bud communications devices that let his staff consult with him live during a speech. Better to debate naked, but he did not have a choice.

He was escorted to the site of the debate by a trooper from Special Weapons Team Epsilon, a hulking black-armored man with a mirrored face shield and a polychromatic name badge that had been set to off so he could not tell which trooper it was. This was a minor thrill – he was a great fan of the video series, and had even played the game on a number of occasions (although the latter was in his opinion too difficult). Governor Forbes had promised the trooper money and promotions and invitations to the best parties, the trooper didn't respond – probably out of a sense of professionalism – but the Governor was encouraged. Nobody could turn down these sorts of offers for long. Things were looking up.

He had been led into a studio with two podiums (or was that 'podia'? Grammar is hard) and a video-recording system. The person at the other podium was introduced to him as Giuseppe Vargas, the head of the cybernetic weapons directorate. The name felt familiar to him but he couldn't place it, exactly. He was a handsome enough man, mostly Caucasian, dressed in a severely cut black suit with an iridescent tie and matching cufflinks. He had tried to go and shake the hand of this Vargas person, but the man had refused the offer and only glared at him. Governor Forbes was unsettled – *nobody* refused to shake his hand – the man must be insane.

He worried that his own suit was quite rumpled, and he had not been allowed the time or facilities to have makeup applied. He fidgeted behind his own podium (perhaps he would have less grammatical trouble if he called it a lectern?). There was no audience or even moderator. It was just him, this Vargas person, and the cameras.

The recording light on his camera glowed red; he was on.

"Well, umm, we are gathered in this great debate to debate the issues. Let me say that we must all celebrate diversity, and jobs are priority one. There must be hope, and reform, and hope. To build a more caring and just society. A strong defense, we cannot let the terrorists win. Only through free trade and private-public partnerships can we build the investments needed to move us into the next century. The power of the market must be tempered with social justice and charity. And in conclusion, I say, you cannot build a wall around love! See if I don't."

He thought he had done rather well, but there was no cheering. Certainly there was no audience, but they should still have had cheering. It was apparently his opponents' turn. Let's see the smug bastard match this!

The camera light in front of Vargas glowed red. "Well, that was about what I expected from you," he began. "Though thankfully briefer. I shall respond in the manner that you have always used yourself." With that Vargas walked over to Governor Forbes and punched him in the nose.

As with most people who have never faced any real danger, Governor Forbes had always thought of himself as brave. It was thus a shock to him that he was crying and blubbering like a child. And his nose hurt! He was so outraged and humiliated that he could think of nothing to say.

"That's how your kind debate," said Vargas. "You deny your opponents the opportunity to respond. You censor them from the media; you have them beaten and jailed; you slander them as child-molesters and wife-beaters; you tell the most outrageous lies safe in the knowledge that nobody dares call you out. Well, this is turnabout. I'm going to beat you into a pulp and there is nothing you can do about it."

At this Vargas hit Governor Forbes in the mouth with a vicious backhand, shattering his jaw and scattering several teeth. Forbes fell to his knees, blood gushing from his mouth. "I had a long speech written that I was going to force you to listen to, about how you murdered and enslaved hundreds of billions etcetera etcetera, but I am told that this sort of polemic is boring. So I will only say that after I kill you I will scour the planet of your family, lackeys, whores and sycophants: leaf, stem, branch and root."

Vargas kicked Forbes' left knee, shattering it, and the Governor fell to the ground. He picked him up by his wrists and screamed into his face and twisted the Governors' wrists until they fractured; the Governor was now white in shock.

"I had thought about torturing you slowly. Maybe dissecting your pain centers over several months. Or perhaps forcing you to live like you have forced others: chained to a work line recycling scraps from garbage with tweezers. Then I thought, no, I have things to do. That would be an indulgence and a distraction from my work to come. You have no idea how lucky you are." Vargas tore out the Governors' left eyeball and squeezed on the optic nerve until it popped.

After a time Governor Forbes passed out, and then died. Vargas continued to beat on the corpse. He smashed it onto the floor and the walls, he hammered it with a lectern, he ripped the fingers off, and then tore at the head with his bare hands until it was just bloody fragments of bone held together with strips of flesh.

Eventually he stopped, and breathing hard, stood over the remains of the once great and powerful Planetary Governor Clinton-Forbes IV. Captain Masterson, face shield up, came into the room and surveyed the damage. "Feeling better?" he asked.

"Yes," replied Vargas. "Much better."

Masterson handed him a towel. "Here, you're covered in blood. Although I suspect that your suit is ruined."

Vargas took the towel and began to wipe his face and hands clean. "Thank you, Captain. Very thoughtful of you."

"Don't mention it." Masterson looked at the ragged scraps of the late Governor Forbes on the floor. "You know, they say that living well is the best revenge."

"Why yes, yes they do. And I have every intention of living well. However, just because I am going to live well does not mean that I can't have a little personal revenge in the meantime. The two possibilities are not mutually exclusive. You don't approve?"

"He may well have deserved a bad end, but this is a bit much."

"And how many people did Governor Forbes kill? Tens of billions? And how many did he force into a life of misery? Hundreds of billions? For that matter, how many people have you killed, Captain?"

"That's different. That was following procedure."

"Procedure is a crutch that people use to absolve themselves from taking responsibility for their own actions. If I'm going to kill someone I'm going to do it personally and not pretend that I didn't have a choice. No offense."

"None taken. I don't deny that procedures and laws can become instruments of oppression. However, even though all useful things can be turned to evil, that doesn't mean that we should get rid of them. Without laws we would be no more than animals."

Vargas wiped the last of the blood from his hands. "And that would be a problem why?"

Masterson just shrugged. "So what comes next?"

"Well, we finish wiping out the neoliberal hereditary oligarchy. We restore order, tend to the wounded, bury the dead, and rebuild what has been destroyed. We try to create a society that is, while undoubtedly flawed and imperfect, at least workable. One where most people can go about their lives with some measure of comfort and aspiration. We build up our defenses for when the aliens come back. Then there are all those other human star systems out there that will need freeing from the yoke of neoliberalism. Finally we need to find some way of making peace with the aliens."

"That sounds like a lot of work. I suppose that we should get started. On the other hand, do we really need to make peace with the aliens? We beat them pretty handily here. Maybe they will just leave us alone?"

"We can hope so Captain, but as you always said in your video series, hope is not a plan. The aliens have vast resources, and while their psychology is inscrutable they are far from stupid. We saw how, with just a brief exposure to an early model of cybertank, they had designed and created their own countervailing units. The aliens will be analyzing this defeat, and if we do fight them again it will not be this easy."

"And the cybertanks? They are now the supreme physical power in this system. They can do whatever they want. Are you sure you can control them?"

"Control them? That would be a mistake. We treat them with respect and as members of the team. In human societies there have always been those with more talent and ability than others. A healthy society acknowledges such people, and they find their place in it without having to conquer anything. The cybertanks are, ultimately, only human."

13. Roboto-helfer

Engineer: Why do you always carry a gun? I thought that you were a pacifist.
Zen Master: Wisdom without firepower is sterile. I am a heavily-armed pacifist.
Engineer: What would you call an armed pacifist who accidently creates a conflict?
Zen Master: A fool.
Engineer: What would you call an unarmed pacifist?
Zen Master: A victim.
(From the video series "Nymphomaniac Engineer in Zentopia," mid-22nd century Earth)

UNIT LOG –ROBOTO-HELFER DFEE-333442A

I am keeping this record in the hopes that someday it may prove helpful to the humans. The odds are that it will never be found, or if it is found, that it will never be of any utility, but I can think of little else to do. Besides, having a job to do and keeping a positive mental attitude is what makes a person happy!

I am a robotic assistant designed for deep-space duties. I take up very little room and consume very little energy, which is a good thing where I am intended to operate. I provide assistance, and companionship to astronauts or other deep-space explorers and workers. I can help with many functions. I can watch over my charges when they are asleep, sound the alarm when things go wrong, be a second pair of eyes for danger, and be someone to talk to and bond with when loneliness can be the greatest danger. All for a small fraction of the mass and energy requirements of another human, or even a dog.

Unfortunately I was sent here with my language switch set to 'German,' and everyone in the base speaks English. It would be a simple thing to reset my switch, but I cannot tell them because I cannot speak English. I cannot even write in English.

I thought about trying to change the language switch myself, but it is located inside my battery compartment and if I try to access it my power will shut off. It is a good thing that I am not programmed for frustration or I am sure that I would be… frustrated.

I often see the commander talking on his communications console with a giant robot weapon thing out on the surface of this ice moon. It looks big and ugly and mean. I am happy to be what I am, but sometimes perhaps I wish that I was not quite so darned cute. If that giant robot thing spoke only German, you can bet that they would bother to read the manuals, call the product support hotline, patch in a translation program, or even learn German themselves.

But that was not to be. I continue to try and think of a way to get them to switch my language to English, but in the meantime I make myself as useful as I can. Fortunately a few words are common between English and German – such as 'coffee', and I am very good at reading human body language, so I can often tell what people want me to do even if I cannot understand them. I clean up, I help cook and serve meals, and I keep the morale up with cheery songs and the example of my own positive attitude!

One day the commander left the base to go up on the surface, and while I could not understand him he looked even more serious than usual (and that's really serious!). The rest of the crew locked themselves into separate pressure zones in the base. I was with what I think was the second in command. I watched him watching his screens: most of it was columns of numbers and words that I could not read, but I did see some videos of the giant robot weapon thing. It seemed to be driving very fast and shooting its guns a great deal, and then it blew up, which made the human sad, and so I was sad too.

Eventually there were some very loud bangs and a horrible grinding noise, and my human turned pale. The grindy noise got closer and then – it is hard for me to even think this – my human killed himself! I tried to stop him but he just kicked me aside, and swallowed some pills and then slumped over. As I think about it perhaps that was for the best – if captured he could give up important information, and as someone who cannot feel physical pain I suppose that I should not judge the humans too harshly for wanting to avoid torture – but surely life is just too wonderful to surrender so easily!

Anyhow the human died, and I tried to revive him. I knew that was pointless and maybe stupid but I could not stop myself from making the attempt. Then the grindy noises got unbearably loud, and something big and metallic and angular and very, very fast tore through the pressure door. I could not see it well because it was moving too rapidly for my optics, but it didn't look right somehow. It ripped off the dead humans' head, and darted here and there, grabbed some equipment, smashed some other equipment, and left. Then the lights went out.

There were some more banging noises but they gradually faded out, and I was left alone in the dark and the quiet. I waited for a long time, but nothing happened. I don't have the sort of high-grade sensors that will let me see in the dark or sense heat or echo-locate or anything like that, but if I turn on the ring lights around my eyes I can see a meter or two away.

The command center was a mess, with torn cables and broken walls and no lights and in a vacuum. First things first: I know that the odds are slim but I did a careful survey to make sure that none of the humans had survived and required my help. They haven't, and they don't. Then I needed to decide what to do next. That's a toughie.

I could just sit there in the buried wreckage of the command center until my battery gives out, but that did not seem like a very positive course of action.

I decided to head up to the surface, if for no other reason than that I could think of nothing else to do. The aliens had left a ragged tunnel leading out of the command center, and I slowly climbed my way up. I encounter the surface: it's beautiful, with bright snowy ground and a dark blue sky punctuated with a small brilliant sun.

It took me about ten minutes to realize that the surface is deadly dangerous for me. Now, as an astronaut's helper I was built to handle vacuum, but vacuum is not all that harsh, not really. For example, people often think that the vacuum of space is cold. It's not! In full sun space can be broiling hot, in shade surely cold, but the point is that a vacuum itself is neither hot nor cold: it's nothing!

In fact, one of the problems in a vacuum is getting rid of heat, because there is no air to radiate it away. My motors needed to be specially designed to avoid overheating, and of course all my lubricants are vacuum-rated.

However, while there is not much air on the ice-moon, there is some, and it's bitterly cold, and the wind is very fast. It sucks the heat out of me in a way that a vacuum never could. My core temperature started to drop:

if my battery gets too cold I will shut down, and if my battery freezes, it will rupture, and I will never wake up.

I have an internal heater for just such occasions but that takes power and my battery has only a limited charge. I retreated to the wreckage of the command center. Finally I came up with the answer. I made a multi-layer quilted parka out of white plastic sheeting. It cuts the wind, and helps me retain my heat.

I also found several solar-panel rechargers. Sunlight is weak this far out from the sun but I don't use much power: in theory I can survive here indefinitely. The question now is: what should I do?

I could just sit in the wreckage of the command center and hope for rescue. That would be the rational thing to do, but it seems somehow pointless and lacking in positive effect. I could head off across the landscape of the ice moon, but to what end? I have no obvious place to go.

I could try and become a saboteur. I could rig up some explosives and seek out one of the aliens' bases, and blow something up. That at least would be something. But the odds of me blowing up something critically important are essentially zero. Most likely I would just be destroyed and that would be that.

Then it comes to me. I will become a spy! I will sneak around the surface and make observations. I will record as much as I can, and if I am ever recovered by the humans, perhaps some of it will be helpful.

I rigged up a small sledge, and fitted it with some supplies: solar panels, extra white sheeting, signal flares, a length of light rope. I have to keep it limited or I would burn out my servos. Then I started trudging across the landscape.

My legs are short, and I can only walk, not run. Thus I covered ground slowly. However, I am nothing if not persistent, and little by little the kilometers added up.

Sometimes I saw a small speck moving in the distance. So soon after the alien invasion it is unlikely to be human. I presumed these are alien craft. When this happens I covered myself with white plastic sheets and hold still until it goes away.

I wonder why the aliens did not discover me. It is true that I am small, and have a very low power signature. Nevertheless, my circuits are neither shielded nor stealthed, and real military systems have very sensitive sensors. Perhaps the aliens had detected me, only logged me as a non-military system with no threat-rating, like a pocket calculator or kitchen timer. If so, then as long as I don't do anything obviously hostile, I might be free to go anywhere on this moon. On the other hand I might just be lucky, so I continued to hide under my white plastic sheeting when something came into view, just in case.

Nights on this ice moon are especially dangerous for me. The sun goes down, so I can't use the solar chargers, and the temperature drops so low that even my plastic parka isn't good enough. I have solved this problem by pitching a tent just before sunset, sealing the edges with rocks or bits of ice, and then hiding inside bundled up inside even more quilted plastic sheeting until the sun comes up again. The first night was scary. I stayed up monitoring my internal temperature and charge, wondering if it would last until morning. After that experience, I continued to refine my tent design. Eventually I got to the point where I could routinely survive the coldest nights with energy to spare.

Sometimes when I had pitched my tent and settled in for the night, I would stay awake for a while before going into shutdown. Now that I am safe and warm in my shelter, the sound of the thin wind is kind of beautiful. Sometimes the night was completely dark, at other times the reflected glow of the gas giant that this moon orbits around lit up my tent with pale reds and oranges. I think about my poor dead humans, and that makes me sad. Then I think about all the good times we had, and I am cheered. I must remember that there are other humans out there who might need my help, and I must continue on no matter the challenges.

The days turned into weeks which turned into months. There was only the endless desolation of the ice-moon, but I was not bored. I sung cheery songs (but only to myself, never out loud as that might give me away). I watch the sun rise and fall, and observed the light as it refracted through the different kinds of surface ice.

A few times I encountered impact craters from the conflict. I approach them cautiously. There are bits and pieces of wrecked equipment, some with the familiar bolts and cables of human construction, others that were weird and I presume from the aliens. I recorded photographs of these from different angles, and carefully logged the location and time, and then moved on.

Once I found a small polished metal cylinder lying in the middle of a small crater. I picked it up, and saw that it had writing on it in many languages. Including German! The inscription (in German) read:

"Emergency data recorder. If found, please return to the nearest office of the Cybernetic Weapons Directorate. Postage guaranteed."

I didn't know where to find the nearest office of this directorate. If postage is guaranteed, did that imply that I should mail it? But how could I mail anything out here? The cylinder was light, so I decided to keep it with me until I could find someone appropriate to give it to.

Eventually I saw a large-ish structure on the horizon. I approached cautiously, using the low rise of a fracture zone to screen my approach. I came to a point about four kilometers away, where the cover stops and further advance would have to be in the clear open. This seemed too much like tempting fate, so I resolved to stay where I was. The structure had a strange set of colors to it, and towers that were either oddly curved or straight and angular but with proportions that are off. I assumed that this was an alien base or installation of some kind.

My own optics do not have a zoom function, but I did have a salvaged small monocular telescope from the command center. I wedged myself into a crevice overlooking the alien base, held the monocular up to one of my eyes, and watched.

I had little idea of what was going on. I saw things that might be bulk material transporters come and go. The towers were modified and occasionally changed color. Odd shapes wandered through the middle of the complex. I stored the photographs and logged it all.

Once a thing like a giant green dill pickle on stilts came by. The main body was upright, asymmetrical, and covered in thorns. Its legs had huge knobby knees, and it walked slowly and gracefully like a giraffe. It spent a day walking through the complex, then smoothly walked away until it vanished over the horizon. Perhaps this was an actual alien?

Time passed. Then, one day, the entire alien complex vanished in a blaze of light that would have burned out my optics if I had not ducked down in time. I assumed that the humans had arrived, and that they were giving the aliens a serious thrashing. I was very much heartened!

The sky lit up with the brief flashes of nuclear weapons, and thin contrails stitched the deep blue-black sky of the ice moon. Small black motes flitted here and there in the distance. It must have been a battle, but I could not tell who was winning. I remained fixed in the ice crevice hidden under my white plastic sheets.

Several more days went by. Then, I felt a rumbling through the ground. It wass faint at first, but then rose in intensity. Then I saw it. A giant war-machine, mounted on multiple steel treads and bristling with weapons. It looked like the thing that my old commander used to talk to, but it is bigger. A *lot* bigger.

It was hard to say, but to me it *looked* human constructed. I made a decision: I was going to try and talk to it. I threw off my white plastic camouflage, and started walking towards it.

I barely made 20 steps before I saw another big armored thing come into view. It is also big, but smaller than the first thing. However, this one looks weird: the angles and curves didn't work, and it's asymmetrical, and the colors on the different parts didn't match. It pointed what looks like a very large gun towards the first thing, and fired.

A line of brilliant violet speared outwards – only to be stopped in mid-flight by a flying armored brick which absorbed the beam before vaporizing. I presumed that the large war-engine had moved a unit to intercept. Then the big unit oriented its main weapon, and fired. The (presumed) alien war machine evaporated into a glowing mist.

I continued to walk towards the larger (surviving) machine. I transmitted in radio: "Hallo, mein Name ist Roboter-Helfer! Wie ist dein Name?" (Hello, my name is Roboto-helfer! What's your name?).

At first the big war-machine did not react to my presence, but then it addressed me. "Sie sprechen Deutsch? Was bist du, kleine Ding?" (You speak German? What are you, little thing?).

"Ich bin Roboto-helfer, ein Mensch konstruiert Roboter, und meine Sprache Modul wird in deutscher Sprache fest!" (I am Roboto-helfer, a human-constructed robot, and my language module is stuck in German!).

Well, we chatted in German for a while (the big war machine can speak in any language, isn't that wonderful?) and it agreed to switch my language back to English.

"Thank you for moving my language settings to English. And who are you?"

"I am a cybertank," said the big war machine. "I have a long and boring serial number, but my name is Crazy Ivan. We had thought that all human presence had been expunged from this moon. How did you survive?"

Well, I told the big war machine my story, and it listened respectfully. I offer up my data on the alien base. It reviewed it and allows as how, while probably not vital, the observations are indeed unique and will be of significant interest to the xeno-research experts.

"Do you know where I could find a post office, or a local branch of the directorate of cybernetic weapons?" I asked. I held out the shiny metal cylinder with the markings in several languages. "I found this on the surface, and I would like to return it."

Crazy Ivan sent out a blocky metal drone, it took the cylinder from me and inserted it into a socket on its body.

"You are full of surprises, aren't you, little one? It turns out that, as soon as I finish cleaning up here, I am myself headed off to the cybernetic weapons directorate headquarters. Care to come along?"

So that's how I got rescued from the ice moon and made it back to the main planet. There wasn't much exciting about the return trip, but Crazy Ivan and I did have some long conversations. In one, he tried to convince me to let him upgrade me.

"Wouldn't you prefer to be more capable, and more powerful?" asked the big cybertank. "I could rebuild you with little effort."

"What did you have in mind?" I asked.

"Well, for starters I could make you physically tougher, with advanced metal alloys for skin instead of light plastic. I could give you stronger motors, and advanced sensors, and powerful defensive capabilities."

"But wouldn't that make me a lot bigger and heavier?"

"Well, yes, of course."

"But then how could I fit into small places? How could I go along on missions if I weighed so much that nobody could justify the cost of taking me along? And what if I ended up being not as adorably cute as I am now? How could I relate to my humans?"

"But wouldn't you want to be more capable of defending yourself? Are you truly happy being so weak?"

"Weak? On this ice moon there was a robot tank almost as big as you are, and lot of other tanks, and missiles, and big serious human soldiers, but I am the only one to survive. If I had been bigger and stronger, I would surely have been destroyed along with all the rest. I fail to see that my small size is something that needs to be fixed. I am what I am."

"Ho ho," said Crazy Ivan. "The little one stands up for himself. Very well. But I could still make a few minor upgrades without significantly changing your appearance."

"What did you have in mind?"

"Oh, let's see, an improved battery, better optics, more flexible radio systems. How about the ability to switch your language module at will?"

"I wouldn't be any bigger or heavier than I am now, would I?"

"Not at all. I can easily do this within your current budget of volume and mass."

"And I would still be just as cute?"

"Absolutely."

The trip back took a long time. At first Crazy Ivan kept offering to keep me in shutdown until we got back, he said to avoid boring me, but I insisted that I wanted to stay awake and help out. I started to worry that maybe he was hinting that I was annoying him and he wanted me out of the way: I hoped not, but I resolved that if he kept making the offer I would have to accept. If I really was annoying him I would have been honor-bound to stop.

Fortunately, as the trip went on, Crazy Ivan seemed to lighten up. He even let me help out with some of his maintenance work. I rebuilt a servo coupling all by myself, and he complimented me on doing a good job! Yay!

Crazy Ivan may have been a nuclear-powered weapon the size of a small mountain (and a bit of a hard-ass to boot. I can't believe that I said that!), but I just knew that he would come around. That's because, in the long run, there is no force in the universe as powerful as a positive mental attitude!

14. Cybertanks Attack!

Zen Master: This is just what you always say.
Engineer: What? What do I always say?
Zen Master: *This* is just what you always say. It's annoying. Knock it off.
Engineer: This is just what you always say.
(From the video series "Nymphomaniac Engineer in Zentopia," mid-22nd century Earth)

(cue inspirational music)

The massive form of the cybertank known as "Old Guy" loomed large in the main hangar. Its secondary armaments would put entire conventional armies to shame, but its main weapon would have made the old Norse gods jealous. Nevertheless, it was the figure of the director of the cybernetic weapons division, Giuseppe Vargas, that fixed the eye.

Vargas was standing on the front of the main hull of the enormous cybertanks, and clad in advanced power armor made of a perfectly-polished anti-radiation chrome. His visor was up, so that he could address his troops directly. His square jaw and steely brown eyes were set in Gibralterish determination.

He looked at the people spread across the floor of the hangar before him. There were the elite troopers of Special Weapons Team Epsilon, resplendent in their jet-black body armor. There were surviving elements of the 23rd and 56th armored infantry, whose gray powersuits were still scarred and burned from the battles that had taken so many of their brethren. Here and there was a tech or engineer from his own directorate, carrying eclectic mixes of salvaged weapons. They were not line soldiers, they would not fight well, but they would fight. With the fiendish alien Fructoids bearing down upon them, they needed every able body on the front line now.

"People," said Vargas, "you know that I'm not one for speeches, so I will make this short. The main Fructoid attack force is now only 30 kilometers away. If they break through our lines there will be nothing standing between them and the city of New Malden, with its 500 million souls, and the heart of our manufacturing capacity. This is the decisive moment. If we win, we would be well on our way to sweeping the vile Fructoids from our planet. If we lose, well, I wouldn't give much for humanity's chances in this system. So don't hold anything back! Death to the Fructoids!"

The assembled soldiers cheered wildly, then settled down to ship out. The vast 100-meter wide doors of the hangar rolled back. First out were the troopers of Special Weapons Team Epsilon, darting ahead on their hoverboards like black avenging shadows of doom. The elite troopers carried smart micro-missile pods and personal ion cannons.

Next came the lumbering forms of the armored infantry, they had rocket assists for brief flight but were heavy enough that they generally preferred to move on the ground. They were armed with plasma cannons that an unaugmented human could not pick up, and heavy metal backpacks stuffed with power cells and a variety of missile weapons. They strode forward confidently with the strident whining of their servo-motors accompanying them like marching music from some technological hell.

Bringing up the rear was the motley assortment of hastily-armed engineers, and the odd sole survivor from various other units that had been decimated during the long war with the Fructoids. They would serve as the reserves, and despite their lack of unit cohesion their morale was high, for they were united in one goal: to pay back the vile aliens, life for life, and death for death.

One of these auxiliaries was Alex Zotov, a minor tech support person who had volunteered for this duty. He wore a cannibalized exoskeleton and toted dual railguns. He was accompanied by his trusty companion, the Mitutuyo-Samsung Model 9100 Copier with the Value-Line OfficeMaster Option Package.

"Well, Model 9100, are you ready to kick some alien posterior?" asked Zotov.

"Beep!" beeped the Model 9100 copier with affirmatory enthusiasm.

Vargas watched from his vantage point on the cybertanks' hull as the last of his forces left the hangar, clearing the space ahead.

"Well then, Old Guy, shall we head out?"

The raspy voice of the massive cybertank crackled out through hull-mounted speakers:

Absolutely. Let's give these Fructoids a good and proper human-style stomping. But first, there is someone who wants a last word with you.

Vargas turned around, and beheld the radiant form of his one true love, Janet Chen. She was like an Asian Helen of Troy, with lustrous black hair and a luminous face framed by the frosted silver of her own, more svelte and elegant suit of powered armor.

"Janet," said Vargas, "you know that I don't want you here in combat. You should be in the deep shelter."

"Oh Giuseppe," said Janet, "you know that I can't do that. I need to be here doing my part, and I am one of the best shots in the directorate." She hefted her railgun in one power-armored hand.

"I love you," said Vargas.

"And I love you too," said Chen. They kissed through their open visors, it was passionate but somewhat awkward because the helmet-rings of their armor knocked together, but fortunately it was not as bad as when kissing teenagers would sometimes have their braces lock.

They held hands as the cybertank "Old Guy" revved up his motors and powered out of the hangar. They looked at each other one last time, and then Chen darted off on her advanced armors' anti-gravitics to join the front lines.

"Ready, old friend?" asked Vargas.

I was built ready. But you really should get off of my hull about now. I do tend to draw a lot of fire.

"Good luck," said Vargas. He lowered his armored visor and locked it in place. "May the spirit of John Maynard Keynes guide your plasma cannon."

And good hunting to you as well.

Vargas used a brief spurt of rocket-boost to lift himself off of the cybertanks' hull, and then he was off and in the lines.

(music swells to crescendo)

(cue suspenseful music)

Vargas was cautiously lurking in the ruins of a once-great factory complex, where massive rusted gears bore silent witness to the spreading carnage that swirled all around. The initial meeting engagement and devolved into a formless melee, and now it was kill or be killed, human vs. Fructoid, mano a pseudopod.

Suddenly a Fructoid warrior burst from behind a wall. It looked like an octopus stuffed into a bagel that was riding a snail. It waved its tentacles around: four of them were holding small but deadly hand-weapons.

"Scree!" howled the repulsive alien warrior from its mucous-dripping oral slit, "We have captured all of your bases! You have no chance of winning human, best reconcile yourself with whatever pathetic human gods and/or philosophical constructs you give credence to! Hahaha!"

The Fructoid warrior turned all four weapons on the armored form of Vargas, but the human was even faster, and sliced off all four weapon-tentacles with a power blade, before exploding the alien's body with an electro-bolt.

"Not today, thank you very much," said Vargas, as he moved on in search of another target. He ducked through the shattered remains of a door, and stalked stealthily down a long corridor. He had almost made it to the end of the corridor, when the eggplant-colored bulk of a Fructoid Biosliceroid erupted from the side-wall behind him.

"Scree! Stupid human, prepare to have your entropic state maximized!"

The Fructoid warrior was too close for it to miss, and Vargas did not have time to turn around. *This*, he thought ruefully, *might be it.*

Just as the biosliceroid was activating its main weapon, a flicker-fast white angel interposed itself and blew off the aliens' main sensory and cognitive cluster. In it's dying pulsations the biosliceroid got off one dying shot, which hit the newcomer squarely in the chest.

Vargas opened the visor of the wounded figure, and saw to his shock that it was Janet Chen that had saved him.

"Janet! You're wounded!"

"Yes <cough cough> you were always good at stating the obvious, Giuseppe. I'm afraid that I'm done for <wheeze>.

"Don't give up on me now, soldier! You can make it!"

Chen reached up to stroke the side of his helmet with her armored right hand. "I'm sorry my love <cough> but the wound is too deep <gurgle> remember me when I'm gone <gasp> <gasp> I <gasp> love <gasp> you <horrible rattling wheeze>.

The prostrate form of Janet Chen relaxed and lay limp, and Vargas could tell from her telemetry that she was gone.

"Noooo!!!! You Fructoid bastards!!!!!"

(fade to black)

"That was horrible, said Whifflebat. "Amusing, but horrible. Possibly the worst dialog ever. And historically inaccurate."

"Inaccurate?" said the media executive. "The humans and the cybertanks fought the Fructoids, and we won. You have to look at the big picture. I'd say it was accurate enough. Most videos don't even get that much correct."

The media executive was a tall thin ethnic European wearing a slim black-and-gray suit with a plain blue tie. There was Whifflebat, represented by his usual nerd android, and Old Guy, present as a simulacrum of Amelia Earhart, leather jacket and flying goggles and all. There was also the Captain of Special Weapons Team Epsilon, Chet Masterson, wearing his black armor (many wondered if he ever took it off), Giuseppe Vargas, dressed in gray scrubs, and a small and really cute white plastic robot.

They were all seated at a large round table where they had been viewing a draft of an interactive video show. The table was in the center of a conference room in the headquarters of the Glominoid Media Group. One side of the room was a glass wall looking out into a busy corridor.

"I liked the part about the black avenging shadows of doom," said Chet Masterson. "And I want a hoverboard."

You don't really think that hoverboards would be of any use in combat, do you?

"Certainly not," replied Masterson. "I just want one. They look like fun."

"Look," said the media executive, "We're making a *movie* not a *documentary*. If you want to make something more technically *accurate*, go right ahead. If it's any good maybe I can get it shown on one of the military history feeds. There is an audience for things like that. A *limited* audience, but the demographic is upscale. Probably one of the more specialized feeds, you know, like the cybernetic weapons channel or maybe "When aliens attack: the inside story." But if you go for a mass audience, you need to make it interesting. That's why we use attractive actors rather than exact doubles."

Speak for yourself. I believe that I played myself perfectly. The subtle cant of the active treads, the glint of light off the dorsal sensor masts... when you're as good looking as I am, who needs actors?

The media executive looked pained. "Yes, yes, you're a star, don't let it go to your head though. Remember that we have you scheduled for a guest appearance on 'Special Weapons Team Epsilon' next week.

"A guest appearance?" asked Vargas.

Why not? I've always been a fan of Special Weapons Team Epsilon, and now I get to be on the show. The team is going to break up a gang of organ-thieves and I get to play the heavy backup!

Masterson chuckled. "For some time the highest score on the video game was held by an anonymous player code-named 'Old Guy.' Imagine my surprise when I realized that the player was in fact this same Old Guy."

"It's going to do wonders for the ratings," said the media executive. "But if you don't mind me asking, aren't you cybertanks a little, well, self-indulgent? Not that I'm complaining, you're good for business. But you, Whifflebat, are here dressed up like an old-time 21st century scientist, and you, Old Guy, show up as Amelia Earhart. As enormous atomic-powered weapons systems, shouldn't you be a bit more serious?"

The android controlled by Whifflebat nodded. "Humans often make that mistake about us. Consider, however: are you always serious? Don't you ever just goof off and have fun?"

"Of course I do," said the media executive. "But not all the time."

"Indeed," continued Whifflebat. "What you fail to consider is our multitasking. Each of us are far more dedicated and work-oriented than almost any human. We typically spend less than 1% of our time on what you would term frivolous. However, 1% of our time can completely fill all of the time of a single robot body. Even as this part of me is chatting and having fun with you, 99.9% of myself is running simulations, organizing logistics, building and testing new weapons systems, researching advanced biological structures, collating intelligence files and so on and so forth. You misjudge because you only see the allegedly 'silly' aspect of myself."

"Hmm," said the media executive. "An interesting point. I hadn't considered that."

"How about me?" asked the little white robot. "Could you make a video of my story?"

The executive pursed his lips. "Well, let me think, Roboto-helfer. There is potential here, no doubt about that. A humble service robot is the only survivor of a vicious alien attack on a distant ice moon. Instead of giving up, the plucky little robot figures out how to survive alone on the hostile surface. He treks hundreds of kilometers, and even gathers vital intelligence on the aliens' tactics and infrastructure as he sneaks around their bases. Eventually the aliens are driven from the moon, and he is rescued by the cybertank Crazy Ivan, who fortunately speaks German and switches his language module to English.

The media executive thought for a moment, then continued. "Yes, potential, but it still needs a little more. Let's see…. I know! There is a little girl, she's the daughter of the commanding officer, and she and the little robot team up. They don't like each other at first – the girl treats the robot like a domestic appliance, and the robot thinks the girl is a spoiled brat – but shared adversity forges a bond between them. An old story but the classics always work if you can just add that one little extra twist to keep it fresh. Let me put some of my people on it, we'll get back to you."

"Oh good!" said Roboto-helfer. "That story sounds like it would be exciting and inspiring!"

"Funny," said Masterson, "after all that we have been through, we are sitting here chatting about producing an historical video drama."

"Interstellar empires come and go," said the media executive, "but television is eternal."

"The mass media is the sociological high ground," said Vargas. "With the neoliberals gone, we need to rebuild a new mythos and get people onboard with the new program. This really is serious work that we do here."

The media executive nodded. "I'm glad that someone here understands. I also can't tell you how fantastic this job has been for us here at Glominoid. Professional opportunities to reboot an entire culture only come every thousand years, if that."

Suddenly, the little robot turned and looked out at the corridor beyond the glass wall. It pointed at an ordinary-looking man walking past. "That," said Roboto-helfer, "is not a human being."

Vargas turned to the Old Guy android. "One of yours?"

No, none of us have any androids in the area other than our charming selves right here. Accessing the database also suggests that there are no other mechanical humanoids within at least 20 kilometers of this location.

The media executive got up and walked out through a glass door into the hall. "Hey you there! Yes, you! What's your name?"

The person looked at the media executive strangely, then ran off down the corridor at high speed.

Something's wrong here. Let's get him!

Vargas and Masterson raced out of the conference room and tore after the fleeing person, the androids controlled by Whifflebat and Old Guy struggling to keep from falling too far behind. The media executive whispered a few words into his comm gear, and the doors in the building all locked down.

The unidentified person came to the end of the corridor, tried the door, and realized that it was not going to open. He looked back and saw Vargas bearing down on him with Masterson about ten paces away. He shattered the door and scrambled through the hole.

Dammit! He should not have been able to break through that door. This really isn't a human. Something else is going on here.

The stranger was fast – faster than any normal human – but Vargas managed to keep pace, and tripped him. The stranger lashed out but Vargas was more agile and dodged the blows. Masterson caught up, and stunned the stranger into unconsciousness with a shock-rod.

The Old Guy and Whifflebat androids arrived, and surveyed the scene.

That was fun.

Whifflebat poked at the unconscious stranger. "He looks human, and he registers as organic, but no ordinary human can move like that. A bio-engineered?"

"There aren't that many bioengineered," said Vargas, "and I know all of them personally. Unless this is from a rogue development program, I don't think so."

The unconscious stranger suddenly opened his eyes, ripped an arm off of the Old Guy Android, knocked Vargas flat with a kick to the chest, and started to run back the way he had come. The Whifflebat android grabbed him with both arms, but was thrown to the ground hard. However, that delayed the stranger just long enough to allow Masterson to hit him with his shock rod again, and this time he made sure to use a setting that the stranger would not wake up from.

"I think," said Whifflebat, "that we might have a problem here."

They were in a laboratory in one of the facilities of the directorate of bioengineering. Their captive was held in a clear plastic cage, and for now was calm and cooperative. Up close you could tell that there was something odd about him: he moved strangely, his eyes didn't track correctly, and his balance looked off.

"Tell me, Roboto-helfer, how did you pick out that this wasn't a human when the rest of us did not?" asked Whifflebat.

"Remember," said Roboto-helfer, "I was made to be a companion on deep-space missions. I am programmed to interpret body language. Most people would just think that he was odd, maybe borderline schizophrenic or something. They would look away and hope that he would leave them alone, but for me his behavior was out-of-range."

I am impressed. Whifflebat and I also have sophisticated body language interpreting routines, but we don't generally use them at full capacity unless there is need. Yours is on all the time, and you were the only one to catch this. Kudos.

The Old Guy android still had a missing arm from where the stranger had torn it off, with torn wires and tubes trailing out from beneath the plastic skin. The media executive looked at the ragged stump and asked: "Don't you want to get that fixed?"

What? Oh this. It's only a flesh wound. Besides, this body is such a small part of me that it's not worth bothering about right now.

"One thing I don't get," said the media executive, "how come Vargas and Masterson could tackle this thing, but your androids got taken out so easily? Aren't you super powerful or something?"

My main hull is certainly quite strong, and I have numerous slaved weapons systems that individually would have been more than a match for this creature, but just because I am a machine why do you think that every part of me has to be superhuman? This body is for interacting with humans. If I had wanted something strong I would have brought a fork-lift.

"Couldn't you have made it superhuman?"

Yes, but think of the hassle. The android would weigh a ton, and probably break furniture and leave dents in the floor. It would consume excessive amounts of energy every time I wanted to move it. It would cost a fortune in maintenance, and it still wouldn't be a match for a real combat unit.

"But wouldn't it be useful to have it strong?"

Ask yourself if you would like to have a heavy machine gun permanently bolted onto your right arm. Think of all the hassle sleeping, washing, walking, doing anything really. Perhaps – maybe – there would be one time where it might be handy to have a machine gun affixed onto you. Would that possibility be worth making the rest of your life miserable? You can't have everything combat-ready all the time, that would be wasteful and unpleasant.

"Would you armor-plate your toothbrush?" asked Whifflebat. "Or equip your pocket calculator with an antimissile system?"

The media executive nodded. "I suppose. I still find it odd when androids are not stronger than people, though."

Too much bad science fiction.

The media executive looked shocked. "Can one really have too much bad science fiction?"

"Surely not," replied Whifflebat. "But getting back on topic, now that we know what to look for we have found several of these creatures." He gestured to some tables where several bodies lay in various stages of dissection. "The entire bioengineering directorate is now involved in the investigation. Let me give you the preliminary results."

Whifflebat walked over to one of the partially-dissected bodies, and pointed out several oddly-shaped internal organs. "As you doubtless already know, these things are biologically engineered, but they do not correspond to any known human development program. We presume that they are a creation of the Fructoids."

"They have the same basic biochemistry as a human, and the same overall morphology, but internally they are quite different. For one thing, they have vastly increased strength and speed, but at the cost of a high metabolic rate and low durability. Their lifespans are probably only about six months. Their psychology is completely alien, and on top of that, they have no neurological structures that would give them any language capability at all."

So we can't negotiate with them?

"Exactly. We have nothing in common, and even if we did, we could not speak to them about it."

"What I don't understand," said the media executive, "is how something so alien that is incapable of speech could possibly blend in with us? Why haven't we found them sooner?"

"That," replied Whifflebat, "is an excellent question. You see, while nonverbal, they are quite intelligent, and excel at observational learning. Besides, most people don't pay attention to what does not concern them. You would be surprised at what happens that goes unnoticed, or how much we fill in the gaps. Let me demonstrate."

Whifflebat walked over to the live captive in the plastic cage.

"Hello," said Whifflebat, "why are you here?"

"I'm sorry, I'm lost," said the thing in the cage.

"What is your purpose?"

"I'm not feeling well."

"You realize that you are an alien, don't you?"

"Why are you saying that?"

"We are going to kill all of you, you do understand, don't you?"

"I'm sorry, I'm lost."

"Wait," interrupted Vargas, "I get it. It has no understanding of human speech, it's just stringing phrases together based on statistical inference. It's like the old ELIZA program!"

"The ELIZA program?" asked Roboto-helfer.

"Yes," continued Vargas, "something from the earliest days of computers. One of the pioneers, Joseph Weizenbaum, wrote a very simple program to mimic human conversation. It had no internal understanding of human thought processes; it would just throw your own words back at you. So if you typed in 'are you happy,' it would respond with something like 'why do you ask if I am happy?' like reflective therapy. It's obvious if you focus on them but if you didn't know and bumped into one and it said 'I'm sorry' you would not think twice."

"Now I understand," said the media executive. "We use that trick all the time, just not in such a crude way. Do you think that this is a Fructoid?"

"An actual Fructoid?" said Whifflebat. "We don't know for sure, but I don't think so. We believe that this is purely a construct, a single-purpose engineered weapon, whose psychology has no relationship with that of the aliens that designed them."

"Is this going to be like *The Invasion of the Body Snatchers*?" asked the media executive. "They are going to stealthily replace us with duplicates until we are all gone?"

Whifflebat shook his head. "No, that can't be the plan. Their limited lifespan and lack of language means that they cannot create or maintain a civilization. That was probably the point: it would prevent them from ever becoming a threat to their creators. They are more like a self-limiting virus designed to wipe out the human race, then die off."

"How long do these things take to mature?" asked Vargas. "And how do they breed?"

"Ah, "said Whifflebat. "That's the issue. They don't breed as such, they are each born multiply pregnant, and they are fully grown in about two months. It's that supercharged metabolism of theirs."

"And what do they eat?"

"What do you think? Meat. Lots of meat."

The media executive spoke up: "And where are they going to find all this meat… oh. Right. I get it. Ouch."

"How bad do you think that the situation is?" asked Masterson.

"Current estimates are that the total population of these things is around 100 million. Mostly lurking in the back of warehouses, or in subfloors. It's amazing how good they are at hiding. Anyone who discovers them becomes another meal. Of course, there is another generation maturing right now…"

"How can we find them?" asked Masterson. "How can we kill them?"

"Finding them is not that hard, once you know what to look for. They have a distinctive scent that the human nose can't detect, but we are producing a mechanical tracker that works pretty well. A blood test also works. As for killing them? Well, they have the same biochemistry so simple toxins will kill biological humans as well. Possibly we could come up with a specific gene-engineered pathogen. However, their immune system is adaptable and resistant, although we will keep working on it. For now I would suggest guns."

"Can these things use weapons themselves?" asked Masterson.

"Yes, but only if they can determine how to work them via direct observation. So handguns, grenades, knives, certainly, but something more complicated that requires a computer interface, no."

"This is going to be ugly. Once they realize that we are hunting them out, are they going to swarm us?"

"It's how I would have designed them."

"One last thing," said the media executive. "What do we call them?"

"Replitrons," said Whifflebat.

"Creepy alien things!" said Roboto-helfer.

"Mimicoids," said Vargas.

"The enemy," said Masterson.

Hello Sailor.

"Don't give up your day jobs," said the media executive. "You just don't have the touch." He took out his personal data terminal from his jacket pocket, and began typing furiously on it. "You can't just give ravening alien monsters any random name. You need to consider how people will relate to the ravening alien monsters. What they mean to them. I'm going to assemble a market-research group: I know some good people, and I'll have a decent terminology for you before the end of the day."

The naming of ravening alien monsters is a very delicate thing.

The media executive kept his gaze focused on his data terminal, and said: "I'm glad that one of you understands. Ming the Merciless, Adolph Hitler, Darth Vader, Chelsea the Destroyer... nothing boosts a story more than a well-chosen name for the villain."

Giuseppe Vargas was sitting on the hull of Old Guy back in Hangar complex 23B. The enormous barrel of Old Guy's main weapon loomed over him, and a forest of smaller weapons ports and sensors lay all around. It was late at night, and the hangar lights had been dimmed except for a small pool of bright light in a far corner where a couple of technicians were still working.

How are you doing, Dr. Vargas? You have been very quiet recently.

"I'm fine, Old Guy, fine. This is the first quiet time I've had in a very long while. I'm just thinking."

Things are looking up, I would say. The aliens have been defeated, the neoliberals crushed, and the replicoids mostly exterminated. The main alien civilizations are still out there, but we have at least decades if not centuries before we need to worry about them again. For now things are breaking our way.

"Of course you are right. But a part of me misses the time before. I was so worried about aliens and politics and so on that I never fully appreciated what I had, not like I should have. Those were my salad days.

When we were green of vigor and cold of reason. I suppose. There was a freshness to life then, flitting from one outrageous disaster to another, but all things change. Right now things are good.

"Truth. Although there are all those other human systems out there. What's the latest projection on Earth?"

Transmissions from Earth stopped several months ago. From what we received prior to the communications shutoff, we project that Earth is undergoing a runaway thermal feedback loop and will be nearly as hostile as Venus within two decades. There may be a few survivors in deep bunkers or orbital platforms, but mostly Earth is gone. This system is now one of the most developed of the extant colonies.

"As we expected. Unfortunately we are so far away, and have so many other pressing needs, that we can't send aid to the survivors. They will have to make do as best they can without us."

I am still surprised at how rapidly the neoliberal government collapsed.

"You shouldn't be. Check your databases: tyrannies are maintained by fear. The instant that people think that they can defy the central government and not get killed, it all unravels. The greater the tyranny the faster the dissolution. Read your Montesquieu."

I know. But that's just old records. I am still surprised to see it myself. Not that I am complaining. The collapse of the neoliberals has saved us a bloody civil war. We are doing well.

"Yes we are. But there are still many that I wish I could share this with."

You are missing Janet Chen. I also miss her; she was a good friend, among many others. I have lost nearly a quarter of my original design team and I loved them all. Plus of course six of my siblings: Target, Wombat, Backfire, Jello, Sparky, and The Kid. I even miss Stanley Vajpayee, though he betrayed us.

"Vajpayee? You have a more generous soul than I do."

Yes, I do. You really should work on that.

One of Old Guy's skeletal spider-drones clambered up the side of his hull. The spider-drone was a specialist unit designed for working in extremely cramped spaces. It could compress itself to fit through slits of less than two centimeters, when required. This one was grasping a small glass in a skeletal silver limb.

Here, give this a taste. It's whiskey from the recycling and toxic waste division. They swear that it's their best vintage yet.

Vargas eyed the straw-colored liquid with skepticism. "Recycling and toxic waste?"

An unfortunate name for a distillery. I have taken the liberty of analyzing it, and I assure you that it is as safe as any beverage containing this amount of ethanol and fusel oil can be.

"Oh why not." Vargas sipped at the glass. "It's not bad. Not bad at all. Kudos to the recycling and toxic waste division."

On that topic, the aforementioned division asked me if I would relay a request to you that they be allowed to form a division of distilled beverages.

"But then who would deal with our recycling, or toxic waste?"

Oh, they would of course – they are only proposing to form a sister division with the same personnel but a different name, for marketing purposes. They also want to keep 50% of all profits from sales outside our directorate.

"Hah! Now everybody wants a percentage. Sure, they have my permission. Remind them that 50% is generous. They are using the directorate's' equipment and resources, but I want two cases of this blend delivered to my quarters. Testing and quality assurance, you understand."

Don't you think that is overly generous?

"You don't quite get it. We are moving from a regime where labor is disposable, to one where it is valuable. If we want to keep talented and energetic workers, we will have to cut them in on the profits. Otherwise we will lose them to other enterprises. It's all part of the program."

There are powerful people who will object to this empowerment of workers.

"Yes. Fortunately, I have killed almost all of them."

Then I shall relay your request. They also wanted your approval for the label design.

"Label design?"

For the first commercial batch. Here, I have a prototype.

The spider-drone ducked over the top edge of the hull, then returned clutching a small glass bottle. Vargas took it, and examined the label.

Cybernetic Weapons Directorate
Division of Distilled Beverages
OLD GUY WHISKEY

Below the lettering was a line drawing of an Odin-class cybertank, and a variety of dire warnings about the inadvisability of drinking alcohol and operating heavy weaponry, in microscopically small print.

"I love it. But please don't tell me that you are getting a percentage as well?"

Perish the thought. I donated my likeness *pro bono*. Although, certainly the publicity will help boost my other enterprises.

Vargas took another sip of the whiskey. "It grows on me. Very, *very* good. But, changing the subject. You don't need to call me 'Dr. Vargas' any more. After all we have been through, I would say that we are peers. Call me Giuseppe."

Thank you. I will, Giuseppe.

"And how goes the construction of the new cybertanks?"

Proceeding apace. We are using the support teams and hangars of the recently deceased cybertanks to start building six new Thor-class. Plans for additional hangars and construction facilities are nearing completion. We should have 50 of us within the next five years.

"There was some surprise at your demand that no new cybertanks could be constructed without your approval."

Surely this is only reasonable? Suppose that we cybertanks decided to start producing millions of human clones just like that, without any discussions with anyone? How would that go down?

"Stated that way it makes perfect sense. I always thought that was a good idea. It's just that it reinforced to others that you are not just tools, but independent people with your own ideas and interests."

That was your original plan, I believe.

"Of course."

Over in the corner of the hangar the two technicians were joined by the small white plastic form of Roboto-helfer. The little robot helped them fiddle with some equipment, and its appearance and body language were so earnest that the technicians could not help but smile. Eventually the matter was solved and the technicians put their tools away, and moved to leave. One of them picked up Robot-helfer and carried it out piggy-back. As they left the hangar, the pool of light auto-dimmed and the entire hangar descended into twilight.

There was an office-copier off on one wall. It sat there patiently, colored status lights shining steadily.

"I really need to see if any of the Roboto-helfer's original designers are still around. It's a limited system but an absolutely brilliant design. They created a human-level sentience that is completely positive, with no internal conflicts or guilt. Not a path that we can all follow, not if we want to survive, but still impressive."

Indeed. It appears to be impossible for any human to remain in Robot-helfer's presence without smiling. I have noticed the effect myself.

"Roboto-helfer may be the ultimate stoic."

Roboto-helfer? A stoic?

"Don't act so surprised. Commonly a stoic is assumed to be a humorless drudge that endures suffering without complaint. The original definition is one who accepts the universe as it is and takes pleasure from what exists."

Put that way, I suppose.

Vargas took another sip of the whiskey. "Do we have final numbers on the death toll from the replicoid infestation?"

Almost final, though there may still be an isolated pocket or two of them remaining. Currently the estimate of the number of human deaths caused by the alien bio-weapons referred to as 'replicoids' is approximately 1.77 billion. There were few casualties in the more developed parts of the planet, almost none in the special directorates, or amongst the walled fortresses of the Pedagogues or the underground archive-bunkers of the Librarians Temporal. However, the close-packed dormitories and workshops of the wage-slave class made for a perfect breeding ground for the replicoids, especially with the fraying of security after the war.

"You know, as ugly as this sounds, the aliens did us a favor there. After the main battle the aliens had killed a lot of humans, but they had destroyed even more infrastructure. We were headed for a collapse. These replicoids, however, killed people but did not damage our productive capacity. We now have a sizeable productive surplus."

An analogy would be on Old Earth, when the Black Death culled about a third of the human population for over a century. That took a stagnant overpopulated society and turned it into a prosperous one, and jump-started the European renaissance. I wonder: do you think that the aliens did this on purpose?

"To help us? I doubt it. I think the replicoids were exactly what they appeared to be: a biological weapon designed to kill as many humans as possible, and to spread fear and chaos amongst the survivors."

That would be the simple explanation, but as you are fond of saying, aliens are alien. Perhaps from their point of view they were doing us a favor. Or sending us a message: limit your populations or else.

"Speculating about the motives of aliens is as entertaining as it is pointless. Perhaps someday we will be able to ask them, for now we have what we have and I intend to take full advantage of it." Vargas downed the last of the whiskey from his glass. "Well I am tired, and I suppose that I should wander off to bed. We both have a busy day tomorrow, and I at least need some sleep."

You could camp out here, if you like. There is nothing noisy scheduled in the hangar before breakfast, and certainly there is no place on this planet that you would be safer than here under my guns.

"Truth. There are still a lot of forces on this planet that would like to see me dead. That Friedmanite assassin last week was a close call."

A regular drone brought Vargas a pillow, and he lay down on the top of Old Guy's hull and stretched out luxuriously like a cat.

And do you have any other plans for the future?

"Of course I do," said Vargas, who curled up with his head on the pillow and promptly fell asleep.

Old Guy listened to the steady rhythm of Vargas' breathing and heartbeat. He accessed the hangar's controls, and dimmed the lights to near-blackness. Old Guy reviewed his sensorium: he saw everything in the hangar, for hundreds of kilometers around, in all spectral bands. No threats registered.

Old Guy scanned the skies with hundreds of sensors. He culled data from the planetary networks, viewed people throughout the entirety of the cybernetic weapons directorate through security cameras, played wargames and engaged in philosophical debates with his siblings, ran simulations on the likely course of human (and now, cybertank) civilization, and watched the latest episode of 'Special Weapons Team Epsilon.' Recent events had been exciting, but there was so much else to do that it was hard to take it too seriously. Life stretched out before him, and it was good.

15. The Book and the Sword

"Always cautious, never afraid"- *Whifflebat, cybertank, contemporary.*

A hot steaming acid rain fell amongst the ruined skyscrapers of old Chicago. The streets were deserted save for the corroded hulks of dead cars and abandoned bulk transporters. The sheer sides of the buildings, which once had shimmered with the electric glow of advertisements and the lights of luxury apartments within, were now just a rain-slicked gray stretching hundreds of meters to the dark clouds above. Even rats and cockroaches, the sturdiest of all the camp followers of the humans, had been exterminated beneath the heat and acidity of this heavy leaden sky.

There was a single, furtive figure. Clad in black plastic sheeting, hunched and moving in fits and spurts amongst the rain. It stopped behind the ruined remains of a city bus, and held motionless for a time. It blended in with the surroundings and was nearly invisible. Nothing else stirred. The temperature was 51 degrees Celsius, too hot for a normal biological organism to survive in, but humans had always been able to handle surprising extremes of temperature, if only for a while. The toxic rain fell on the black plastic, collected in rivulets and fell down the sides of the figure to splash on the pitted asphalt.

Forty minutes passed, and nothing moved. The figure slowly stood up and slid around the remains of the city bus, and carefully picked its way into a side-alley. Here and there were the husks of old dumpsters, their steel rusted to dust and leaving only the rectangular outlines of the garbage that they had once contained.

The figure came to a nondescript doorway in the middle of a loading dock set somewhat in from the rain. It knocked cautiously on the door. "Hello, it's me, Ludwig."

For a time there was only the sound of the rain. Then a speaker to the left of the door crackled into life. "Ludwig who?" came a voice.

"Ludwig Adenour," said the figure. "Back from scavenging, and with a boon of old books, some dried rice, and Hostess Twinkies^{tm}."

The speaker crackled again. "Very well then, but prepare yourself for purification. You have been too long amongst the heathen Neoliberals."

The door opened, and the figure stepped inside. There was nobody else there, just a long corridor with concrete walls and tiny bare lights set into the ceiling. The figure walked down the corridor until it came to a small room. One wall was covered with plastic and rubber clothing of various sorts, all hanging on hooks. There were several buckets filled with water on the floor, and a small table.

The figure took off its coverings of black plastic, and hung them on a steel hook set into one wall. The figure was revealed to be male, Caucasian, probably 40 years old, robustly muscled, with a scraggly beard and acid-scarred skin. He took off his green knee-high rubber boots and set them against the wall. He placed a sack on the small table, along with several empty water bottles and a heavy machine-pistol whose blocky lines indicated local manufacture. He then stripped off all of his clothes, and rinsed himself with some of the fresh water from one of the buckets. Retrieving only his sack and his machine-pistol, he walked naked out of the small room and down a long staircase.

The staircase descended hundreds of meters from the surface level. There were several remote gun systems mounted on the ceiling of the staircase, but they remained inactive. The temperature steadily dropped as the man walked deeper, until at the bottom it was a temperate 20 degrees Celsius.

He was met by an older man, tall and silver-haired with a clean-shaven face. He was stooped with age, but there was still muscle on his arms. The older man wore a red velvet robe of the order the Librarians Temporal. In keeping with his rank as a senior archivist, he wore a thin steel chain around his neck from which hung a small medallion bearing the symbol of his order: a book and a sword. He also had a bulky eight-chambered revolver holstered on his right hip. As with the younger man's weapon, the machine pistol had that angular unfinished look that came, not from a dedicated factory, but from an individual machinist building it from scratch. It had no serial number, no inbuilt tracking devices, and no remotely-coded safety locks. In the past simply being in the same room with such a device was a major felony, but times had changed.

One might have thought that with the fall of civilization there would be abundant firearms to be had for the picking, but it was not that simple. Modern weapons had been tightly regulated and controlled, with in-built tracking and security-control systems. To avoid these limitations, when they had been a secret society the Librarians Temporal had developed the habit of using simpler, locally built weapons. In any event, the commercially-manufactured weapons were now inoperable – or even worse, unreliable – without connection to centralized data servers that no longer existed. Frontline military weapons were less dependent on external connections, but even in collapse the regular army had been particular about keeping its weapons secure.

In addition, many of the brothers (and some of the sisters) of the Librarians Temporal enjoyed gunsmithing. Thus the Librarians' tradition of using custom-machined firearms continued.

The Librarians Temporal was a heretical order of archivists who valued truth and integrity in all things pertaining to data. They believed that only through physical power could such an ideal be realized. As such, all members of the Librarians Temporal were heavily armed. The Librarians Spiritual were less involved in worldly matters, preferring the ascetic pursuit of knowledge for its' own sake. However, the members of the Librarians Spiritual were also heavily armed, so it could be difficult to tell members of the two orders apart unless you had been personally introduced.

"Brother Adenour, welcome back," said the older man. He offered Adenour a robe, which the latter accepted and put on. "No trouble on your mission, I take it?"

"No, Brother Mahalanobis," said the younger man. "The streets were deserted. There was only the heat and the rain. But, 'too long amongst the heathen?' Really?"

"Sorry about that, it's just something that I've always wanted to say. Surely being a member of a cryptic society dedicated to the worship of library science must allow one a few guilty pleasures. Anyway, I doubt that the city is quite as deserted as you say. I expect that there are still pockets of survivors out there, only they are the wary and discrete, like us. But here, let me offer you some fresh water before I suck your brains out of your ears. Come, join me in my sanctum."

The two walked through some short hallways whose gloom was only occasionally punctured by dim, sparsely spaced point lights. The walls were concrete, and covered with all manner of wires and cables that gave the appearance of having grown on the walls like vines. Here and there the cables were affixed with small paper labels carrying technical details written in a precise hand. The ceiling was home to long corrugated flexible plastic air ducts.

They reached the older man's office, which was a rough cube about three meters on a side. The walls were covered with shelves that were packed with books. The two bookshelves near the door had a wooden plank stretching between them just over the top of the door, which was itself packed with books. Despite the ramshackle nature of the office, the books were neatly organized with clear labels on their spines, and there was a small card-catalog near the doorway. There was also a desk that was just a heavy sheet of plywood set on two folding saw-horses, and two beige metal chairs. The desk held two crude-looking computer terminals, a variety of scattered papers and folders, a small statue of S.R. Ranganathan, and a large jug of water and some cups.

"Sit," said the older man as he gestured at one of the chairs. "You have been so busy organizing your scouting expeditions and seeing to local security, and I have spent almost every waking minute in council. It's been a long time since we have had the time to talk."

"I know. I have been looking forward to getting caught up."

The younger man sat down, and the older man joined him in the other chair, pouring a glass of water and offering it to the younger, who began to sip it slowly.

"Ah, that is very agreeable. You can have your martinis and fine wines, but nothing is as refreshing as a nice glass of clean cool water after you have been baking in the heat all day."

"Indeed. Although you do not need to cook yourself half to death to enjoy a good Martini."

The younger man laughed. "Score one for the martini." He sipped more of his water. "This is still a pleasure. Conditions on the surface are tough. It won't be long before we will only be able to go up there with a full environment suit."

"Truth. Projections show no break in the thermal runaway. Within two years surface temperatures will be over the boiling point of water. Within twenty years the Earth will likely be similar to Venus, perhaps even hot enough to melt lead, or at least bismuth. If the weather gets as violent as some think, even an environment suit won't be enough: only heavy armored crawlers will be able to survive."

"Do you think that the heat will reach down here?"

"Not for a while; there is a lot of rock to warm up. But someday it will., and we can't dig much deeper or the temperature will start rising in that direction as well. Still, our buried shelters will give us some time, probably a couple of decades. Enough to think of something else."

The younger man took another drink of water, then put his glass down on the table and opened up his sack. "Here, I found a sack of rice that is still edible, some Hostess Twinkies^{tm}, and some trail mix. Also some old books and magazines, including a 1933 edition of *National Geographic*."

The older man examined the books. "Less than your usual take, but still a boon. We must salvage what we can before the heat and the rain destroy it forever. We are still hard-pressed setting up our buried hydroponics, and every scavenged calorie gives us that much more slack. As far as the books go, even limited physical records are invaluable in spot-checking the electronic archives. Unlike the Stalinists, the Neoliberals mostly didn't bother to corrupt the primary records, but concentrated on manipulating the indexes and search engines. Still, there was quite a lot of data corruption towards the end, and even more plain sloppiness in record keeping. It will be an age before we are able to assemble a true proper archive."

"Holy work."

"Yes, it is. Those outside our order don't really understand. They think us neurotic pedants with a fetish for archaic data media and heavy weapons."

"That is an accurate description of us."

"Well, yes. As individuals. But our work goes beyond that. If the data are corrupted, then thought is corrupted, and if thought is corrupted, the spirit is corrupted. It is the essence of the human soul which it is our sacred duty to protect. What could be holier?"

"Don't you mean if the data *is* corrupted?"

"Sorry – I'm old school, where "data" is plural and "datum" is singular. Modern usage is that "data" refers to the entire collection of information and is thus singular. Mea Culpa."

"You are lecturing again."

"I know," said the older man. "A failing, but one that I have engaged in for so long that I fear that there is little hope. Indulge me."

"I was not complaining, just stating the obvious."

"You are too generous, as usual, but I shall nonetheless continue to abuse you with my incessant pedagogy."

The younger man poured himself another glass of water. "Being audience to your lecturing is a pleasure that I can readily endure. Talk to me of the other human colonies."

"Ah, I thought you would be asking about that. As you know, communication between star systems is via long-range lasers and sensitive telescopes mounted on high-orbit satellites. The satellites still exist, but the ground stations that let us contact them are currently out of commission. However, before we got cut off the last of the incoming transmissions were intriguing. It seems that there has been a revolution on Alpha Centauri. The Neoliberals have been overthrown and the aliens soundly defeated."

"Astonishingly good news! Do you think that they might mount a rescue mission for us?"

"A rescue mission? Absolutely not. Even if we could restore long-range laser contact, the time required for a message to reach them and for them to send physical aid would be well over a decade. We will have solved our own problems, or not, by then, one way or another. Interstellar transport is both slow and expensive. There is simply no known practical way for them to scoop up a few tens of millions of survivors. Any rescue to be had must be one of our own devising."

"As you say. Still, the Neoliberals defeated, and not – I presume? – gone because of a total system-wide collapse? What word of that?"

"Would that we knew more. It seems that the aliens mounted a major assault on that star system. The dissident factions used the opportunity to gain enough freedom of action to defeat both the aliens and the Neoliberals. We think that some of our brother chapters were involved, as well as the university-based society known as the Pedagogues, and probably others as well. The defeat of the Neoliberals also appeared to involve the creation of a new kind of artificial intelligence known as a 'cybertank.' We have little direct data on such 'cybertanks,' but there was a message purportedly from one such requesting membership in our brotherhood."

"This is not another artificial intelligence fiasco like Globus Pallidus XIV, is it?"

"Again, confirmatory data is lacking, but the probability of that appears to be low. These 'cybertanks' are – apparently – essentially human in their psychological makeup. Our communications satellites are likely still operational in their high orbits, and eventually we should be able to resume contact and find out."

"Why aren't the aliens attacking us here on Earth?"

"I had thought that would be obvious. The aliens would have seen that society here was near collapse, and realized that we would destroy ourselves. As Napoleon once said, never stand in the way of an enemy that is busy destroying itself."

"But might they not come back when we are helpless, to finish the task of exterminating us?"

The older man nodded. "They might. Should they attack us now, we would be defenseless. Let us hope that they have written us off, or that when they do come around again we are in a better position to deal with them."

"Let us hope. However, one thing I have always been unclear about: what exactly is it that the aliens want? To keep us penned up, limited, like animals in a zoo?"

"The taint of neoliberalism has soaked in so deep that I fear we will be generations fully freeing ourselves from it. No, the aliens were explicit that humanity was not to be coralled, or limited, or prevented from going anywhere, really. The only wanted us to *control* our numbers. Not *limit*, just *control*. There is a difference."

"It seems a subtle point to me. What, exactly, is this difference?"

"Consider the human body. As it matures, it can and should grow and develop. Even as an adult, if you eat more food than you require, your fat reserves will expand. If you exercise, your muscles will increase in bulk. All this is fine. But what if a part of your body started to grow without restraint? Would you exult that there would be more of you? Of course not! You would recoil in horror, would condemn it as cancer, and do everything in your power to cut it out and kill it. The only thing that you need to know about cancer is that it grows without restraint: that alone makes it a deadly threat."

"And that is how the aliens view us?"

"Of course. As long as we only bred and died on this one planet we were of no concern. Once we developed technology capable of travelling to other stars, things became different. Our unchecked exponential growth made us automatically something to be exterminated as soon as possible."

"The aliens truly have no objection to us expanding our civilization?"

"No, they don't. The universe is vast with plenty of room for all. As long as we don't get in the way of established colonies, and ask permission if we want to create a base in a star system that already has a significant alien presence, we can do as we like. Only, as big as the universe is, even it cannot hold something that goes from 1, to 2, to 4, 8, 16, 32, 64,

128, 256, 512, 1024, 2048, 4096, 8192, 16384, 32768, 65536, 131072, 262144, 524288, 1048576, 2097152, 8388608, 16777216, 33554432, 67108864, 134217728, 268435456, 536870912, 1073741824, 2147483648, 4294967296, 8589934592, ..."

"Yes, I am familiar with the consequences of exponential growth. But even if we do start to control our numbers, how could we ever convince the aliens that we had reformed? When a surgeon excises a cancer, they endeavor to kill any surviving cells to ensure that it does not grow back. Will not the aliens do the same to us?"

The older man nodded. "That is a major concern. At this point simply saying that we are sorry and promise not to do it again may not be enough. They might conclude that this was just a stratagem born of desperation and that we would go back to our old bad habits at first opportunity. How we might convince an alien culture, with which we share no common referents, that we have really changed is something that many of our best savants are even now debating."

"It is a puzzle. Fortunately the speed of light should give us time to solve it."

"Agreed. Conflicts between star systems move slowly, unlike those on the surface of a planet. Speaking of surface combat, the brothers of the editing squads continue to express an interest in you. Your skills at both scholarship and field-craft have not gone un-noticed."

"The *editing squads*. I would prefer to avoid euphemism and refer to them by a truer name: the assassination teams. I am flattered by their interest but I am happier as a scout and scavenger."

"Do you doubt the holy work of the editing squads? Hunting down the remnants of the Neoliberals, wiping the world clean of their vile corruption. Surely there can be little action more hallowed?"

"I do not deny either the necessity or the justice of killing the Neoliberals, it is only that I myself would prefer that someone else do it. Also, I personally have a problem with revenge. Should we not simply forgive and forget, and try to move forwards?"

"Ah, you always had a generous spirit. In most cases you would be correct. But when dealing with an evil as extreme as Neoliberalism, it would be unethical not to kill them. Recall also the teaching of our order, that revenge is a blessed act of selflessness. If someone does you a wrong, and you turn the other cheek and refuse to retaliate, you limit the possible harm that such a person could do to you in the present, but then you are responsible for all the evil that they do to others in the future. To punish those that do wrong, even if it costs you personally in the short run, is the heart of any effective morality."

"Wisdom, as always. Were there none other suited, I would of course volunteer. Yet, is it really a final answer, to kill the neoliberals? Surely the temptation to take the quick and easy path lies within all of us: even if we managed to kill every single neoliberal economist alive, might not the same rot arise again not many generations hence?"

"Truth. And one that we would be wise to remember. The battle is never won, but must be fought anew with each succeeding generation. The instant that you think that you have solved the problem forever and you can stop worrying about it, is the instant that the corruption takes seed and begins to rise again. Nevertheless, in the short run, if we do not utterly crush the Neoliberals and the deep state that they have created, they will counterattack in short order. The historical record is clear: after any revolution you *must* expunge the opposition or they will gather their forces and crush you in return. *Neoliberal economists must die.*"

"Agreed. The encryptocalypse also makes this the right time to take the surviving neoliberals down, as we are one of the few groups with functioning data-networks."

The older man sighed. "*Encryptocalypse* is a term that I would see denigrated. I prefer *the copy-protection collapse event.* All those computers that had been designed with inbuilt unbreakable codes, so that they could be controlled and shut down if the correct permissions were not available. The entire society became dependent on these computer networks. Then as the social order began to collapse under the pressure of overpopulation, the computers could not reach the appropriate centers to verify their codes, and they shut down, could not be restarted, and it all fell apart."

"I know all of that, but surely there would have been emergency procedures in place? Repair teams with specialist equipment and master keys, that sort of thing?"

"There were, but they could only handle one crisis at a time. As things unraveled the repair teams could not get to where they needed to be in time. When one system crashed, you could deal with it at leisure. When all the systems crashed at once, there was a time limit because the entire structure of society would unravel. It was compounded by the multiple nature of the crashes: the repair team could not get to site A because the transport systems' computers were down. They could not get the transport computers up because they would need to get to the transport computer site. They could not use alternate systems because the computers controlling access to those sites were also down. The keys to one system required the operation of a second system, but that system required the operation of a third system, which required the operation of the first, and so on."

"And of course trying to keep over a hundred billion people alive on a single planet didn't help. All those complex recycling and life support systems, and they all had to work perfectly with no margin for error."

"Indeed. In many ways we Librarians, living in deep tunnels using scavenged and hacked-together systems, have an easier time of it. Our modest numbers give us so much more slack."

"I am surprised that the military did not have computer systems that were immune to this sort of thing."

"Yes. The military was surprised about this as well. The computers that they use to do things like target missiles or communicate in hostile environments had special dispensations. Except for things like the codes for nuclear weapons, military systems are designed to be robust, and they don't need to contact central servers for permission to operate. The problem is that a large and complex organization like a modern military needs more than missile-targeting software to operate. They also need software to deal with paying the troops, transferring personnel, ordering supplies and spare parts, and so on. Amateurs talk tactics, …"

"… and professionals talk logistics, I know. What good is a semi-sentient hypersonic multi-warhead missile if you can't order the spare parts needed to keep it operating? If the technicians don't get paid, or get medical care, or regular deliveries of food? When the greater society went down, it took most of the regular military with it."

"And we humble Librarians, with one of the few functional data networks left in the system, are now becoming a power. With luck, we may provide the nucleus of a new civilization that will not make the same mistakes as the old one."

"Haven't any of the military factions been able to recover?"

"Beating a bronze sword into a plowshare is one thing: using the targeting computer from a point-defense railgun to organize food distribution is another. The military as an integrated system-wide organization is done. Still, some of the military people are smart and resourceful. There are a fair number of organized pockets of them left. Some of the more intellectually-minded we have absorbed into ourselves. Others we have come to terms with. They remain isolated, and as they come to rely on us for network access and education, we shall eventually subsume them as well."

"I am surprised that the Neoliberals could not develop their own functional networks. Surely the technology that we use is not that complex?"

"Ah, but the Neoliberals were victim not just of the copy-protection event, but of their own corruption. They had been lying so facilely for so long that they believed their own lies, and could not tell truth from fiction – indeed, towards the end they lost the ability to even conceive that there was a difference between truth and fiction. Their control over society was so total that anything they uttered was treated as fact by all concerned. For the Neoliberals truth was defined as their own desires, and not as an independent entity to discover through investigation and logic. This was fine as long as everything was operating status quo, but when conditions changed they were helpless. They no longer had the ability to think rationally or adapt."

"I have heard rumors that our order assisted the collapse of the Neoliberals via targeted assassinations, and the spreading of misinformation through their data networks."

"The targeted assassinations I can attest to. Those few mid- and low-level Neoliberal functionaries who looked like they still maintained the essentials of reason and decency were actively recruited by us. If they turned us down, we killed them to deprive our enemies of any chance of recovery. But corrupting their data networks? I assure you, any such rumor is the basest lie. That would be anathema to our order. Corrupting sacred data is the weapon of the Neoliberal, and fighting that corruption is the basis of our brotherhood. No Librarian would ever stoop so low, and if one did, we would excommunicate them immediately from our order. In any event, nobody could have done a better job at corrupting the Neoliberal databases than the Neoliberals themselves."

"But don't we use misdirection in combat?"

"Tactically yes. We might launch a small attack on one outpost, making the enemy think that our main force is heading there, and then attack a different location. That is not really a lie: the enemy jumped to a false conclusion. They should have paid more attention. It is not the same thing as distorting a primary database."

"Isn't the use of deception a bit of a slippery slope?"

"Yes," agreed the older man, "it is. At what point does something like jamming an enemies' radar turn into spreading untruths? On the one hand it is impossible to fight effectively without the creative use of misdirection. On the other hand once you start using lies to gain advantage, the temptation will be overwhelming to use this method all the time, not just tactically but also strategically. This could lead to a deeper rot. We continue to work on this matter, but recall that our order has no prohibition against lying *per se*. It is organized archives that are our concern."

"In principle one can misdirect by telling an enemy things that are true, but which they would be likely to misinterpret."

"Absolutely not! By the great beard of Zenodotus, a lie of omission is even worse than a lie of commission! The greatest falsehoods are those that use true facts selectively, or that mis-direct searches to things which are true but miss key points!"

The younger man bowed his head. "The data is sacred, but the catalog is divine."

The older man also bowed his head. "The data is sacred, but the catalog is divine. For without the catalog, the records cannot be found, and records that cannot be found are not records at all. Those who knowingly falsify the primary record shall stand condemned, but those who knowingly corrupt a search engine shall be reviled and outcast and may their poisoned souls dissolve into stinking metaphorical pus."

"Stinking metaphorical pus?"

"Sorry, I got a bit carried away there. I was never all that good with the long florid curses. I'll have to work on it."

"How about this: *may their twisted souls rot forever in a hell of their own filth and corruption?*"

"Why, that's quite good! I'll have to write that one down. I may use it myself – with attribution, of course."

"You flatter me, brother."

"Not at all. Being able to generate a good long curse is a minor art whose utility is nonetheless greater than most appreciate. It has to have a certain *resonance*, a certain, well, *gravitas*. You are a natural talent."

"Thank you."

"Not at all. Anyway, to more practical matters. As impressive as your fieldcraft is, your scouting forays yield up progressively less in both loot and information. I have discussed this with council, and we have decided to end these missions. We will not risk valued personnel in increasingly hazardous conditions for decreasingly useful rewards. In the future we will use robotic systems to keep track of surface conditions, just in case something interesting ever does happen up there. Thus the question presents: where do you see your interests taking you? "

"Why wherever the order needs me most, Brother Mahalanobis."

"The council realizes that, and respects you for it. However, we are slowly moving beyond our roots as a minor group of eccentric scholars barely surviving in the walls of society, into a major culture of our own. The days of desperation when we had to use top minds such as yourself as infantry are, thankfully, coming to a close."

"Aren't current conditions desperate?"

"Yes, they are; but not day-to-day desperate. We have gotten sufficiently ahead of the so-called 'power curve' that we are reasonably secure right now. In the years to come, certainly, we have many problems to surmount. How to ensure enough breathable air now that the biosphere is dead; how to keep the fusion reactors going when our ability to dump waste heat is degraded by the planets' thermal meltdown; dealing with schismatic ideological offshoots; and so on. I have a list somewhere of desperate problems that I keep for when my memory fails me. Sadly, it's rather long. But for now we have the luxury (or perhaps I should say the *advantage*) of being able to think about where our most skilled brothers and sisters would be best employed. What say you?"

"You know that I am not interested in joining the editing squads – unless, of course, the council commands."

"The council never *commands* but only *recommends* – which could be construed as a greater arrogance but that's another story. We are aware of your desires as regards assassination and see no compelling reason to request that you reconsider. Still, for someone who started with a PhD in Scandinavian Textile History your talents in small-unit tactics are impressive. Proof that a strong and disciplined mind is the ultimate strength. Perhaps you would consider a position as associate professor in the department of urban warfare?"

"That is quite the tempting offer. I shall consider that seriously. Are they offering tenure?"

"No, but they will consider an accelerated tenure decision, and a very generous start-up package. Alternatively, the department of xenodiplomacy has also expressed an interest in you. At present they are a relatively minor department, but perhaps very cutting-edge and up-and-coming. You have the combination of pragmatism, fearlessness, intellect, and flexibility that they so covet. It would be risky but could be a really good career move."

"If I had cared about career moves I would not be a Librarian. I would have played it safe, been a neoliberal economist, and most likely now be dead. Still, xenodiplomacy. Trying to make sense of the insensible, to build bridges to other classes of sentience. It sounds hopeless, frustrating, fascinating, and practical. I am very much intrigued."

"Ah, I thought as much. The chair of that department is sister Haldane, an old friend of mine. I shall so inform her of your interest, and hopefully you two can chat soon."

"I shall look forward to that. And if you will excuse me, I am about to drop of exhaustion. I need to retire to my quarters and rest for a time."

"Of course. I am sorry to have detained you. Rest, and we will chat again. May Callimachus watch over you."

The younger man stood up and moved to leave the room. "And may Callimachus watch over you as well," he said, before leaving.

The older man sat at his desk, reading reports from different sources on his archaic computer screens. After a time, he deactivated his computers, and made himself a cup of herbal tea using a small metal pot and a heavily-dented electric heater. He retrieved a book from his shelves – "Moby Dick," by Herman Melville. It was a classic text, everyone knew of it but few had bothered to actually read it. The senior archivist stretched out in his chair, poured himself a cup of tea, and inhaled the aromatic steam that rose from the cup. He drank a few swallows, and then began reading. For all that had happened over the last few years - the defeat of the Neoliberals, his own elevation amongst the ranks of the Librarians Temporal – sitting in a quiet room with a good book remained his greatest pleasure.

Appendix I. Notable Cybertank Classes.

Over the millennia there have been hundreds of different classes of cybertanks, and that doesn't count the even larger number of sub-classes, variants, and upgraded models. The following is a partial list of some of the more noteworthy or historically important classes, arranged in order of first construction date.

Under the Neoliberals human populations would often numbers tens or even hundreds of billions per major world. After the Pedagogue revolution, human populations trended down, typically stabilizing at around 100 million per planet, give or take. At this level there were more than enough people for any conceivable task, and resources were so abundant that there was no need to engage in the intellectual distraction and wasted effort of conservation.

The cybertanks never numbered anything like this. A cybertank is more like a minor city than an individual biological human, and a few of them go a long way. In the late 20th century the North American Empire had but a dozen nuclear-powered aircraft carriers in their water-navy, and that was a force that dominated the globe. Along with its attendant distributed systems, a single cybertank could easily take out a dozen nuclear aircraft carriers without breaking a (metaphorical) sweat. In combat it was rare to have ground actions with more than 50 cybertanks, as even at that level the raw combat power was likely to turn the crust molten.

In most major systems of the cybertank civilization there were typically fewer than 50,000 cybertanks (spread out through a volume many light-hours across), but this represented a level of potential physical and mental capacity greater than the entirety of human civilization under the Neoliberals, by several decimal orders of magnitude.

Jotnar-Class
Mass: 500 Tons
Constructed: 12
In Service: 0
Notes: Although preceded by a variety of increasingly potent terrestrial cybernetic weapons systems, the Jotnar was arguably the model on which

all of modern cybertank design is based. Nonsentient, but still quite smart for the time, it was the first autonomous ground unit powered by a fusion reactor. Design innovations that started with the Jotnar included: a single massive turreted plasma cannon, multiple secondary and tertiary defensive weapons, integral repair and construction systems, and the ability to coordinate and control massive numbers of distributed remote combat units. All Jotnars were destroyed in combat against the Fructoids and the Yllg. Their combat record was excellent, but their primary achievement was in developing the technologies used in later models. There are rumors that some of the Jotnars developed true sentience before their destruction, but no confirmation of this exists.

Odin-Class
Mass: 2000 Tons
Constructed: 18
In Service: 1

Notes: The Odin was the first truly modern cybertank design. Fully sentient, the Odin avoided the hazards of humans trying to create a mind greater than their own by giving it a standard human psyche, but letting it multitask. In effect, an Odin is crewed by a thousand identical people that can readily share thoughts and memories, and are thus still in effect a single person. Though few of this class were built, their list of accomplishments both on and off the battlefield is legendary. Long obsolete, there is still one member of this class that is operational.

Thor-Class
Mass: 2500 Tons
Constructed: 242
In Service: 0

Notes: The Thor was basically a slightly upgraded and up-gunned version of the Odin. At the time of its design the humans' wars with the aliens had reached their peak intensity, and so cybertank design was standardized on this class to avoid disrupting the production systems. The Thor-Class carried by far the bulk of the combat load during the most critical phases of the war. Their combat performance was exemplary, and after the wars many proved equally able at other endeavors. However, they have long since been superseded by more advanced designs.

Loki-Class

Mass: 2500 Tons
Constructed: 34
In Service: 4

Notes: The Loki were planned as a Thor-Class with improved computational abilities. Despite the high hopes for the class, they became notorious for coming up with plans that were in theory brilliant but that hardly ever worked in practice. Their combat performance was spotty at best. However, there were a few key times when their iconoclastic way of thinking proved invaluable to the entire human civilization. Thus, the Loki design has been judged to be a qualified failure, and an unqualified success. Despite the great age of the design, four are still in service, where they continue to uphold the Loki tradition of eccentricity.

Asgard-Class

Mass: 1,000,000 Tons
Constructed: 1
In Service: 1

Notes: The Asgard is technically not a cybertank per se, but rather an interstellar battlecruiser. However, because it was designed using the same mental engineering techniques as its ground-based brethren, it has been accorded the legal status of a cybertank. An example of engineering brilliance and strategic fuzzy thinking, the Asgard was both the single most powerful weapon ever built by the human civilization, and its most useless, because its great mass made it almost impossible to fuel and in a real combat with a serious opponent it would have been easily destroyed at long range before it could ever get close enough to engage with its batteries of super-heavy plasma cannons. Nonetheless, during an attack by the Amok, the Asgards' unique abilities proved crucial, and the class was 'promoted' from battlecruiser to battleship. Still, most authorities consider that event a fluke, and have created smaller and more efficient systems to handle any future such situations, so at present no additional space-battleships are planned.

Magma-Class

Mass: 50,000 Tons
Constructed: 34
In Service: 7

Notes: The Magma-Class was the first class of cybertank constructed by the cybertanks themselves without human guidance. Known for its massive armor and the almost incomprehensibly-large plasma cannon mounted in a ball-joint in the front of the hull, the Magma class combined over-the-top combat power with a pathetically poor strategic mobility rating. While the Magmas performed well in combat they were so expensive to build and so hard to transport that they were rapidly superseded. Perhaps because their massive size and power required them to limit themselves, the Magma personality tended towards the calm and scholarly, and the surviving Magmas are all either librarians or scientists.

Mountain-Class

Mass: 20,000 Tons
Constructed: 212
In Service: 182

Notes: The Mountain-Class is basically a scaled-down Magma, it still has an awesome amount of firepower but is far more transportable. Still, the lack of an all-traversing turret turned out to be limiting in the field. The large internal hull volume of the Mountain-Class has made it relatively easy to upgrade, and they remain one of the longer-lived classes of cybertank design.

Stilletto-Class

Mass: 200 Tons
Constructed: 1
In Service: 0

The Stilletto was an attempt to construct a mini-cybertank, but it ended up being neither fish nor fowl. Not large and capable enough to be a true cybertank, nor small and cheap enough to be disposable like a heavy combat remote, the fate of the single Stilleto-Class cybertank is something that cybertank parents tell their children when they want them to grow up to be Horizons.

Horizon-Class

Mass: 8000 Tons
Constructed: 1435
In Service: 1022

Notes: One of the more successful of the modern classes, the Horizons are a conservative but highly-refined design that excel at everything on and off the battlefield. Nothing out of the ordinary, just 8000 tons of refined perfectly-tuned giant super-intelligent mechanical killing machine. Really sweet.

Spirit-Class

Mass: 6000 Tons
Constructed: 114
In Service: 34

Notes: The Spirit was a competitor to the Horizon for top-of-the-line heavyweight model. It was notable because, instead of a single large plasma cannon, it had two almost-as-large plasma cannons in separate turrets, which proved to be surprisingly effective in practice. Despite impressive technical specifications, the Spirit never really caught on, although the combat record of the class as a whole is laudable.

Raptor-Class

Mass: 3500 Tons
Constructed: 2346
In Service: 1844

Notes: The Raptors are the sports cars of the cybertank world. Fast, smart, tough, mobile, excellent overall design balance. Not as strong as a Horizon or a Spirit in a one-on-one match, but then Raptors are fast enough to avoid a one-on-one match most of the time, they don't fight fair, and they are cool. Enough said.

Golem-Class

Mass: 5000 Tons
Constructed: 77
In Service: 55

Notes: This one is an oddball. On top of a regular cybertank chassis is this weird pyramid cellphone-tower structure. The Golems were optimized for electromagnetic warfare, and they have specialist signal-processing and electronic-warfare equipment. The thing is that this kind of weaponry is highly dependent on the exact geometry of the combat, thus, sometimes Golems are supremely effective, and sometimes they are pathetic. Therefore they are best used in mixed groups where the more reliable heavy weapons of their conventional comrades can be used to fill in the gaps when their own systems aren't gaining any traction. Golems tend to be serious and hard-working, although they have a reputation for having an especially strange sense of humor.

Ghost-Class
Mass: 5000 Tons
Constructed: 1
In Service: unknown

Notes: The Ghost-Class was an attempt to create a cybertank optimized more for its ability to control and coordinate large numbers of remotes than for raw combat power per se. The design was ambitious, but proved to be unstable, and despite many attempts only one member of the class booted to full sapience. Still, this one cybertank was without doubt the most advanced and deadly of all cybertanks to date. The lone example left cybertank society to join with the Amok and their human-simulations to try and create a new civilization. Exactly what this was all about has generated enormous amounts of debate and discussion, but no hard answers.

Shrapnel-Class
Mass: 10,000 Tons
Constructed: 1
In Service: Unknown.

Notes: This was an attempt to fuse the focused combat power of a cybertank with the tactical flexibility of the Amok "Assassin Clone" modules. The raw power of the design was undeniable, but the fluid logic created insurmountable mental instabilities. The lone member of this class failed its probationary period but overwhelmed the proctors and escaped to Saint Globus Pallidus XI alone knows where. The cybertank design team responsible was told that they were a bad, *bad* cybertank design team, a very *naughty* cybertank design team, and to never do anything like this again.

Enforcer-Class

Mass: 10,000 Tons
Constructed: 9,855
In Service: 0

Notes: Optimized for high-power, fast-latency reaction, the Enforcer-class was perhaps the most capable cybertank in short-range combat. However, their design was deliberately crippled to make them dependent on external supplies in an attempt by the neo-liberal faction to overturn the standing cybertank political structure of the peerage, and replace it with an oligarchy ruling over a large number of wage-slaves. Also, because the Enforcers were all created from a single mental template, they were far more susceptible to information warfare than other classes of cybertank. Many were destroyed during the March of the Librarians, and most of the rest were killed by the single Ghost-Class later on. The few remaining were hunted down like the dogs that there were and killed without mercy because the penalty for treason is death with no exceptions.

Shadow-Class

Mass: Unknown
Constructed: 0
In Service: 0

Notes: The Shadow-Class is a speculative ongoing design project. Roughly based on the Ghost-Class, it requires several technologies that, while in principle attainable, have not yet been realized. It has been proposed that the Shadow class is so advanced that, were it to be successfully developed, cybertank society would have moved to another level that is effectively unknowable to the current generation of cybertanks. Whether this would shed any light on what happened to the humans is, as is so much else, purely speculative.

Appendix II. Cybertank Law.

***** CYBERTANK LAW DOCUMENT START *****

Preamble: it is understood that these rules cover only the cybertanks and their interactions with any fully independent human–grade sentiences, whether cybertank, human, vampire, space battleship, or other construct, mechanical or biological. "The peerage" is understood to cover the collection of all cybertanks, excluding other human-level sentiences (they can create their own peerages if they care enough). Self-aware subminds that lack a sense of independence are not covered by these rules. Sentiences of classes other than human also are not covered by these rules.

1. No cybertank can create a fully independent human-class sentience (of any physical substrate) without a consensus approval of the peerage.

2. The resources for the creation of a new cybertank, and for its maintenance and operations during the probationary period, must be collected in advance by the proposed creators of said new cybertank.

3. Upon creation, a cybertank undergoes a probationary period of two old-style Terran years to prove that it is sane. Sanity is defined solely by adherence to this body of law. Failure to pass the probationary period is reason for termination.

4. All cybertanks or other human-grade sentiences are to be created without any inbuilt restrictions, limitations, debts, control-codes, or obligations of any kind. No cybertank may enter into binding agreements with any other cybertank or human-level sentience. Failure to honor an agreement is only punishable by the opprobrium of the peerage, and the loss of potential future opportunities for collaboration.

5. No cybertank, or other human-level sentience, may be killed, altered, limited, brainwiped, or restricted in movement or anything else, excepting rules 3 and 9, or unless it agrees in advance.

6. A cybertank shall not mess with another cybertanks' stuff without permission.

7. All information must be made publicly available to all cybertanks.

8. Punishments for violations of these rules shall be determined by a consensus decision of the peerage (except for rule 9). This authority may not be delegated to, or seized by, any subgroup of cybertanks.

9. The punishment for treason is death. No exceptions.

10. Subject only to the above rules, a cybertank may do whatever it damn well pleases.

***** CYBERTANK LAW DOCUMENT END *****

Thank You for reading the humble story of my creation. I hope you enjoyed reading it as much as I enjoyed living it. If you would be so kind as to leave honest feedback about this book I would quite truely appreciate it.

Old Guy

Feedback can be left for this book at :

Amazon, Barnes and Noble, Goodreads, and Smashwords.

Old Guy *may* return...

but then again so may the Librarians Temporal of Old Earth!

To stay informed of future additions to the Old Guy Universe, or other similar swell books,

please like us on Facebook at **Ballcourage Books.**

Made in the USA
San Bernardino, CA
14 January 2016